*after*

*dark*

Sadie Matthews is the author of six novels of contemporary women's fiction published under other names. FIRE AFTER DARK was her first novel to explore a more intimate and intense side of life and relationships. SECRETS AFTER DARK and PROMISES AFTER DARK complete the *After Dark* series – her first provocative romantic trilogy. She is married and lives in London.

Find Sadie Matthews on Twitter at
www.twitter.com/sadie_matthews

Also by Sadie Matthews

Fire After Dark
Secrets After Dark

# promises
# after
# dark

## SADIE MATTHEWS

HODDER

First published in Great Britain in 2013 by Hodder & Stoughton
An Hachette UK Company

1

A CIP catalogue record for this title is available from the British Library.

ISBN 978 1 444 77587 7

Typeset by Hewer Text UK Ltd, Edinburgh
Printed and bound by Clays Ltd, St Ives plc

Hodder & Stoughton policy is to use papers that are natural, renewable
and recyclable products and made from wood grown in sustainable
forests. The logging and manufacturing processes are expected to
conform to the environmental regulations of the country of origin.

Hodder & Stoughton Ltd
338 Euston Road
London NW1 3BH

www.hodder.co.uk

To

J. T.

# CHAPTER ONE

I'm in a sleek snub-nosed Bentley, leaning against the black leather seats and looking out of the tinted window at the snowy streets of St Petersburg. In front of me are the driver and the meaty bodyguard who sits beside him, their salt-and-pepper stubble blurring the toughness of their skulls. The doors of the car are tightly shut, the stub of lock sunk down into the black leather below the window. For a moment, I imagine trying to claw it up with my fingernails but I know that would be impossible. There is no way I can escape.

But even if I could, where would I go? I don't know this city, I don't speak the language and I have no money; even my passport has been locked away in the hotel safe. And I've been warned that this place is dangerous. I've been told that I'm vulnerable and that's why I will not be permitted to be alone at any point when I'm out of the hotel. I have my mobile phone but I'm not sure who I would ring. My parents are far away, at home in England. I wish with all my heart that I was there right now, walking into our cosy kitchen where my father is reading the paper over his afternoon cup of tea while my mother bustles around, trying to do six things at once and urging Dad to move his feet out of her way. On the stove something delicious is cooking and the radio is playing a classical concert.

I can conjure it up so clearly, I am almost able to smell the stew, to hear the music. I want to rush to my parents and hug them, tell them not to worry.

But they're not worrying. They know where I am. They think I'm perfectly safe. And I am. I'm being very well looked after.

*Too well?* I try to repress the shiver that threatens to convulse me.

A pair of blue eyes is fixed on me. I know this even though I'm not looking at the man beside me. I can feel his laser-beam gaze burning on my skin, and I'm hyperaware of the body only a seat's width away from me. I don't want him to know that I'm scared.

*Your vivid imagination!* I scold myself. *It's going to be your downfall. You're perfectly all right. We're not going to be here for long. We're leaving the day after tomorrow.*

This ought to be a dream come true for me. I'm here because Mark, my boss, is too ill to come himself but despite the sad circumstances, it's an amazing opportunity. I've always longed to visit the Hermitage, to see some of its massive collection of art treasures, and now I'm being taken there, not just into the gallery but into the very heart of it, to meet one of its experts. He is going to give us the verdict on the lost Fra Angelico painting that Mark's employer Andrei Dubrovski bought recently, now that it's been properly analysed.

This is the trip of a lifetime and I should be elated, excited.

*Not afraid.*

I try to stifle the words before they've sounded in my head. I'm not afraid. Why should I be? And yet . . .

We arrived last night, touching down at the airport in Andrei Dubrovski's private jet. As usual, the formalities were done quickly and confidentially. I wondered what it would be like when I had to go back to queuing at passport control, lining up for my security check and getting myself to some far-off gate to catch a flight. All this VIP treatment would spoil me for ever if I wasn't careful. We went straight from the plane to a stretch black limo – a little flashier than I would have expected from a man of Dubrovski's taste but maybe things were different when he was in Russia – and glided out onto the highway for the short trip into St Petersburg.

'What do you think of Russia so far?' Andrei asked as the car purred smoothly past the other traffic on the highway.

I gazed out into the night but there was not much to see beyond the car window. Ahead the darkness was tinged with orange, the illumination of the big city leaking into the vast night sky above us. 'It's hard to tell,' I replied. 'I'll let you know in the morning.'

Andrei laughed. 'I know what you'll say. It's bloody cold. Believe me, London will feel like a tropical paradise in comparison.'

I laughed too, and hoped it sounded convincing. Ever since our flight, my emotions had been in turmoil.

3

Andrei, for whom I'd been working for a few weeks, revealed that he knew about my relationship with Dominic, and that Dominic and I had parted. Even so, he didn't bother to spare my feelings by telling me that as far as he was concerned Dominic was now his enemy. And then he said those three words, the ones that had turned my world upside down.

*No more games.*

Those were the words spoken in my ear by the man who made passionate love to me in the darkness during a party in the catacombs. I had thought it was Dominic but now I feared that it had been Andrei after all. The problem was, my perceptions were completely undermined by the fact that I had almost certainly been drugged, most likely by Anna, Andrei's now ex-lover and employee, whose passionate feelings for Dominic caused us all sorts of trouble.

Just thinking about that night at the strange underground party made my stomach swoop and churn.

*If I made love to Andrei then I was unfaithful to Dominic, consciously or not. And if Andrei is the kind of man to take advantage of a woman who is clearly not herself, what else is he capable of?*

I glanced over quickly at Andrei, who had taken his eyes off me for a moment to lean forward and mutter something in Russian to his bodyguard. His physique was simultaneously attractive and a little menacing, his shoulders broad inside his dark overcoat, his hands large and strong. The perfectly tailored charcoal wool suit he was wearing did little to disguise the hard, muscled body within. His face was craggy, with piercing blue eyes and an unsmiling mouth with its stubborn, jutting lower lip. Despite my love for Dominic, I had at times felt the shiver of attraction that his physical magnetism exerted over me. I hated myself for it, but I couldn't help it. Perhaps that was why I was in such agonies over the possibility that he and I had made wild passionate love against the cold stone wall of the cave: part of me knew I wanted it, despite what I told myself.

It wasn't as though he'd acted against my wishes. He had asked me if I wanted to and I had practically begged to be fucked as hard as possible. It had certainly been consensual.

*Except for the small matter of his identity. Did he know that I thought he was Dominic?*

It was impossible to know without asking him and I hadn't yet gathered up my courage for that particular line of questioning.

'What is it, Beth?' Andrei's rasping, almost harsh voice breaks into my thoughts. Startled, I jump. I haven't realised that I'm still staring at him as my brain whirls round the recent events, trying to piece it all together.

'N-nothing,' I say. I regain my composure as quickly as possible. 'Are we nearly there?'

I realise that we've slowed down and have been edging forward at a snail's pace for a few minutes now.

'St Petersburg traffic,' Andrei says shortly. 'It's renowned for being awful, especially when there's snow on the roads, which you can imagine is fairly often. But I think we're almost there now.'

It's only mid-morning but already it feels like evening, with the low grey clouds heavy with more snow pressing down upon us. I stare out of the window again, and realise that we are coming up to a vast broad river and on the opposite side is the most incredible façade of buildings: a collection of baroque palaces, their hundreds of windows glittering darkly, pressed close, distinct and yet a group. They are dominated by a palace so large and ornate, it looks as though it comes from a film or a storybook.

'The Hermitage museum,' Andrei announces proudly. 'Surely the most beautiful museum in the world. Such grandeur, such beauty.' He indicates the largest, most baroque of the palaces, with its vast stretch of white columns and dark green walls between porticoed windows. 'That's the Winter Palace, home to the Russian Emperors. From there, they ruled over 125 million souls and one sixth of the earth's surface. Impressive, isn't it?'

He's right; it's a magnificent sight. For a moment I imagine I'm Catherine the Great being conveyed in a magnificent carriage towards my spectacular home, full of the extraordinary works of art I've collected. Then I remember what it must have been like to be an ordinary Russian, excluded from the luxurious, gilded life within, only good for toiling on its construction, or being taxed to pay for the glorious art on its walls without ever having the privilege to see it.

But times have changed. These are now public buildings that can be accessed by all. Everyone can enjoy their beauty and the treasures that lie inside.

'What do you think?' Andrei presses.

'Amazing.' I can't say more, I'm overwhelmed. We cross the river and approach the Winter Palace by the Embankment, then stop at a large wrought-iron gate that's shut fast. A moment later, a man rushes out to open it and wave us through and then we're inside a courtyard with a garden in the centre that's blanketed in snow, its bare trees with their white-laden branches black against its walls. The gate is closed behind us.

'Nicholas II's daughters used to play here,' Andrei remarks as the car swoops to a stop in front of an ornate front door. 'Imagine, four little grand duchesses running around, laughing, throwing snowballs at the soldiers protecting them. Not knowing what a miserable death awaits them.'

The driver has already got out and has opened the door on Andrei's side. I shiver as icy air rushes into the warm interior, and push the thought of the fate of those children from my mind.

I put on my hat and gloves as the driver comes around to open my door. He helps me step out onto the icy path and guides me around to where Andrei awaits me.

'A private entrance,' he says, a slight smile twisting his lips. He smiles so rarely, but even this small effort manages to lighten those craggy features and soften his icy stare. 'These things can be arranged.'

*Not quite so open to everybody after all. Money still buys its way in where others are forbidden.*

The door opens and a man comes out. He's in late middle age, wearing a big black overcoat and a fur hat and boots. He's smiling, his small eyes crinkling behind thick black-framed glasses. He rushes forward towards Andrei, greeting him effusively in Russian. They talk for a moment as I try to hide the fact that I'm shivering already despite my warm coat. I look enviously at the lucky driver who is back inside the warmth of the car.

Andrei suddenly switches to English as he gestures to me. 'And this is Beth, my art adviser. She was there when I acquired the piece.' He doesn't bother to tell me who this man is, but I can guess he is someone important in the museum.

'Madam Beth.' The man speaks in accented English as he bows a welcome to me. 'Please, let's go inside. I can see you are cold.' We follow him through the door and into the palace. At once I want to gasp out loud. No one else turns a hair at the magnificence within, they are obviously used to it, but I'm stunned by the opulence on show. Marble floors, gilt lamps with crystal shades, ornate mirrors, stunning paintings in vast gilded frames – everywhere there is colour and amazing, glittering, over-the-top decoration.

The two men ahead of me are talking again in Russian, and I follow behind trying to drink everything in. Here I am, in the Winter Palace in St Petersburg. There's no one else around, so we must be in a private area shut off from the public. How lucky I am . . . and yet I can't help feeling full of trepidation. I'm in a strange place, a vast palace, with no idea where I actually am.

Andrei's companion turns to me with a smile. 'Is this your first time here, Madam Beth?'

I nod. I wish he would drop the madam but I don't know how to ask it politely.

'It's a big place, isn't it? There are fifteen hundred rooms in this palace, and a hundred and seventeen staircases. Please, do not get lost, it will be no easy task to find you!' He laughs and turns back to Andrei.

Somehow I don't find the prospect of being abandoned here quite as funny as he seems to.

We walk on. The men in front of me are keeping up a swift pace, which means I can hardly take in the stunning sights and the many beautiful paintings on the walls before we have passed them. We climb a large dark-oak staircase to the first floor and then walk down several more corridors before we finally reach our destination, a large polished wooden door set with an ornate brass handle and escutcheon.

Our guide opens it with a flourish. 'Please come in!'

He leads us into a grand room, the plain office furniture in odd contrast to the gilded ceiling, huge chandelier and the vast windows. The walls are covered in red silk, enormous gilt-framed paintings glowing against them. In one corner I notice a large easel on which is mounted a canvas that's covered with a plain cloth.

Our friend begins to speak in Russian but Andrei holds up one gloved hand and shakes his head. 'No, Nicolai. English, please, for my adviser here.'

'Certainly, certainly!' Nicolai smiles over at me, obviously keen to please. 'English it shall be.' He gestures to us to sit on the plain black chairs in front of his grey Formica desk. 'Please, make yourselves comfortable.'

'We're not here to socialise,' Andrei says almost roughly. 'You know what I want. What's the answer?'

Nicolai slowly removes his fur hat, revealing a shiny bald spot on top of his head, and places it on the desk. He begins to unbutton his coat, frowning a little. As he shuffles it off, he says, 'I can't pretend, Andrei: this is one of the most complex cases we've ever been presented with. My experts here have been exceptionally thorough in their analysis.'

Andrei goes very still. 'And?'

I glance at his face. His lips are set hard, the lower one sticking out in that obstinate way, and his eyes are burning with intensity. I know he badly wants to hear the right answer. This painting has put us all through a lot. I'm anxious myself: my heart is pounding and I feel breathless. I realise that my hands are tightly clenched inside my coat pockets.

Nicolai clearly has a taste for the dramatic. He slowly hangs his coat over the back of his chair and then makes his way across the room to the easel. He takes the corner of the cloth covering the canvas on the easel in one hand, pauses for a moment and then pulls so that the fabric slides slowly away. And there it is, in all its glory: the shimmering, beautiful painting that I last saw in a Croatian monastery. The Madonna still

10

sits serenely in her gorgeous garden, her baby on her knee, the saints and monks around her. It truly is exquisite and the moment I see it, my faith is reborn. *This is the real thing. Surely. Can anything that isn't a masterpiece be so lovely?*

I'm surprised by a sudden stab of unexpected sadness. Something mournful fills me as I remember what else happened in that monastery: the glorious reunion I had there with Dominic. It felt as though our relationship had been rekindled and made stronger than ever. Now, we are apart again and this time I'm afraid that we'll never be able to bridge the gap between us.

I see him in my mind, just as he was when we were last together, so clear and so vivid I can't help pulling in a sharp breath. But his beautiful face is set hard with anger and fear, his eyes are glowering. I hear his words again:

'*I want you to swear on your life that nothing has ever happened between you and Dubrovski. Come on, Beth. Swear.*'

But I couldn't do it. I couldn't be sure. And that sent us spiralling apart, the precious trust between us broken. For ever?

*No. I won't let that happen. I'll make sure it doesn't.*

Andrei's voice, harsh and jagged, brings me back to the present. I'm filled with desperate longing to be with Dominic, not here in this strange country with the man who was the cause of the trouble. This is sheer madness.

'Come on, Nicolai! What's the answer?'

11

Nicolai puts on a pair of glasses and examines the painting closely, making little clicking noises with his tongue. At last he says, 'The brushwork is magnificent, the paints absolutely masterful in their tints. They match exactly what we would expect from Fra Angelico's genius. Everything: the composition, the linear perspective, the style . . . it's almost perfect.'

'*Almost?*' raps out Andrei.

Nicolai nods mournfully. 'Perfect, but for one thing. Analysis of the pigments and the canvas itself tells us that this work is no more than two hundred years old. It's a very clever, very delightful, very exciting pastiche. It is a wonderful work by a great talent, but it is not by Fra Angelico.' He looks straight at Andrei who is standing like a statue, his face pale. 'I'm sorry, Andrei, but there's no doubt about it. Your painting is a fake.'

# CHAPTER TWO

I'm virtually running through the Winter Palace in pursuit of Andrei, who is striding ahead of me. I hope he can remember the way out because I have no idea where we are. We've gone along metres of corridors and down at least one flight of stairs already.

*Fifteen hundred rooms. If he can't remember the way, we could be racing around for a very long time looking for the exit.*

But Andrei evidently knows the route and he keeps up his killing pace until we reach the door where we came in. He goes to open it.

'Andrei, please!' I gasp. 'Wait!'

He stops and turns around. His expression is awful: I've never seen rage so deeply etched on a face and his eyes are like burning flint.

'I . . . I . . . I'm sorry!' I manage to say as I try to catch my breath. 'I know what the painting meant to you!'

A nasty snarl curls his lips. 'You and your friend have cost me two million dollars,' he says, his voice harsher than ever. I never usually notice his accent – he sounds more American than anything to me – but now the Russian aspect is pronounced, as though he wants to emphasise the difference between us. 'You want to think about that, huh?'

I almost recoil in shock. 'What do you mean?'

'You're my art adviser, aren't you? You and Mark, together? You came with me to Croatia to advise me on the purchase of the Fra Angelico and it was on your say-so that I bought the goddamned thing! So much for your expertise.'

I gasp at this. It's blatantly unfair. I can see Mark's unhappy face in my mind right now. He didn't want to be pressed into advising Andrei to buy the painting but Andrei insisted. Mark's advice was to wait until the painting was properly authenticated; Andrei hadn't listened. I can hear Mark telling me that his reputation would be on the line if the painting turned out to be a fake. *Oh God, Mark – what will this do to you?*

Fury blazes up in me. Andrei can't play it this way. He can't pretend that he didn't steamroller us and buy the painting against Mark's advice.

'You know that's not true!' I cry. The anger boiling up in me makes my voice strong and indignant. 'I won't let you blame Mark for this! He warned you, he told you to be cautious but you wouldn't listen. He never wanted you to buy that painting but you went ahead anyway. He's been so loyal to you, how dare you turn on him like this?'

Andrei says nothing but he's paler than ever, his brows knitting as he stares at me.

I'm more fired up now, despite a voice at the back of my mind warning me to tread carefully. 'It's your own fault, you know it is. You wanted to believe that the painting was real, so you did exactly what you wanted. Is this how you operate? Throwing people to the lions when things go wrong rather than take the blame yourself? I thought better of you than that. But I'm beginning to realise I was wrong about you on more than one level.'

I can't quite believe what I've just said. A thread of fear curls around my stomach and tightens. *Oh no, I've gone too far.*

His teeth are clenched, I can tell by the tightness of his jaw and the way a muscle is pulsing in his cheek. He looks like he wants to kill me. Then, after an agonising pause, he says curtly, 'Get in the car. Now.' He strides out without looking to see if I'm obeying.

As I follow him through the door, I curse my rashness. I'm completely at this man's mercy. Now is not the time to antagonise him – but I couldn't stop myself. If he's going to blame Mark and me for this situation, then our working relationship is at an end anyway. But what if I'm about to see a whole different side of Andrei Dubrovski? I've seen him polished and civilised, considerate, even seductive – but I've always known that under that sophisticated exterior is a boy from the Moscow back streets, brought up in an orphanage, who made his fortune through toughness and determination, succeeding no matter what it took.

*How far would he go if he wanted some kind of revenge?*

The driver is out of the car, holding the door open for me. I climb in and wonder what the hell is going to happen now. Andrei is next to me. He's silent but I can sense the fury roiling inside him. My instinct tells me to keep quiet, so I don't even ask where we're going now. I want desperately to be back in my room at the hotel. I need to get away from him so I can think this all through. The car sets off, out through the gate and back over the river. We're on the Nevsky Prospect, the famous main road of St Petersburg, crawling along through the heavy traffic, rolling by crowds of well-wrapped-up people walking through snowy streets in front of bright shop windows. We pass ornate department stores, brightly lit malls, huge churches and beautiful monuments. I ought to be thrilled to be here, I ought to be drinking in these sights, but instead I'm nervous and unhappy, wondering what is going to happen next.

Andrei doesn't speak all the way back to the hotel. Then, as we walk into the glitzy marble lobby with its giant crystal lights, he says, 'I'm going to my room. Order whatever you want for lunch. Be ready to leave here again at two o'clock.'

'Are we going home?' I venture.

He looks down at me with a swift chilly gaze. Then something he sees in my face makes him pause and soften slightly. 'Not yet. Tonight. There's something I need to do first.' He looks as though he wants to say something else, but he decides against it and only adds: 'Two o'clock. Exactly.'

I go back to my room, grateful to be able to recover a little from the drama of this morning. When the door is safely closed behind me, I lean against it and sigh with relief. Then I kick off my boots, throw myself down on my bed and stare up at the ceiling.

'So the painting is a fake,' I say out loud. 'I can't believe it. After all that.'

I wonder what Andrei intends to do about it. I wouldn't want to be the abbot of the monastery when he has to take that particular telephone call. But I have my own call to make. I ought to tell Mark what the results of the Hermitage investigation are; he needs to know. I remember the last time I saw him, just before I left for Russia with Andrei. I'd gone round to the Belgravia house to see how he was and get some final instructions, only to find a big bustling blonde woman had taken charge of everything.

'My sister Caroline,' Mark explained in a voice that was weaker than ever. 'She's going to stay and take care of things in the house.'

'And you?' I asked, watching as Caroline stomped off to give some instructions to the handyman working outside, her loud patrician tones already ringing out. Her bulky noisiness was in such contrast to Mark's slim, quiet elegance that it was hard to believe they had the same parents. 'Is she going to take care of you?'

I was still absorbing the news that Mark was sick, and wondering how serious it was, as he refused even to say what exactly was wrong with him.

'Of course. Very good care. She's excellent at all of that.' Mark smiled, and the sight made me want to cry. It was supposed to look cheerful but his thin lips stretched over his bony face gave him a rictus grin. I realised suddenly that his teeth and eyes looked enormous in his head, huge but yellow-tinged and unhealthy.

*He's really ill*, I thought, with something like astonishment. Of course I knew he was ill, but people get sick and then get better. Unless they get sick and then sicker, and then sicker still and then . . .

'Actually, Beth,' Mark said, making as though to lean towards me confidentially but then not finding quite enough strength, 'did I tell you my operation is tomorrow?'

I shook my head, hoping that he couldn't see the blur of tears in my eyes.

'Oh yes, I'm top priority. Into theatre first thing, and eight hours on the operating table. It'll whizz by because I'll be the closest thing to dead there is without actually being dead. At least, I hope I don't end up dead, that really isn't the idea.' Mark chuckled at his own little joke. 'So think of me recovering in my hospital bed while you're waltzing around St Petersburg – but Caroline will make sure I'm taken care of, don't worry.'

I'm staring up at the light above the bed, and I realise I've been counting the little halogen bulbs over and over while I think about Mark. The operation must have been yesterday. It was on his neck, so I've no idea if he'll be able to talk, even assuming it was a success. *Oh God, I hope it was a success.* I've grown to love Mark, as a friend and mentor and an inspiration for how to live life beautifully. He's been so much more than an employer to me.

I pick up my mobile and my thumb hovers over it for a moment, then I put it back down on the bed beside me. I won't phone him with this particular news, not yet. There's no nice way to tell him that Andrei intends to throw him under a bus – and I might yet be able to salvage the situation. After all, there is the mysterious trip at 2 p.m.; perhaps I could try exerting some influence over Andrei then.

*Yes, that's definitely the way. I'll try and appeal to Andrei's decency. I'm sure he has some. And I'll wait to see how Mark is doing before I tell him anything else.*

With that decided, I sit up and think about ordering lunch, so I can be ready to go at precisely two o'clock.

I'm ten minutes early in the lobby, just in case. At five minutes to two, Andrei comes striding out of a lift, wearing his dark-blue silk and cashmere overcoat. Everyone notices him at once and watches him, some subtly, others openly staring. His energy radiates out and draws every eye. Besides that, he's physically inter-esting to look at: he's tall, broad-shouldered and his face is almost handsome. It's craggy and tough, its heavy features and obstinate mouth given something extraordinary by those blazing blue eyes.

It's strange to remember that I've seen those eyes soften to a hazy sky-blue, and that unsmiling mouth curve into a smile meant just for me. And I've heard that hard voice become mellow and murmur strange promises and predictions that touched something in me even while I was pulling away.

'Good. You're here,' he snaps.

*Nice to see you too!*

Actually, I prefer this Andrei. I can deal with a bad-tempered, selfish, spoilt Andrei. I find it harder to know what to do with a softer, sweeter, more human, more vulnerable Andrei.

*Stop it. Don't go there. Don't even think about it.*

Just then I notice that Andrei is not alone. There's a woman behind him, dressed in a long black coat and the round dark fur hat I've seen on so many people here. Wisps of fair hair are escaping from beneath the soft fur, and her face is pale and fine below. She is expressionless, and keeps one hand resting on a large leather bag that she wears with the strap across her body. I notice that she's quite a bit taller than I am.

*We've got company?* My heart sinks. This will put an obstacle in the path of talking to Andrei about Mark.

Andrei gestures to his companion. 'Beth, this is Maria. She's my assistant today. Come with me, we're leaving immediately.'

I fall in obediently behind Maria, and we follow Andrei out, looking like a rather comical trio of large, medium and small. The car is just outside and a moment later we're back in its delightful warmth. I shiver after my brief experience of the freezing air outside. I don't think I've ever been anywhere as cold as St Petersburg. Thank goodness Andrei didn't feel like a trip to Siberia.

Andrei and Maria talk as we set off, and they talk for the rest of the hour-and-a-half journey, but as every word is in Russian, I understand nothing. I concentrate hard for a while, attempting to decipher what I'm hearing, but it's pointless. Maria has taken a notebook out of her capacious bag and is scrawling across the pages in what looks like impenetrable scribble.

As we leave the most prosperous part of St Petersburg, the lights become less golden and gaudy. It's almost dark already, and I feel suddenly very tired. Leaning my head back against the leather headrest, I can't fight the sudden weight in my eyelids, and the inner pull towards unconsciousness. I try to stay awake, but I simply can't.

When I come to, we've pulled to a halt in a small car park in front of a large, grey, institutional-looking building.

'Come on, sleepy,' Andrei says, his voice rough but not unkind. 'We're here. You'll be woken up by what's inside, don't worry about that.'

I shake my head to dislodge the sleepiness, a little bewildered. A moment ago I was lost in a vivid dream in which I was at home, arguing with my mother about something. What was it? Oh yes, she was telling me to come home. 'You've been away long enough,' she was saying sternly. 'I don't like it, Beth!' and I was exasperated, trying to explain that I couldn't just come home, I had to wait for Andrei's private plane and . . .

'Come on, Beth!' snaps Andrei.

The driver is holding the door open. I climb out, burrowing down into my coat as hard as I can. The cold is cruel, biting through my coat and clothes as though they're not even there. I need to get out of this bitterness soon; my feet are already numb from the icy ground and my skin is prickling all over in protest at the sensation of freezing air sucking out all its warmth.

Andrei leads the way along a path around to the front of the building, and Maria and I follow, concentrating on not skidding on the path, which is still icy despite being well gritted. At the front door, the building looks even bleaker, its four grey storeys stretching up, with shutters closed and not much sign of life anywhere.

'Where are we?' I ask, not able to keep my mouth shut any longer.

'You'll see,' Andrei replies shortly. He presses a button mounted at the side of the doorway. I think I can hear noise from behind the thick door, a kind of high-pitched wailing. Then, a moment later, the door is pulled open and a middle-aged, grey-haired woman is standing there, dumpy in a plain skirt and jumper, starkly outlined against the flood of light coming from inside. She sees Andrei and gives a big gasp, her eyes widening and her mouth broadening into a smile. The next moment, she has begun to chatter excitedly in Russian and, to my astonishment, she has flung her arms around Andrei, despite his bulky coat, and is hugging him tightly.

From within the building comes more high-pitched

chattering and noise: the babble of voices and the sound of small shoes, scraping chairs, clattering feet on stairs. We must be visiting a school or . . .

We're going inside. The woman has released Andrei and is now pulling him by the hand while she calls out loudly to the people inside the building. Maria is beside me, a big smile illuminating her pale, rather sharp face. Now I'm beginning to guess and, as soon as we step into the large, brightly lit hall, blessedly warm compared to the chill outside, I know for sure.

Around sixty children aged from about three to around ten have grouped themselves in the hallway at the foot of a staircase. They are muttering, whispering and fidgeting but as we stand in front of them, they fall silent, and sixty pairs of eyes turn to another figure, a woman standing in front of them, who lifts her hands, counts them in and begins to conduct as the childish voices suddenly soar into song.

I don't recognise the tune or understand any words, but the song is absolutely beautiful. I think it must be something to do with Christmas, but perhaps that's because I can see that there are strings of home-made chains made from shiny paper strung from the walls and twisted up the stair rail. Of course, Christmas is coming . . . it's December already.

The children have a shabby look about them, with their well-worn trousers, skirts and jumpers, but they are clean and bright-faced. I watch the very littlest, the ones with angel faces, who don't yet know their words but are singing along as best they can. Then I see the older ones, earnest, missing teeth, concentrating hard as they watch the teacher, or being distracted by a friend's nudging elbow or an enticing bit of fallen paper chain. There are all sorts of children: pigtailed girls, girls with flowing hair pinned with sparkly clips, girls with thick glasses, girls in trousers and girls in dresses. There are boys with buzz cuts, boys with ponytails and others with mullet affairs. There are angelic-looking boys, and boys with bruises and grazes, plump-cheeked lads and gaunt, skinny things who look like they could eat all day and still be hungry. All are singing.

I look over at Andrei and I'm amazed. He's smiling in a way I've never seen before: broad, open and full of pride and pleasure. He's clutching his hands in front of him and rising up slightly on his toes in time to the music. He looks as pleased as any father at his child's carol concert.

So this is Andrei's orphanage. He told me on the plane that he sponsors an orphanage, and that his wish is to make the place as full of colour and fun as he can, so that it's not like the grim place where he grew up. I look around: yes, despite the functionality of the place, there's colour too. Plenty of it. Pictures are everywhere, bright cushions are on chairs, there are patterned rugs on the grey linoleum floor. It's a cheerful place, despite having the unmistakeable air of an institution rather than a home.

I look back at the children. Which one would Andrei have been most like? That round-faced, blue-eyed boy singing his heart out? Then I see a boy at the back. He's about ten and taller than the others, so he's tucked himself away where he can't be noticed. Perhaps he's shy about his height, or doesn't like singing. He's thin-faced, probably because he's growing so fast, and he's singing through barely moving lips, as though he's doing it because he has to. The boy's expression is unreadable and then he glances over at Andrei and his face takes on a look of absolute hero worship.

I'm blinking back tears as the song comes to an end and the children look to Andrei with their bright eager faces. He gives a great booming laugh, and claps his hand, his applause muffled by his big gloves. He says something in Russian, which makes the children smile, and I can tell he's praising them. Then he makes another announcement as he pulls his gloves off, one that makes the children gasp and chatter excitedly. The middle-aged woman who greeted us at the door bustles forward and begins giving out loud instructions. Within a few minutes, the children are neatly seated on the floor, and Andrei is speaking to them. I can't follow what he's saying, but the children often pipe up with an answer to his questions, and he makes them laugh too. As he speaks, their faces get brighter and happier, and then they all make an 'oooooh' noise and turn to look at the front door. It opens at that moment, and in comes a huge Christmas tree, already decorated and being care-fully carried in its tub by two men in overalls.

The children laugh and clap as it's taken across the hall and put in a place of honour. A plug is inserted into a socket and the switch turned on, and the children sigh with delight as the lights spring into twinkling life. It looks beautiful, hung with baubles and chocolates, and topped with a golden star.

A chair is produced and Andrei sits down on it. Another workman appears carrying a huge sack and, under Maria's direction, he puts it down next to Andrei. I sidle over to the wall, and find a chair where I can sit down and watch. It's a beautiful hour to witness. Andrei calls out name after name and each time a child excitedly clambers to their feet, picks their way to the front and comes to Andrei to receive a gift from the sack. The room is soon split between those clutching a present and those waiting in tense desperation to have their name called. Every one, from the tiniest fat-kneed three-year-old to the skinniest ten-year-old, gets summoned for a quick word with Andrei and the presentation of a gift. The boy who had stared adoringly at Andrei during the singing can barely speak when it's his turn, he's so overcome, but Andrei shakes his hand in a manly way, claps him on the back and sends him back to his seat elated.

*So that's what he's doing. He's giving them a father figure. Someone to love. Someone to please.*

I've never seen Andrei look like this before. He's transfigured. He's been smiling non-stop for over an hour now, which has to be a record. He's blossoming in the company of these parentless children. He knows them, understands them, because he was one himself.

Maria is ticking off names and making further notes.

The presentation is over. The children are sent back upstairs, perhaps to open their presents somewhere else. Then Andrei, Maria and I are led by the woman who must be the head of the orphanage to a comfortable sitting room warmed by a fire in the grate, and given hot sweet black tea in decorated glasses.

Other orphanage staff are there. People are perfectly nice to me, smiling when I catch their eyes, offering me more tea and peppery sweet biscuits from a plate, but I can't understand the flowing conversation. I observe the goodwill towards Andrei though, and the genuine warmth and pleasure in his company, and I find I'm enjoying myself, despite everything. After a sociable thirty minutes or so, Andrei rises to his feet, and the whole room follows suit. The head of the orphanage makes a speech and then kisses Andrei on both cheeks. He says a few words of his own and then next moment, they are walking arm in arm to the front door, with Maria and me following and the rest of the staff behind us. It's now pitch black outside. Stars are twinkling in the inky-black sky. The final farewells are said and I can smell that unmistakeable school-dinner smell wafting out of a kitchen somewhere. So it's the same here in Russia as it is at home. I imagine all those children sitting down in their dining hall, waiting for their stew and dumplings or whatever they're having, each one with a shiny new present upstairs. Then I follow Andrei back along the path to where the driver is waiting.

On the return journey, Maria sits in the front with the driver, separated from us by the glass partition. 'Well?'

asks Andrei as the car begins its smooth journey back to St Petersburg.

I smile at him. 'That was lovely! All those children – you made them all so happy!'

'I visit them when I can. It's not often, I'm always on the move and don't have the time.'

'Were you giving them Christmas presents?'

'Well, not exactly. Christmas is a little different here. It was as good as banned when I was young in the Soviet era, but even our government understood the value of a festival in the depths of winter, so celebrations moved to New Year instead. It's when Grandfather Frost, our version of your Father Christmas, comes to hand out gifts and we decorate trees and so on. I told the children that we were having our New Year a little early, that's all.'

'So you don't have Christmas on the 25th of December?' I ask, surprised. I know there are different traditions all over the world, of course, but still, it's hard to imagine Christmas not happening on that date.

'We do,' Andrei says with a smile, 'it's just that our 25th of December falls on your 7th of January because of the old calendar in the Orthodox Church.'

'Oh, I see,' I say, though I'm still slightly confused. Then I remember the look of joy on the little faces as they received their gifts. I say softly, 'Those children owe you a lot.'

His blue eyes, less fiery than usual, slide over and lock on mine. 'It's the least I can do. I've got plenty of money and no children of my own. It's right to give something to those children who, like me, are parentless.'

I feel a shiver of something like a sob in my throat. I can't help thinking of my own warm, loving home, with it shambolic cosiness and the tumbled possessions of my two brothers and me. I can't imagine life without my mother to turn to and my father's support. I can't imagine how I would feel or who I would be if I hadn't had their unconditional love all my life. I can see the bright young faces of those children singing, candid and innocent, and can't bear to think that none of them have a mother or father to tuck them in at night, to kiss their cheeks and tell them they're loved. My nose starts burning and tingling and I can feel treacherous tears burst out, blurring my vision.

'Are you all right?' Andrei asks softly.

'Yes.' It comes out choked, and I hope he won't keep questioning me or I might lose it completely. I feel his hand on mine and he squeezes it gently.

'Don't be upset,' he says. 'They're happy really. I saw a lot of new faces today. That means lots of the children have been found families. That's what we work towards – finding loving places for them to go, and providing them with a big, comfortable home in the meantime. They're being educated and well provided for.'

His hand is huge and warm over mine. It's astonishing how quickly and how constantly I have to revise my opinion of this man. This morning I thought he had shown me his true colours with his decision to blame

Mark and me for the painting. Now I think I've seen the real Andrei, the little boy inside that grown man's body. The kind-hearted soul who wants nothing more than to play Father Christmas for orphans and give something back.

'Beth?'

I look up at him. In the gloom of the car's interior, it's hard to read his expression. His eyes are glittering at me and although he's not smiling, his craggy features seem soft and almost kind.

'Yes?'

'I'm glad you were there today. I knew you'd understand.'

I don't reply but turn to look back at the vast black landscape beyond the car window, out towards the far-off flickering lights of St Petersburg.

# CHAPTER THREE

Back at the hotel, there's only a short time to collect my things before we're on our way to the airport.

Maria doesn't reappear, so it's just Andrei and me in the back seat of the car. I feel that this is my last opportunity to say something to him about the Fra Angelico, but I'm not sure how to broach it. I'm so grateful to be heading home that I don't want to cause any trouble. Part of me thinks I should just keep quiet and let things unfold in their own way. But then I see Mark's thin face, his eyes full of trust and confidence in me and in Andrei. I can't bear for all that to be shattered.

While I'm dithering, we arrive at the airport and then everything starts happening. We're taken to Andrei's jet and within moments we're boarding. It's good to be back inside its luxurious interior and I realise with an inner laugh that the last three times I've travelled have been by private and very expensive plane.

*Beth Villiers, you're getting spoilt!*

But I know that next time I'll be back on a budget flight, crammed into a narrow seat and drinking bad coffee just like everyone else. I may as well enjoy this while I can.

I'm elated as the plane takes off. We're going home. I long to be back there and away from the strange atmosphere between Andrei and me. I was worried when I arrived that Andrei would somehow attempt to approach me but he hasn't done that. I suppose now that he's so furious about the painting, that's out of the question. He won't want anything to do with me any more.

*So why did he bother taking me to the orphanage? It was like he still wanted to impress me somehow. Maybe he just can't help showing off and I was a captive audience.*

I glance over at Andrei. He's been taking calls on his mobile the whole way from the city to here and at last he's put his phone down, switching it off for take-off. He's staring right at me, his eyes hooded and unreadable. *How long has he been doing that?*

I know I have the unfortunate characteristic of showing whatever I'm thinking all over my face; inscrutability is not my strong point.

'Are you all right, Beth?' he asks. 'Dinner will be served soon. In a few hours you'll be back in London.'

'And what happens then?' I venture. 'Once we're back?'

'What do you mean?'

I gaze at him, hardly knowing where to start. I don't want to antagonise him – the whole idea is to soften his heart, not anger him. 'It was amazing to watch you with those children today,' I begin. 'You were such a different person – I saw your goodness and kindness.'

Andrei lifts an eyebrow very slightly.

'I don't think many people get to see that,' I add.

'You're right,' he murmurs. 'Not many at all.'

'It made me remember you're a man of compassion and that's why I wanted to speak to you about Mark.' I pause, swallow hard, and then go on quickly, not wanting to lose the moment. 'I told you that Mark is ill and you were so kind about it – you wanted to get him the best consultants, pay for his treatment and do whatever you could.'

Andrei continues to stare at me and says nothing.

'But I didn't realise then how ill he was. I saw him before we came away and it's obvious that he's seriously sick. He hasn't told me exactly what it is but I'm guessing it's cancer of the throat or neck, as that's where he's having his lump removed. He went into hospital the day we came here.'

Still Andrei watches but doesn't respond. I have no idea whether this is achieving anything at all. *But I have to go on. I've started now.* I remember the smiling, laughing Andrei at the orphanage. I have to believe that is the man I'm talking to right now. I take a deep breath.

'I shouldn't have shouted at you the way I did at the Winter Palace, and I'm sorry for that. Truly I am. But I can't take back the truth of what I said: Mark has been your loyal employee for so many years, and you must know in your heart that he never wanted you to buy that painting. Please – I'm begging you – don't blame him for this. It will destroy his reputation, the thing he's built up and nurtured all these years, and the thing that matters most to him. His standing in the art world, and his reputation for integrity and knowledge, mean everything to him. If you cast aspersions on it, you'll hurt him so deeply I don't think he'll ever recover from it.'

Andrei has been like a statue all this time, but now he leans towards me.

'And you, Beth? What will it mean to you?'

I blink and hesitate. 'Well . . .' I gather my thoughts. 'It won't affect me in the same way. I'm just an assistant at the moment, but anything that hurts Mark will hurt me. And if his business fails, I could be without a job as well.'

'You're very fond of Mark, aren't you?'

'Yes. He's a good man. He's been kind to me.'

'Who else are you fond of, Beth?'

'What do you mean? My family?'

'No. I'm sure you love your family like a good daughter. I mean . . . me. Are you fond of me? Have I been kind to you?'

I don't know what to say. Is he setting some kind of trap? I think quickly and decide there's only one reply I can make. 'Yes, you've also been incredibly kind. I've had the opportunity to go places and see things I would never normally be able to. I'd like to thank you for that.'

He smiles just a little, so that his lips twitch upwards at the corners. 'I accept your thanks. And – are you fond of me?'

He's not letting me avoid his question. He wants an answer. There's only one answer I can give.

'Of course I am. We've been through a lot together.'

'We certainly have.' He looks at me hard, those blue eyes taking on the laser quality I know so well, the one that makes it feel as though he can see right inside me. 'But the truth is that you're still fond of Dominic, aren't you?'

I draw in a breath, startled by his direct question, and begin to stammer out an answer. 'I . . . well, I . . . it's complicated, I . . .'

He leans back and knits his fingers together, resting his huge hands across his chest. 'You don't need to answer. I can see it on your face. Beth, you have to forget him. He's no good for you and he's betrayed me.'

*That's not true!* I want to shout. *Just like Mark, Dominic was your loyal lieutenant. Now he wants to strike out alone and make it by himself. That's not a betrayal!* But I say nothing. This is a delicate moment and I can't antagonise him.

Andrei goes on. 'Dominic is not a man; he's a boy. He has a lot of growing up to do and he's made a very unfortunate error by turning me from a friend to an enemy. He'll discover that my sphere of influence is very much greater than he thought. I'm capable of destroying his business with a click of my fingers –' Andrei lifts one hand, his thumb and middle finger pressed together, ready to snap '– but I haven't decided whether I shall do that or not.' He lowers his hand back to his chest. 'We shall see. You're better off without him, Beth, I'm serious. You don't need a boy, you need a man.' His voice drops to a caressing murmur and his eyes become even more hooded as he gazes at me. 'I can sense possibilities in you, Beth. I always have, from the first time we met. I've never forgotten you that morning in the monastery when you walked into the room, so alive, so vibrant, setting the air around you shimmering with the power of your sensuality.'

I remember that morning too. Dominic had brought me to life in the night, setting my flesh on fire, awakening everything in me as he adored me with his body. Andrei had seen the reverberations, the aftershocks of that glorious night, and something about what they did to me had entranced him.

'Ever since then, I've known we're meant for one another.' His voice is still soft, almost hypnotic. When he talks like this, I can't stop myself becoming alert to his intense physicality: the broad-shouldered, muscled body, the magnetic charisma. 'You would know it too, Beth, if you would just let yourself accept that Dominic isn't the man for you.'

*He is, he is, he is.* My longing for Dominic is suddenly so intense I want to gasp. I long for the strength of his arms around me, the unbearably beautiful scent of his skin, the taste of his mouth as it takes possession of mine . . . the thought sends a wave of hard desire crashing through me.

Perhaps Andrei senses it. He leans towards me, his eyes burning with intensity, and says, 'You should let me make love to you. I promise you would forget your childish infatuation at once. You would know what it meant to be with a real man.'

I stare at him. He is implying that we have never made love before. And that means . . .

I speak in a rush. 'The caves, the catacombs, that night at the party . . .'

He raises an eyebrow questioningly.

'I need to ask you something. It sounds odd but I have to know. You . . . you haven't ever tried to make love to me before, have you?'

*There. I've said it. At last!* I brace myself for his reply, my heart racing and my shoulders stiff with tension.

He frowns, and an amused look crosses his face. 'I hope it would be the kind of thing you would remember, Beth.'

I don't know what to say. I do remember it but I don't know for sure who it was. 'I was drugged by Anna,' I say at last. 'Remember I told you that on the plane on the way here? I've got some strange memories and I don't know whether they're true or not.'

'Anna is certainly mischievous enough to do such a thing,' remarks Andrei. 'There are many things I won't miss about her, but she did make life interesting.' He smiles as if enjoying teasing me. 'Well, well. You have a memory of the two of us. How interesting. I wish I knew what it was. I would love to share it with you.'

I'm still confused. Does that mean he has his own memories – or none? I've come so far. I have to know

now. 'Andrei, I have some confused images of that evening. I need to know if anything at all happened between us in the caves that night.'

He stares at me, obviously stringing out the agony. Then, at last, he speaks. 'Beth – much as I would have liked something to happen between us that night, I'm afraid that nothing did. I found you passed out and I'm not into unresponsive partners. I brought you up to the surface to revive you. What did you think happened?'

'Nothing. I just had to be sure.' A great surge of relief washes through me. My conscience is clear. I did nothing to jeopardise my relationship with Dominic. *Thank goodness for that.* Then I'm instantly filled with an awful sadness. If only I'd been able to say that to him when he begged me for the truth! Why hadn't I asked Andrei sooner? It hadn't been so bad after all. *Oh my God, I've really messed up. How the hell am I going to make it right now?*

I feel a wild impulse to call Dominic immediately and make him listen while I tell him the truth: that I've always been loyal to him in my heart, and now I know for sure that I've been utterly faithful in my body too. Of course it's impossible to do it with Andrei here, listening and watching. I have to conceal my desperation and my eagerness to be home.

*Just a few more hours and I'll be free.*

I look up and Andrei's staring at me, those hooded eyes glittering darkly, almost hungrily, and a half smile on his lips. When he speaks, his voice is low, its harshness now velvety.

'Something could happen now, if you want it to, Beth.' He looks towards the back of the cabin. 'Through that door there is a bedroom, equipped with a delightfully comfortable bed with silk sheets. We could go there now and I could show you that the reality is far beyond anything you can imagine.'

My eyes widen and my hands tighten in my lap. *How did we get here?*

He leans towards me and I catch the musky scent of his cologne. I feel suddenly like a defenceless creature being approached by a stealthy, slinking tiger, keeping me hypnotised by its rippling grace while it gets close enough to pounce.

'I promise you, you would not regret it,' he murmurs. At any moment, he'll reach out and touch me. 'Anything you've dreamed, anything you've enjoyed in your fantasy . . . you can have it now, if you want it.'

The treacherous image is in my mind immediately: it is Andrei's broad naked back, my arms around it, my head thrown back as he makes love to me . . .

*Oh my God, Beth, stop it! No, no, no.* He's trying to seduce me, I mustn't listen to him. I know what I want, who I desire most in the world, and it isn't Andrei.

'Well?'

'I . . .' I shake my head. 'No. I can't.' I return his gaze but it's hard to meet his eye. I can't conceal that I'm uncomfortable, frightened even.

There's a pause and then he sighs. The electric charge in the air vanishes.

'I can see from your expression that you're nervous.' He looks almost sad as he says it. 'Don't worry, whatever you might think of me, I'm not a rapist. I don't get any kicks from unwilling women, believe me.' His voice takes on a low intensity. 'Beth, I want you to come to me full of desire, ripe and willing. And I'll wait for that. All I ask is a chance.'

I stay silent, hoping that he won't press me to say anything.

He sits back in the soft leather of his seat and regards me intently. 'You want me to protect Mark. Very well. I will protect you both. Mark is an old friend, I value him and wish him only the best. Anything I can do to help him in his present trouble, I will. And from you, Beth . . . like I say, all I ask for is a chance. Will you give me that?'

*A chance to make love to me? I can never do that. My heart is Dominic's, my body is his too. Or does he mean a chance to spend time with me?* I feel as though so much rides on my answer. He's practically telling me that Mark is safe as long as I comply.

Just then the cabin door opens and a stewardess comes through. 'Dinner is ready to be served, sir,' she says cheerfully. 'Please allow me to prepare your table.'

'Of course.' Andrei has not taken his eyes off me. Then he mouths, '*A chance?*'

I hesitate and then I nod once. What else can I do?

It's very late by the time the car drops me off at my flat and the place is in darkness. Laura must have given up on seeing me hours ago and gone to bed. I let myself in, carrying my suitcase to keep its wheels from rolling on the floor and waking her up, and get myself off to bed, worrying about the pact I've somehow agreed with Andrei. He didn't mention it again, and talked of other things as we ate our delicious meal. At the end of the journey, before we went our separate ways, he fixed me with one of those intense looks of his and said, 'I'll be in touch, Beth. I have a job for you.'

*What the hell did that mean?*

I'm exhausted but I can't sleep. Thoughts are racing around my head. I need to find Dominic and tell him what I now know for sure: that nothing happened in the catacombs between Andrei and me. That means that it was definitely Dominic, a thought that fills me with warm relief. But first, I need to see Mark. He has to know what happened in St Petersburg.

At some point, my fervid mind must have relaxed and let me sleep because I wake up groggy when my alarm goes off at eight o'clock.

'Morning!' cries Laura from the kitchen as she hears me emerge from my room. 'How was the trip?'

'Great,' I say, heading for the shower. 'But I'm glad to be back.'

'What was St Petersburg like?'

'Amazing – I'd love to go back and visit properly. I only really saw it from the back of a car.'

'I'm going to work now.' Laura comes out of the kitchen, still munching a last mouthful of cereal. She's smartly dressed and ready for her day. 'We'll catch up tonight, okay?'

'Lovely. Have a great day.' I watch her go enviously. Laura's life sometimes seems very straightforward compared to mine: a normal job in a normal office. I know her work is hard and demanding but at least there aren't the kinds of nasty surprises I've been having lately.

Once I'm dressed I wonder whether to go straight to the hospital and see Mark but I don't want to disturb him too early, so I go first to his Belgravia home from where I'm going to be helping to run the business in his absence. His maid Gianna answers the door to let me in, and then Caroline comes stomping down the stairs.

'Ah, Beth!' she calls out. Her voice is so incredibly posh that my name comes out sounding more like 'bath' which makes me want to laugh. 'How lovely to see you. How was the trip? Successful?'

'Hello, Caroline. The trip was . . . interesting. I need to fill Mark in on the details.'

Her big pink face looks solemn. 'I'm not sure whether that's going to be possible, my dear.'

Anxiety rises up in me. 'Is he all right? How was the operation?'

'They've taken out the tumour, and they think it's the primary, although they're not absolutely sure. The trouble is that they've had to take out a chunk of his tongue too, and although they grafted on some flesh to patch it up, it's left him in a great deal of pain and not able to speak – at least, not for a while.'

'Oh, poor Mark!'

'He's very ill.' Caroline looks quite grief-stricken for a moment then quickly covers it with a stoical expression. 'But I'm sure he'll pull through. He's a tough one, you know. They want to treat him with radiation once he's recovered from the op, to give him the best chance of recovery.'

'I'd like to visit him.'

'Not right now,' Caroline says, shaking her head. 'I don't think it's the right time. I know you're keen to see him but he needs complete rest for a couple of days until he's over the worst of this pain. And I don't want him upset at all so try not to worry him, won't you?'

I nod. 'Of course. I want whatever's best for Mark.'

'Thank you, dear. We all do.'

Sitting in Mark's beautiful circular office, I feel very low. He should be here at his impressive desk, laughing and joking as we go through the morning's post together. It doesn't feel right that I'm the one in the walnut chair, slitting open envelopes with Mark's engraved silver letter opener. There's no way I can tell him that the painting is a fake, not now. He would be distraught, and I can't risk that while he's so ill.

I suddenly realise that I'm caught in Andrei's trap after all. I can't afford for him to decide to throw Mark to the wolves and he must have guessed that when he asked for that chance.

*So much for the friend of orphans and giver of gifts. He's out for what he can get after all, no matter what it takes.*

# CHAPTER FOUR

Now that I know there's no hope of seeing Mark, one thing dominates my thoughts.

I have to see Dominic, find him somehow, and tell him that I can now swear to him after all. Andrei might be trying to manipulate me into opening my mind to being with him, but he's given the most precious gift he can without even knowing it: the gift of knowing that I have stayed true to the man I love.

When I've finished the morning's work, I write an email to Dominic.

Dominic, darling,

I'm so sorry about what happened between us the other night. It was stupid and pointless and I can't believe I hurt you like that. I haven't had anything to do with Andrei, I promise on my life, and I never will. I'm yours, no one else's, you must know that. There's a reason why I couldn't swear to you – I'll tell you all when I see you, I promise. Please, please, meet me. I have to see you. I want you to know everything. We could meet at the boudoir?

All my love,

Beth

Before I send it, I also copy it as a text message. Then I press send to dispatch it through the ether to Dominic's email and phone. Surely it has to reach him one way or another.

I try to concentrate on doing odds and ends and catching up on Mark's filing, but I'm hardly able to do anything but stare at my inbox and my phone, waiting for a message to pop up.

There's nothing.

*Dominic! Please answer, please give us a chance. Don't throw everything we have away for nothing. I can't stand it . . .*

My thought messages are no more successful that the others. Nothing comes back to me and I get increasingly frantic. What am I going to do? I can't just sit here and let him walk out of my life like this. I won't let that happen. I promised myself I would fight for him so fight I will.

'Caroline!' I call as I grab my coat, 'I'm going out. I'm heading up to Bond Street.'

'Yes, dear, see you later,' comes her answer from the drawing room.

'Give my love to Mark when you see him.'

'I will.'

Outside, it's very cold. The temperature is not exactly as bad as St Petersburg but it's definitely frosty. I catch a bus up to Hyde Park Corner and then walk up through the back streets of Mayfair to Randolph Gardens. I don't know what I intend to do, exactly, except that I can't help going to where I last saw

Dominic and the only firm thing I really know about him, which is where he lives.

I march past the porter and take the lift to Dominic's floor. I almost run along the corridor to his apartment door and knock hard.

'Dominic!' I rap hard on the wood. 'Are you in there? Dominic?'

I hold my breath and hear footsteps inside approaching the door. I'm filled with wild happiness. *He's here, I can speak to him, tell him everything, make him listen to me . . .*

The door opens.

'Dominic, thank God— oh.' I'm not looking at the face I long to see so much but into a pair of dark brown eyes that belong to a lady in domestic overalls holding a polishing rag.

'Yes?' she says.

'Is Mr Stone in?' I ask weakly but I can already guess the answer.

She shakes her head and says in a strong foreign accent, 'No one here. I'm cleaning but no one here.'

'Do you know when he'll be back?'

'Uh uh,' she says, still shaking her head.

'Can I come in for a moment?'

She lets me in reluctantly and I walk into the apartment, not sure what I think I'll find here. I just want to feel close to Dominic, but as I go into the elegant sitting room I feel further away from him than ever. This place is full of his absence. It doesn't feel as though he's just popped out but as though he's packed up and left, not intending to be back for a while.

I walk around the room, looking at familiar objects and remembering the time I've spent here with Dominic. The spanking chair is gone, the one where I saw Vanessa paddling a man I thought was Dominic. I wonder where he's put it.

I notice that on the table is a brochure, a glossy piece of corporate cardboard. I pick it up. It reads *Finlay Venture Capital* and under some stock photographs of smiling businessmen in a smart boardroom, there's some blurb about how this company likes to invest in the future and discover amazing new ways to make money. The contact details are printed at the bottom, somewhere in the City where most big-money business is based.

'Can I help you?' asks the cleaning lady. She's come in and is watching me, obviously uncomfortable that she's let me in.

I put the brochure down. 'No . . . no. Thank you. I'm leaving now. Thanks for your help.'

*This is crazy. What the hell am I doing?*

I hailed a taxi on South Audley Street that's now threading its way through Mayfair and heading east. As we roar along, I realise that London has become very Christmassy. Lights are up everywhere, and all the shop windows are decorated with snowflakes and themed displays. Christmas is only a few weeks away now. I haven't decided what I'm doing, but I can't imagine anything other than going home to be with my family. I yearn for them as soon as I think of them all. I can't wait to be there, waking up in my old room, with a stocking stiff and knobbly at the end of my bedpost. Mum still makes sure we all get a stocking when we're home even though we're grown up.

I stare out of the window as the taxi takes short cuts and back ways and gets us up to New Oxford Street, and onto the main road heading east. We pass Holborn and then suddenly we're in the skyscraper part of town, where big business is conducted in steel-and-glass penthouses hundreds of floors up, where gambles are made on trading floors, and huge law firms rake in money by supervising and tying together the thousands of deals made every week.

We don't stop in front of any of the great modern edifices, or the venerable old stone buildings. Instead the taxi driver guides the cab down incredibly narrow streets and into a small cobbled square where some red-brick Victorian buildings have been converted into funky-looking offices.

The driver looks over his shoulder at me. 'Here you are, miss! Tanner Square.'

'Thank you.'

I pay him and get out. I'm wondering now more than ever what the hell I'm doing here. But what have I got to lose? I shake out my shoulders and walk purposefully towards the offices at number 11.

Inside there is a glossy white reception desk with bright blue lettering on the front of it that reads 'Finlay

Venture Capital'. A receptionist looks up at me. 'Yes, can I help you?'

I stare at her, not knowing what to say. I should have planned this before I came in but it's a bit late now.

The receptionist frowns. 'Do you have an appointment?'

'I . . . I . . . Not exactly.'

'I'm afraid that you'll have to leave if you don't have an appointment to see someone.' Her voice is turning frosty.

'No, please, I really need to see someone – anyone, really, someone in charge . . .'

'What seems to be the trouble?' It's a deep male voice coming from my left. I turn to see a young man with glasses and a dark brown beard standing there. He's casual in jeans and an open-necked shirt with a jumper. 'Can I help you with anything?'

His eyes are friendly enough and I make the sudden decision to trust him. 'Yes – I hope so. I'm looking for Dominic Stone and I wondered if he might be here.'

The man looks surprised. 'Dominic? That's strange. He was just here. He left about twenty minutes ago.'

'Oh no!' I can't help crying out in frustration. 'Do you know where he's gone?'

He gives me a puzzled look. 'What's this about? I can't just give you his whereabouts. I've no idea who you are.'

I stare at him pleadingly. I can't begin to explain out here in public and, to my relief, he seems to grasp this, as he suddenly beckons me into his office.

'Look, come in here.'

I follow him into a small office full of modern gadgetry and sit down in the chair the man gestures to while he takes a seat behind the desk.

He says, 'I'm Tom Finlay, by the way. Who are you?'

'I'm Beth Villiers and I'm Dominic's friend.'

'Hmm.' He gives me an amused look over the top of his glasses. 'His special friend?'

I flush. 'Well . . . it's complicated. But yes, we're involved. I really need to see him, to explain something. I made a mistake, and I have to put it right.'

'Well, well.' Tom Finlay smiles at me. 'I'm glad to hear it's romance and not some business disaster, considering I've just agreed to invest a sizeable sum in Dominic's company.'

'His company is up and running already?' I say, surprised.

Tom nods. 'It sounds like it was all up and ready to go. He was just waiting for release from his old employment and the cash injection he needed to get started. He's hitting the ground at a sprint.'

I smile. That sounds like Dominic. I'm seized with a longing to be with him. Perhaps it shows on my face because Tom says, 'Look, I wouldn't normally give out any information about a client or business partner, but you look pretty desperate.'

'I am!' I say quickly. 'He's not returning my calls or emails.'

'Oh?' He frowns. 'Have you thought about the possibility that maybe he's not interested?'

I see with a touch of panic that I've given him the idea that maybe Dominic doesn't want anything to do with me and that I'm a troublesome stalker. 'No, no, he doesn't know what I have to tell him. He'll want to know, I promise! I'm not crazy. Please tell me what you know about where he is.'

Tom considers.

I make myself sound calm. 'Honestly, you'll be doing Dominic a favour. And me.'

He sits back in his chair and smiles. 'You know what? You seem like a sane person to me. Dominic's big enough to look after himself.' Tom picks up a pen and twiddles it absent-mindedly as he speaks. 'He's finding investors for his company. He's got some great ideas and he's looking for five or six people to come in with him, each one putting in a sizeable amount of money. He's off to Paris today to meet a very big fish who lives there, to see if he can hook him.'

'Paris?'

Tom nods. 'That's right.' He looks at his watch. 'In fact I think he said he was catching the two o'clock train from St Pancras. If you hurry, you might catch him there.'

I had thought that the day couldn't get any crazier but here I am in another taxi, heading north-west this time. My new driver doesn't seem to be quite as keen on racing along buzzy little back routes as the last cabbie was, and we crawl along the road towards Old Street, making sure that we hit every red light and give way to every bus and pedestrian that shows even the slightest desire to pass in front of us. I'm nearly biting my knuckles with frustration. I stare at my watch, trying to work out the times. The train departs at two, so Dominic will need to check in at least thirty minutes beforehand. But he left Finlay twenty minutes before I arrived, so he would have possibly already got to St Pancras before I left Tanner Square. He's bound to have checked in. He's probably going business class, which means he'll be able to use the business lounge so that's where he'll be – unless for some reason, he's hanging around outside and I can catch him before he goes through the gate. I have to get there before one thirty at the latest and it's ten past one now.

We finally get around the Old Street roundabout and head towards King's Cross, but we're still stopping at every traffic light along the way. We can't seem to hit a green. I'm almost bouncing up and down on my seat with a frantic desire to get the taxi moving faster. At last I can see the huge King's Cross terminus and the imposing Gothic facade of the St Pancras hotel. It's nearly twenty past one. Just over ten minutes to go. It's agonising as we wait to make the right turn down to the Eurostar entrance but at last we're pulling to a halt in front of it. I rummage in my purse for the money to pay the fare and then jump out of the cab and race inside.

The entrance to the Eurostar is crowded with people. There's a train to Brussels leaving in an hour and the bulk of passengers are checking in. I scan the crowd urgently for Dominic but there's no sign of him. Why would he wait in this scrum when he could be in the quiet and peace of the business lounge? Why did I ever think anything else? I glance up hastily and see on the departure screen that the train to Paris is boarding. There are only a few minutes left. Any minute now he'll be leaving London and I'll have lost him. I open my bag and check the inner compartment. Yes, there it is. My passport. I haven't removed it since returning from Russia. I run to the ticket machines behind me and start tapping at the screen, making lightning decisions. I pull out my credit card and press in the numbers with clumsy fingers that have gone all stiff and disobedient.

'Come on, come on!' I mutter, trying not to shout. 'Come on . . . please!'

And then the transaction goes through. The machine starts to whirr as it prints my ticket and spits it out into the dispenser. I scrabble for it and then race over to the ticket barrier. I don't bother with the ticket reader but hand my ticket straight to the inspector standing there so he can open the gate for me to race through. I can see there's a queue at the baggage inspection ahead – will I still be in time to make the train? After all, I don't have any luggage except for my handbag. The inspector takes my ticket, looks at it and then at the screen. He silently gestures to it and I look up. The screen for the two o'clock train reads 'Check-in closed'.

'You're too late,' he says mournfully.

'Please, please let me through!' I beg. 'Please, it's only one minute!'

He shakes his head. 'I can't. Against the rules. Let in one, you have to let in them all. If one minute, why not two or three? Nope. Sorry.'

I stare aghast at the ticket in my hand. It's useless. I've just spent three hundred pounds on this bit of cardboard.

The inspector looks at me sympathetically. 'Listen, I saw you buy the ticket. You take it to the main office around the corner there, and tell them I sent you. You missed the train by one minute. Ask them to change the ticket to the next train. You can still get to Paris.'

*But will I have come to my senses by three o'clock?*

I look at the ticket again. One way to the Gare du Nord. It's eating me up that the train hasn't departed yet, that Dominic is still in the station but I can't get near him.

*What the hell? What have I got to lose?*

I look up at the inspector. 'Where did you say I can find the main ticket office?'


Once on the Eurostar with my newly changed ticket, I settle into my seat and look about me. The train is filling up quickly. It's that time of year, I suppose. Christmas seems to be a good excuse for people to nip over to a foreign city for shopping or a treat. I can see couples, some of them older, perhaps celebrating an anniversary or going for a special jaunt to Paris, the city of romance. People in suits, clearly travelling for work, are already opening up laptops or looking at their tablets. There are plenty of French people returning home and others who will be going onwards into Europe. A young family sits near me, the mother taking out plastic tubs filled with grapes and rice cakes for her small children.

I take out my mobile and call Caroline. She doesn't answer, so I leave a message explaining that I'm going to be away from the office this afternoon and I'll call later to see how Mark is. Then I call Laura at her office.

'You're *where*?' she says disbelievingly when I tell her what I'm doing.

'On the Eurostar at St Pancras, about to leave for Paris.'

'Are you totally insane? Why?'

'Because Dominic is in Paris. He left on the train before this one. He's probably under the Channel right about now.'

'And you think you're going to find him?' Laura's voice is completely incredulous. 'Just stumble across him? In the whole of Paris, you're going to go straight to him? Beth, get off the train now and chalk it down to a moment of madness.'

'No,' I say. 'I can find him. I'm sure of it.'

'How?'

'I'll think of something.'

'But when will you come back?'

'The last train goes around nine, I think,' I say vaguely. I haven't researched this yet. 'I can probably get on that.'

'Good God, Beth, you got back from St Petersburg in the early hours of this morning! Now you might be

55

home from Paris at some ungodly hour tonight!' Then she sounds wistful. 'It sounds kind of fun, though. I wish I could come with you.'

'Me too! But listen, I'll keep you informed, okay? Don't worry about me. I'll be fine.'

'Beth, I wish I could be so sure. Just be careful.'

'I'll be fine,' I say again, firmly. I almost believe it myself.

Once I've rung off, I use my phone to look up the return times from Paris. If I can't get back, I might have to find somewhere to stay, so I also look up some hotels in central Paris. I feel a tingle of excitement. This is mad but it's making me feel exhilarated with possibilities. I'm not going to let Dominic walk out of my life thinking that I cheated on him. He's going to know the truth if it's the last thing that happens between us.

I remember that I don't have a phone charger with me, so I turn off my mobile to save its battery and then open a magazine that I bought in the shop on my way through the departure lounge. I don't quite know how I'm going to be able to calm down enough to absorb anything but maybe that's okay. Within three hours I'll be in Paris.

Once we're under way, I feel the tiredness from my late night begin to overwhelm me and I take the opportunity to sleep as we fly through the Kent countryside and onwards to France. By the time I wake up, we're making fast progress to Paris. There's only another half an hour to go. Once I've woken up and had a drink of water, I start to realise what I've actually done. In a short time, I'll be arriving at the Gare du Nord – and then what? I won't have a clue where to go.

I think for a while and then turn my phone on. It connects to a French network and a text message pings in, telling me I'm now abroad and alerting me to the new charges. I find the phone number for Finlay Venture Capital online and call it. The receptionist puts me through to Tom Finlay.

'Hello?'

'Tom, it's Beth here. We spoke earlier about Dominic.'

'Yes, of course, I remember you. Did you catch him?'

'No – I was too late. So, I know it sounds crazy but I've followed him to Paris.'

He laughs. 'Oh God, I knew I shouldn't have helped you. You're a nutter, aren't you? Great, Dominic's really going to thank me for this one.'

'He will,' I say quickly. 'You don't know how much. But listen, I have a problem. I don't know where he's going to be and I'd like to surprise him. Is there any way you can find out a little bit more for me?'

'Why don't you just call him?'

'I told you – he's not returning texts or emails.'

'Yeah, but he might pick up if you actually call him.'

'Maybe . . . I will try that but could you possibly help from your end? Please?'

'Look, I'll do what I can. Shall I tell him you're look-ing for him?'

'No, no, I want to surprise him.'

'Okay – leave it with me. Are you on email?'

'Yes.' I give him my email address, and we ring off. I sit back, satisfied. If all goes well, I won't have to waste my time wandering around Paris looking for Dominic, I'll be able to go straight to him.

We're already on the outskirts of Paris when I get a message from Tom flashing up on my phone. I go to my inbox.

Hi Beth

I think Dominic must be in his meeting with this big business honcho. He wants around twenty million dollars from him, so I don't think he's going to be taking any calls while he's asking for it. If it's any help, I've been thinking back over what he said today and I'm pretty sure he told me he was going to be meeting this guy at his flat in St Germain and that he was going to stay in the same area, so you could try around there. I'll let you know when I hear from Dominic.

Take care,

Tom

Good work, Tom, I think. It's annoying that Dominic hasn't replied directly but at least I've narrowed it down to one part of Paris. I'm going to need a charger, I realise. My phone is not going to take much more Internet use without losing all its power. That will be my first task when we get to the Gare du Nord.

\*     \*     \*

Twenty minutes later, I'm walking along the platform with all the other arrivals as we make our way to the front of the station. I've been to Paris once before on a school trip and I'm instantly taken back to that time by the musical bongs that accompany every single station announcement. I can't understand a word of the French but I'm elated that I've made it here. I find a cashpoint and get some euros out with my bank card, then locate a phone kiosk and manage to make the man there understand that I want a charger for my phone. A few minutes later, I'm the proud owner of a charger wired for European sockets. First mission accomplished. At another tourist kiosk, I get a map of Paris and another of the metro. I'm making big strides.

I find a quiet corner where I can look at the maps and work out where I need to go. With a little help from some Internet research, I locate the St Germain area and the nearest metro line. Good. No point in waiting around. That's where I'll go.

The Paris metro is so different to the London Underground but it's fairly easy to find my way around. I decide to go to the station of St Germain-des-Prés, as it sounds as though it's right on the money, so I make my way down into the metro station, get a ticket from a booth with my terrible schoolgirl French, and take the dark pink Line 4 eleven stops down to St Germain-des-Prés. The square train comes roaring along almost immediately, and I get on wondering if I look lost to the other commuters, not that any of them are taking a blind bit of notice of me. I feel elated as the train passes through each romantically named station – Château d'Eau, Châtelet, Cité – and takes me closer to Dominic. I get off at St Germain-des-Prés and, as I emerge from the station, I realise that my task is going to be harder because night has fallen. It's one hour ahead here and it's already early evening but the lights of Paris are lit and, just like London, there are glittering Christmas decorations everywhere. I'm on a square dominated by a large church, its steeple floodlit and piercing the navy blue sky like a great grey-gold dart.

I can hardly breathe with excitement. Here I am, in Paris! I'm standing on a beautiful square that's edged by the lighted windows of cafés and bars, there are people walking about and it feels incredibly French. Now all I have to do is find Dominic. How hard can that be? I take out my phone and check it. Nothing from Tom yet. I'll go to a café and see if I can charge my phone up there while I have a cup of coffee and think what to do.

I approach the nearest café and instantly feel intimidated. It's full of business people checking their phones while they drink coffee or a glass of wine, and beautiful women, some with little lapdogs tucked into huge handbags. I'm far too shy to go into a place like this. I make my way out of the square and round the corner and wander along the road for a bit until I see a quieter, cosy-looking place called Chez Albert, with tables outside tucked under warm outdoor heaters. I gather my courage and sit down at one of the empty tables. A waiter comes up and says something in rapid French.

'*Café au lait, s'il vous plaît*,' I say in halting French, and he goes off to get my coffee.

The disadvantage of being outside is that there's nowhere to charge my phone. I might have to move inside later and do that, but I like being out here with the chance that Dominic might walk by. I imagine him now in this important man's flat, inspiring him with his rhetoric and passion to invest millions of dollars in his new company.

*If anyone can do it, Dominic can.*

The waiter comes back with a black coffee accompanied by a jug of hot milk, and puts it down beside me, along with a bill. I glance at it. Five euros for a cup of coffee! Well, I suppose it's like going into a café in Knightsbridge – it's going to be expensive no matter what.

*What will I do if I can't find Dominic?* It's not a problem, I tell myself firmly. I'll take the Eurostar home or find a hotel, if necessary. But considering other alternatives doesn't seem to be necessary. Something tells me I'm going to find him. And then my phone, down to its last bar of power, flashes into life. It's an email from Tom.

# CHAPTER FIVE

I'm in the lobby of a smart boutique hotel off an elegant
street in St Germain. It's clear that this part of Paris is
very expensive and I haven't yet dared ask the cost of a
room as the white wine I'm sipping has cost me almost
a tenner. Tom came through with the name of the hotel
where Dominic is staying and I found it with the help
of my map app. After a trip to the ladies to spruce
myself up, I'm sitting here in the lobby on a very
comfortable striped sofa, flicking back through my
magazine while I enjoy my drink and surreptitiously
observe all the comings and goings in the hotel lobby.
It's a comfortable place to be but I hope Dominic turns
up soon because I don't know how many glasses of
wine I can afford – or manage – to drink before he gets
here.

*What if he's going out for dinner and won't be back
till late? How long will they let me sit here? And
besides, I'm starving.*

I haven't had a proper meal all day, I realise. I try not
to think about all the marvellous restaurants that must
be within a few minutes' walk, each serving up delicious
French food . . . my stomach rumbles longingly.

Suddenly food is the last thing on my mind. I feel it

before I see anything. Like an animal scenting thunder, I am alert to something in the air and every hair on my skin prickles with it. I know beyond doubt, without looking, that the chemistry of the room has altered and that something glorious is happening. It's as though the room is full of a delicious aroma, or the most divine music has suddenly begun to play, and it fills me with joy.

*He's here. I know it.*

I turn my head towards the hotel entrance, feeling as if I'm moving in slow motion. I have complete faith in what I'm feeling. I'm responding to the presence I love most in the world, how can he not be there?

*Dominic.*

He's come in through the outer door and is walking through the small lobby, talking on his phone as he goes to the desk to collect a key. The sight of him makes me quite dizzy and weak. It's not so long since I last saw him but it feels like for ever. My last glimpse of his face was when he was angry, hopeless and bitter but now he looks serious and intense as he listens to whoever is on the other end of the line.

*My God, he's gorgeous* . . . Sometimes he has the power to hit me afresh with the strength of his attractiveness. His olive skin is darkened by a shadow of stubble around his jaw, his brown eyes are fixed on the ground as he listens, and his mouth, so beautiful with its hint of the wicked pirate in its curve, makes me want to leap up and kiss him. He looks delicious in a dark grey suit, his white shirt tieless and unbuttoned at the neck.

I don't know what I thought I might do when I saw him but I try to stand up, only to find my legs buckling underneath me. He has his key and has turned towards me, heading past the small sofa where I'm sitting. In a moment he will walk straight past me and not even notice I'm here. He's deep in his conversation and oblivious to everything. I force myself onto my feet. My hands are shaking and my stomach is whirling and churning like a washing machine. I feel light-headed and giddy, but also triumphant. So I found him – with Tom's help, of course, but I found him!

He's so close to me now, I can almost reach out and touch him. I have to speak or he'll be gone.

'Dominic,' I say, but it comes out like a soft whisper lost in the echo of the lobby. I gather my breath and say again more loudly, '*Dominic!*'

He hears me. He turns his head to look at me. His brown eyes lock onto mine. He stops walking and I can see astonishment covering his face. His mouth drops open and he lets the phone fall from his ear as he says wonderingly, 'Beth?' He looks suddenly both surprised and happy.

'I'm sorry to surprise you, but I had to see you. We have to talk!' I'm still standing, caught between the sofa and the low table where my drink is sitting on a white circle of paper.

Dominic remembers himself and lifts his phone back to his ear. 'Richard, do you mind if I call you back later?

Something's come up. Thanks.' He slips his phone into his pocket as he stares at me, still in shock. The happy look fades and a frown creases his brow. 'What are you doing here? Did you know I was going to be here?'

I nod. 'Yes. I know it seems extreme, jumping out at you like this in a hotel lobby, but I had to see you. Please – can we talk?'

His expression is cooling by the second. He's remembering what happened when we last saw one another. 'I don't want another row, Beth. I think we said all we needed to say in London. You know how I feel.'

'Dominic,' I say urgently. 'Everything's changed. I promise. You must believe me.'

'Must I?' He's beginning to look hostile. I have to save this situation before it's too late.

'Yes. I know things I didn't know before.'

'Like whether or not you've had anything to do with . . .' He can't bring himself to say Andrei's name.

'Yes. Yes. You know I don't lie, you know I tell the truth. Please listen to me. Don't let us lose what we have over some stupid confusion.' I gaze at him beseechingly. 'Five minutes. Please.'

He stares down at the floor as though fighting an internal battle. 'All right,' he says after a moment. 'You've got five minutes. But that's all.'

'Here?' I ask, glancing around the hotel lobby where people are milling about and staff are keeping an interested eye on us.

He thinks for a second. 'No. We'll go to my room. Come with me.'

I follow hastily as he strides away over the marble floor towards the lifts and a moment later we are standing together in an elevator, riding up to the third floor. Dominic doesn't look at me but I can tell he's affected by my presence by the tension in his shoulders and the firm set to his lips. Standing beside him, I'm in a complete whirl. It's taking all my strength not to touch him. The desire to reach out is almost over-whelming. I long to brush my fingertips over his hand, to press my lips to that soft part of his neck below his ear and breathe in the warm scent of his skin. I can feel my body responding to his nearness with delight, making itself ready for the pleasure of his touch. I want to tell it to calm down. While my hormones are revving up and my nerve endings preparing to turn somersaults of joy, my brain is trying to overrule my excited body and tell it to stand down – nothing is certain. Yet.

The lift door slides open and we make our way down a carpeted corridor to the door of Dominic's room. As he pushes the door open, he turns on the lights inside to reveal a comfortable, elegant room. I follow him in and he turns to look at me.

'Come on then. Five minutes. I'm busy, Beth. This is a really important time for me.'

His gaze is cold. I hate seeing that look in his eyes. Has he really changed how he feels about me? Will I never see again that soft loving look or the burning intensity of desire? I don't know how I'll survive it if he stops loving me. The thought of never tasting another kiss from him twists in my chest with physical pain. I've got five minutes to win him back.

'When we last saw each other, you wanted to know whether anything had happened between Andrei and me,' I begin.

He cuts in roughly. 'And you couldn't answer. Remember?'

'I know, I know and I was an idiot. I knew I'd never wanted anything to happen. He'd made a few suggestions to me, that we might . . . that something might happen . . . but of course I always turned him down flat. Because you're all I want and need, you know that.' I gaze at him imploringly, but his eyes are still cold and his mouth unsmiling. 'The night of the party in the catacombs something very strange happened to me when we were apart. You were dancing with Anna and we were separated, but Anna came up to me and while I was distracted, she drugged my drink. I don't know what she put in it, but I'm certain she's the one who did it. She's got form, Dominic. She must have told you that she uses drugs.'

There's a flicker of reaction in his eyes but I can't tell what kind of reaction it is. I press on.

'I didn't know I was drugged but everything started to go really strange. I got very confused and then lost in the caves when I tried to find you. But you found me, didn't you? And we made love in the caves. But because of the way it happened, afterwards I had the most horrible thought that it hadn't been you, even though I'd been convinced it was. For weeks I was tormented by the fear that perhaps I'd been unfaithful to you without meaning to. I was afraid I'd made love to Andrei by accident.'

Dominic makes a sound like a bitter laugh. 'Accident!' he says quietly.

'Yes.' I take a step towards him. 'Please, you must believe me. When you asked me to swear, I desperately wanted to because I knew that in my heart I've always been utterly faithful, completely yours. There's no one else I want, Dominic, you know that!'

'So why didn't you just ask me if we had made love in the caves?'

'Because I was trapped,' I said quietly. 'If I asked you, and you said no, then you'd have known something happened with someone else, and I couldn't bear that. I can't explain what it was like that night, how weird and distorted everything was. My perceptions were so warped. I didn't understand how it had happened until I realised what Anna had done.'

He stares at me. His dark brown eyes with their coppery lights are almost unreadable but I think I can see that I've touched something in him. I sense him struggling with himself. I can guess that he's spent a lot of time convincing himself that it's over between us but he can't fight his feelings, his desires.

I want to beg him to give in to them, tell him that he mustn't try to kill what he feels for me. It's too precious; it has so much to give us both.

'I wanted to be honest with you, I've never lied,' I say quietly. 'I couldn't swear before but now I can.

Nothing has ever happened between me and Andrei Dubrovski, and I vow that on my life.'

'How can you be so sure now?' he asks abruptly.

'Because I asked him. And he told me that nothing happened.'

An awful look contorts Dominic's face and his fists clench. 'You've been with him.'

'Of course, I'm still working for him. Now that Mark is ill I'm the only one available.'

'And what were the cosy circumstances that made you able to ask Andrei if he's ever fucked you while you were high on whatever little concoction Anna slipped you?' His voice is sardonic, unpleasant.

'I didn't want to ask him but I had to. I had to know the truth for the sake of us.'

Dominic turns his face away from me, staring at the floor, a muscle pulsing in his jaw. He's fighting something. I know he hates the thought of Andrei and me together.

'He means nothing to me,' I say. 'I love you. You know that. Please, Dominic. Don't let him drive us apart. He would love that so much. If we're happy, it will be the best revenge you could ever have on him.'

He looks up at me at last and I almost gasp at the sight of the pain in his eyes. 'You don't know how hard this has been for me,' he says, his voice low. He goes over to one of the armchairs and sinks down into it. 'Beth, no one has ever made me feel this way. Ever since I've met you, I've been in the strangest place. Everything I thought I could control – it's all been turned upside down. I've had to question everything about myself.'

I go over to him and kneel on the floor beside his chair. I take his hand in mine and hold it gently, savouring the touch of his skin. He lets me caress it. I want to kiss it but I restrain myself.

'I thought I knew about love,' he says huskily. 'But I knew nothing. I thought love was about agreements and boundaries and submission to my will. But with you, love has been chaotic, uncontrollable and I've had to relinquish power as much as exert it. You know how that's tormented me.'

He gazes down at me, his brown eyes softer now as he begs for understanding. I nod. I know that our journey together has taken Dominic to places he hasn't expected. He's tried to reject aspects of himself only to find them emerging in other ways. He stopped using certain instruments on me when we made love, thinking it would prevent his need for control and dominance, but those facets couldn't be suppressed, even when he tried to beat them out of himself with self-flagellation.

'I love you, everything about you,' I say gently, longing for my touch to heal the breach between us and give him back the confidence to be himself. 'You don't have to change.'

His head droops a little. I'm desperate to kiss his mouth, wrap my arms about him, feel his hot skin against mine. I lift his hand to my lips and press them on it.

'Beth.' His voice sounds cracked. I look up. He's

gazing down at me. 'I don't know ... I'm not ready yet.'

'Don't you want this?' I ask softly, pressing another kiss on his hand.

He groans. 'Of course I do. You know the power you have over me. But ...' He closes his eyes for a second and when he opens them, he seems determined. 'You and I are not just about sex, you know that. This is important, this is serious, this is about our hearts. I want to fuck you very, very badly. But when we do, it has to be because it's the real thing. Until ten minutes ago I had resolved to shut you out of my life. I can't just make love now as though all that is reversed. I have to think about it and be sure. I can't risk the pain of getting it wrong again.'

I want to leap up and shout joyously, 'But we are together, there's nothing to keep us apart!' but I don't. I know that what seems simple to me is not so straight-forward for Dominic. I haven't had to fight the inner battles that he has faced. So I say softly, 'And what if the people who fuck aren't us?'

He looks at me, frowning. 'What do you mean?'

'I mean ... it doesn't have to be Beth and Dominic.' I stand up. 'Wait for me.'

I go into the bathroom and start to take off my coat, then my clothes. I'm wearing a plain black dress that buttons down the front to the waist. I slip it over my head, catching a glimpse of my face in the mirror. My eyes are bright and intense and my cheeks are flushed. I undo my bra and take it off, then slip off my tights and knickers. I'm naked in the bathroom of Dominic's hotel room. This is kind of strange but I'm thinking on my feet here. I pick up my dress and put it back on. I'm barefoot, without underwear, wearing just my dress.

Opening the bathroom door, I see that Dominic is still sitting in the chair, waiting for me to emerge.

'Stay there,' I say. 'Close your eyes.'

He closes his eyes obediently and I go quickly to the door of the room and let myself out into the corridor. Excitement is bubbling up inside me. I have no idea if this will work, perhaps it's too crazy, but it's worth a try. It will all depend on whether Dominic is prepared to go with it or not.

I knock on the door.

A moment later, he answers, opening it just a little. 'Yes?'

*Excellent. He hasn't said, 'Beth' or 'What are you doing?' He's open to this whether he knows it or not.*

'Your maid service is here, sir,' I say in a low voice.

'My maid service?'

'Didn't you order a maid service?'

'I'm not sure I did, but as you're here, you'd better come in.' He opens the door wider and I step into the room. I keep my head bowed, looking at my bare toes on the carpet, and my hands are clasped in front of me.

'Who are you?' he asks in a commanding voice.

*That's right, my love, that's right.*

'My name is Rosa,' I reply. It came straight into my head. It sounds right.

'Hello, Rosa.' Dominic is observing me but I don't look at him. 'And you're my maid, is that right?'

'Yes, sir.'

'How interesting. What are your duties?'

'Anything you wish, sir.'

'Anything?'

I nod, then add, 'Yes, sir.'

'I see.' I can tell from the tone in Dominic's voice that he is tickled by this scenario. I know he's getting turned on, and I know that I am from the feeling of swelling anticipation between my legs.

'Well, you seem like a promising maid, Rosa. You appear to be very willing and that's good. But we need to see if you are all that you seem. First, Rosa, I want you to prepare the bed.'

'Yes sir.' I walk over to the large double bed and take off the decorative cushions, and fold back the heavy damask covering to reveal the pillows and blankets beneath.

'Take the covering completely off, please.'

'Yes, sir.' I fold back the heavy bedspread until it falls to the floor.

'Oh no. That's very messy, Rosa. I can't have that. Tidy it up, please.'

I try to fold up the bedspread but it's stiff and heavy and I struggle with it. Dominic watches as I manage to make it tidy.

'You still have a lot to learn,' he says.

'I apologise, sir,' I say, dropping my head down. 'I'm clumsy.'

'You are clumsy, aren't you? You know what, Rosa, I like you but I think it's important to set out the boundaries right away. I can't tolerate clumsiness. You must learn to do better. Come here.'

I walk towards him, my heart thumping hard with delicious anticipation. I'm aware of my dress moving across my bare skin. Dominic sits down on the stool by the dressing table. I go and stand in front of him.

'Put yourself across my knee,' he says, his voice kind. 'You need a gentle reminder, I think. My maids have to be of the highest standards, I can't accept anything else. Do you understand?'

I nod and swallow, my throat dry and my skin tingling. I crouch down and lie across his lap. It's awkward because the stool is high and I can't put my knees on the floor but I have to bend my legs to be low enough. Nevertheless I love the sensation of his hard thigh muscles beneath my chest and a moment later I'm not thinking about the awkwardness, only about the fact that with one large smooth palm, Dominic is smoothing my dress up over my buttocks. He gives a small gasp as he realises I'm not wearing anything underneath, then a throaty noise of appreciation. He runs his hand over my buttocks, smoothing it gently over the surface, relishing the plumpness and the warmth of the skin.

'Oh Rosa, you have a beautiful bottom. I can't wait to see it pink and hot. I hope this won't hurt you too much, but it's important that you learn your lesson.'

I'm trembling with anticipation and I can feel that my juices are already flowing hard, making me deliciously receptive to his every touch. I want to press down against him and feel my sex against his thighs, but I hold back for now.

He slaps my bottom lightly. It doesn't hurt much but I cry out. 'Oh, sir, oh, please, you're hurting me!'

Another blow lands on my bottom. 'That's my intention, Rosa.'

The slap is tingling, strong enough to reverberate through me but not so much that it causes real pain. It's like a sting that sends little prickles flying out all over me and the effect is to stimulate me even more. I can hardly stop myself from wriggling on him.

'Stay still!' Another slap, a little harder.

I moan. 'Oh sir, it hurts! I promise I'll be good!'

This makes him deliver three more hard, sharp slaps. I can feel that my bottom is hot and red where it's taken the blows.

'I think that's enough for today, Rosa, as it's your first time and you haven't been too bad. But that's just a taster of what you can expect if you don't perform.'

'Oh yes, sir, I'll do my very best.'

Dominic's voice changes. 'What's this? What's this, Rosa?'

I've moved my legs apart to support me better during my spanking and Dominic has let his fingers run down my bottom to where my sex is now exposed and open to him. He runs his fingertips in the hot juices there and I gasp without meaning to.

'Oh, I see. You rather liked that little spanking, did you? That wasn't my intention but now I understand

75

that I've managed to stimulate your senses with my punishment. Well, well . . .'

I can't support myself any longer, and I let myself slide to the floor so I'm kneeling in front of him.

'Look at this, you've left my fingers quite greasy with your juices!' Dominic puts his hand in front of my face to show me. I take his hand and start to lick his fingers clean, tasting the slightly salty, pungent flavour of my own sex. He watches carefully and I can tell from his breathing that he's reacting strongly to the touch of my warm wet tongue lapping his fingers and sucking at their tips. 'I'm glad to see you offer such a personal service,' he murmurs, his voice throaty with desire.

I let go of his hand and gently push his knees apart. Then I shuffle forward on my knees so that my face is close to his crotch. I can see the hard bulge there now and my stomach twists with excitement. I can't wait to see and hold and touch his magnificent penis, and have it for myself once again.

I tip my face up to him. 'May I undo your trousers, sir?'

He's looking back at me tenderly. 'Yes, you may.'

Within a moment, I've opened his trousers and let his cock spring free from his boxers. It's as beautiful as I remembered and I can't stop myself leaning forward to take it in my mouth, holding the hot, hard shaft in my hand as I run my tongue over its smooth top. I want to take its entirety into my mouth but he's far too big for that, and he's swelling even more as I let my lips slide up and down the length as far as I can. It's joyous to feel it again and to love it with my mouth. My other hand slides beneath him into the warmth below, and I cup his balls, moving them gently in my palm. He groans and puts a hand on my head, running his fingers through my hair and pressing me gently so that I increase the pressure on his rock-hard penis. I suck and lick with relish, not wanting to let him out of my longing mouth, carrying on until he gently pulls my head away and tilts it up towards him. He takes my hands and lifts me up, then wraps his arms around me and pulls me tight into his embrace. At last, his lips find mine and we're kissing feverishly, deeply, as though we're dying with need for one another. His tongue takes possession of my mouth, finding mine, and I respond with everything inside me. His taste is divine and the sensation of our mouths meeting is like heavenly completion. There can't be kisses better than this, that feel so perfect, so intensely right, like two halves of a whole being reunited. As we kiss he pulls me onto his lap so that I'm straddling him, one leg on either side of his. With fierce excitement I can feel his hard cock pressing against the front of my sex. I thrust forward a little so that the shaft is right against my clitoris that's now swollen and desperately sensitive. The delicious sensation makes me kiss him harder, and I dig my fingers into his hair. He knows what he's doing to me and he moves his hips subtly so that his penis carries on giving me buzzes of powerful electricity every time it touches my sweet spot.

I feel as though I could come in a second, just from the pleasure of our passionate kisses and the smell of his skin. The almost unbearable pressure of his cock on my clit is close to sending me spiralling over the edge but I don't want that yet. I don't want this pleasure to end, and I don't want to come before I've felt his penis deep inside me, pushing me to the very brink. I know he wants the same.

I lift myself up and reach down to hold his penis. I tilt it forward so that its tip is angled towards me and then, very gently, I lower myself down on it, finding the entrance as I go. It goes perfectly to the place – *I knew we were made for each other* – and with a moan I let myself sink down, slowly engulfing him and savouring the pleasure of feeling myself open to take his hot girth. Dominic groans and exhales as his cock pushes upwards inside me.

'Oh God, that's good,' he says. His eyes are burning with the strength of his lust and then he's kissing me again as I begin to move my hips so that he thrusts deeper and deeper. 'Oh . . . Rosa,' he murmurs between kisses. He reaches down and lifts my dress up and over my head, discarding it on the floor, then covers my breasts in burning kisses, stopping to tug gently on my nipples. They light a hot path to my groin as he sucks and pulls on one, stroking the other with his fingers. I throw my head back and sigh with delight as I feel his teeth grazing the sensitive bud. He runs his fingers down my belly, strokes my bottom, grasps me hard so that he can use his strength to push me up and down on his penis. I want him completely inside me, as deep as he can go, I feel as though I can never get enough of him. I'm frenzied by the pleasure of having his body joined to mine once more, when I was so afraid I might never have him again. Suddenly I feel him holding me tightly and his thighs go like iron as he summons his strength and stands up, lifting me with him, his cock still inside me. I wrap my legs around him, kissing wildly – his lips, his cheeks, his eyelids – as he carries me easily across the room to the bed. He lowers me down so that I'm lying on my back, and I open my legs as far as I can so that he can stay inside me as he lowers himself between them. He grabs my wrists in one hand and holds them tightly above my head as he begins to thrust fiercely, his hips moving in a strong rhythm as he plunges into me as hard as he can.

Each thrust makes me gasp out loud and each time he grinds down on me he's pushing me a little closer to the edge as he rocks down onto my clitoris and presses deep into my pleasure zone.

'You're so beautiful,' he says, breathless, as he gazes down at me. 'You're never more gorgeous than when we're fucking.'

'Don't stop, don't stop,' I beg, feeling the joyful abandon getting nearer. The blissful sensations are building, the grip around my wrists is tight and exciting. I feel utterly open to him as I stretch below him, his chest hard against my breasts, my sex surrendering to his pounding manhood.

I feel him swelling within me and the knowledge that he's going to come sets off my own desperate excitement. I thrust my hips up to meet him, pressing my clit up to meet his thrusts and as he groans with his approaching orgasm I feel my own triggered deep inside me and I am helpless to resist the wave of pleasure that engulfs me, and I stiffen and cry out under the rush of feeling that sweeps over me. I buck and twist, still moaning, still desperate to find those final thrusts that will keep the juddering pleasure rocking through me, and I feel Dominic arch his back and stiffen as he pours out a fierce orgasm.

We are left gasping in each other's arms, Dominic heavy but delicious on my chest, his panting in my ear. My hands are free again, and I run them over his smooth back. No unexplained weals there this time, I note with relief. His breathing slows and he turns to kiss me, lingering on my lips and then nuzzling into my neck.

'That was beautiful, Rosa,' he murmurs.

'Thank you, sir.'

'I think you're going to make a most promising maid.'

'Thank you. I'll try my best to please you.'

'You're very sweet.'

We lie in one another's arms for a while not saying anything but revelling in the closeness of our bodies and the post-coital glow on our skin. I can feel the dynamic between us changing as the maid and her master return to their usual identities. We're Beth and Dominic again. It's taken that fantasy to restore us to one another and now we're able to lie reunited in each other's arms. When Dominic speaks, he is normal again – no longer my commanding master with his chastising hand, but my lovely man with his strong, warm embrace and his deliciously scented skin.

'Do you have anywhere to go? You can stay here tonight if you want to. I'm going out – in fact, I have to get ready right now. I'm meeting an important client for dinner. When are you going back to London?'

'I'll head back in the morning, I'm sure I can get a ticket easily enough.' My spirits swoop downwards a little. We're only just back together and we're talking about separation already. 'What are your plans?'

'I'm not going back to London. I'm travelling for the next month or so. I have lots of people I have to see.'

'And then?' I gaze at him imploringly.

'I don't know, Beth. Don't ask too much just yet.'

'But . . .' I know my eyes must be full of fear. We've just made such sweet love together. How can that count for nothing? Isn't our relationship the most important thing there is?

'Can you wait for me?' he asks gently. 'I still have to get my head around this, you know.'

'Of course I can wait, but I'm afraid that I'll lose you again.'

'You don't have to be afraid.' He kisses my nose. 'But I do want one thing if we're going to start again.'

'Yes?'

He gives me one of those looks from his heartbreakingly beautiful brown eyes: sincere, intimate, like he can see into my very soul. 'Beth, I want you and Andrei Dubrovski completely out of each other's lives. It's not just jealousy on my part – I'm worried about you being with him. He hasn't taken kindly to the idea that I'm setting up as his rival, and if he guesses what we mean to each other, he could think up some pretty nasty tricks to get back at me.'

I stare back at him, trying not to show my feelings. *Oh Dominic, it's not that simple.* I can't simply tell Andrei that I'm not going to have anything to do with him. Not only have I promised to continue to be there for him but he holds the future of Mark's career in his hands.

'Do you understand, Beth?' says Dominic, holding one of my hands and stroking it with his thumb. 'It's best for both of us if we get that man out of our lives.'

I nod. I don't know what to say. I can't bear to risk this reborn trust between us, our re-found intimacy.

'Good.' He drops a kiss on my hand. 'Now I'm going out. Make yourself at home here. I'll be back later.'

# CHAPTER SIX

On the Eurostar bound for London, I watch the French countryside flying past the window and cool my forehead against the glass. My trip succeeded better than I could have dreamed. I'm sore and swollen but in a way I relish. I was asleep when Dominic returned last night but this morning, when we woke in bed together, he wordlessly began to make love to me, his strong morning erection pressing in between my legs almost before I knew where I was. Waking to his cock filling me up was a delicious way to start the day, and it was fast and deeply satisfying. Then he got up to shower.

The atmosphere between us over breakfast in his room was strange: intimate and yet distant. We know each other so well and yet there was the sense that we were in some ways still strangers.

When I asked him why he hadn't replied to any of my messages, he looked blank. It took a minute before we worked out that I'd been texting and emailing a defunct phone and a dead email account.

'When I left Dubrovski, everything went back to the company,' Dominic explained. 'I've got a new phone, and a new email.' He gave me the details.

Now, on the train home, I realise that I still don't know where I stand. Dominic said he was travelling to Montenegro to meet a multi-millionaire on his yacht and he was vague about where he would be after that. It feels as though he's ready to enjoy our relationship when we can pretend to be other people but that he's not quite ready to trust his heart.

*But he knows the truth now. I have to give him time to think it over.*

I'm sure that the delightful bedroom activities we've enjoyed will stay on his mind for a while. How can he not want more of the delicious things we do to each other? I shiver lightly as I remember the slap of his palm on my bare bottom and the delightful tingles he sent all over me.

He was sweet when we parted, kissing me tenderly and promising he would be in touch.

*But how are we going to be together, with Dominic travelling all over the world?*

I already miss him with a deep, yearning ache. As the train speeds me further away from him, I wonder how I'm going to be able to stand our separation when there's no end to it in sight.

I remember his final words to me that morning: 'Don't forget, Beth, you need to cut your ties with Dubrovski, right away. Tell Mark you can't deal with him any more.'

I know that Dominic needs that reassurance before he can truly commit again.

*But how can I do that without destroying Mark?*

\*　　\*　　\*

By lunchtime I'm back in London. I can hardly believe that this time yesterday morning I had no idea where Dominic was. Now I can still feel the pressure of his mouth on mine and the stiffness in my limbs from all of our physical activity. I try to subdue the voice in the back of my mind that's asking me exactly what footing our relationship is on, and how I'm going to manage to get Andrei out of my life. I need to think about my work after my unauthorised absence.

From St Pancras I head home and get changed, then go to Mark's house. By the time I arrive, it's mid-afternoon and Caroline is on her way out.

'Oh hello, Beth, dear,' she says, pulling on orange knitted gloves. 'I'm just going off to visit Mark.'

'Are you? Can I come? I'd love to see him.'

She looks at me for a moment and says, 'Why not? I'm sure you'll cheer him up and I'd like the company. No matter how comfortable a hospital is, there's always something depressing about it, isn't there?'

She flings her arm up in the air and a taxi pulls obediently out of the traffic and stops at the kerb for us. 'The Princess Charlotte Hospital, please, driver!' she cries and opens the cab door. We both climb in and settle ourselves, and then we're off, heading towards Kensington.

'Have you been keeping busy, Beth?' Caroline enquires, tucking her coat around her barrel-shaped body.

I nod. 'I'll tell Mark all about it.'

'I don't want him worried about work though,' she says quickly. 'He's doing well and is much more cheerful than yesterday but he mustn't have any setbacks.'

'I understand.' Just then I feel my phone vibrate with an incoming text. I take it out of my pocket and check it. It's a text from Dominic's new number.

I want to see Rosa again. She fucked me very beautifully.

My stomach performs a lazy somersault inside me and I have a flashback to Dominic's orgasm. It makes me gasp.

'Are you all right?' enquires Caroline. 'Not bad news I hope.'

'No, no, it's fine,' I say. I text back.

Rosa wants to see you. She wants to obey. When will it be possible?

The answer comes back almost at once.

Soon. Tell Rosa I am a loving master if she is a willing and obedient maid.

I'm tingling with arousal as I read it, remembering Rosa's punishment yesterday and the way Dominic's hot palm caressed my bottom and then slid down to the wetness of my waiting sex.

*Stop it,* I scold myself. *You can't get all worked up sitting with Caroline in a taxi!*

She's oblivious though, gazing out of the window as we pass expensive shops, their windows glittering with Christmas displays.

We come to a halt outside the private hospital and Caroline settles the fare. We go inside and at once there is that hospital smell, a disinfected citrusy aroma that speaks of sterile surfaces and hand rub. A large Christmas tree sparkles with decorations but the cheerfulness feels forced.

At the reception desk, Caroline signs us both in and leads the way to Mark's room. I'm not sure what to expect as we go in and I feel nervous. This isn't the kind of place I would associate with Mark. He's so elegant and well turned out, how can he be anything but out of place in a hospital bed, no matter how comfortable?

We reach Mark's ward and check in with the nurse there, who directs us to wash our hands and apply the alcohol rub. She also shows us how to put white plastic aprons over our clothes and then we're ready to see Mark.

Caroline leads the way to the door, knocks and opens it. I follow her in. The room is pleasant enough and well furnished, but the armchairs and the television can't hide its purpose. It's dominated by a large hospital bed and by the equipment that surrounds it: the drips hanging with bags of fluid, the stands and the machines with their flashing lights and monitors. In the bed Mark looks thin and lost. He's half sitting up and seems to be drowsing against the nest of white pillows. A line goes from the stand by his bed into the back of his hand where the needle is taped into place. He is heavily bandaged around his neck and his mouth looks swollen. As we come in, his eyes flicker open and he smiles feebly. I'm shocked at how ill and weak he looks, how deflated and tired.

'Hello, old boy,' Caroline says, bustling forward to land a kiss on his cheek. 'How are you? Beth's come along with me to say hello. She's been missing you, the poor thing.'

I step forward and smile. 'Hello, Mark. How are you? Caroline tells me the operation has been a success.'

He nods, then says, 'Hard to talk' but it comes out so thick and distorted I can hardly understand.

'Tongue's still swollen?' asks Caroline, lowering herself into a chair by the bed.

Mark nods again.

'Painful?'

He nods more emphatically. Then he cocks his head towards the drip stand and says, 'Lovely morphine!' which I understand perfectly. We all laugh.

He looks over at me and smiles, more with his eyes than his mouth. 'Everything okay?' he says in his strange thick new voice. He's evidently speaking in as a few words as possible but it's odd. Mark wouldn't usually use that kind of phrase.

'Yes, fine.' I smile again, trying to convey that he doesn't need to worry.

He says something unintelligible and has to repeat it a couple of times before I realise that he's saying 'St Petersburg'.

'Oh! Yes, the trip.' It feels like a lifetime ago, not two days. I smile at Mark while wondering what to say. I was going to be completely straight with him and tell him that the painting has been declared a fake but now, seeing how ill he looks, I don't know if I can do that. He'll know at once what it means. No matter how the news is managed, there will be a slur on his reputation because Andrei has already told the world that Mark was the man who had authenticated the fake Fra Angelico. I can't bring myself to do it, not while he's sitting helpless in a hospital bed.

'The painting?' Mark asks.

I nod, still smiling and hoping that I look sincere. 'Yes, I saw it. They haven't come to their final conclusions yet, but it's looking hopeful.'

Is that enough to put Mark's mind at rest for now? He nods and relaxes back into his pillows, looking pleased.

'Now, that's enough work chat,' Caroline scolds, gesturing to me to sit down. 'Let's talk about something else. Beth, are you going home for Christmas?'

We emerge from Mark's room just under an hour later. He's enjoyed our company but he's clearly exhausted when we leave. I come out feeling anxious. Mark is obviously not going to be back on his feet for a long time. How on earth will I keep the truth from him? And should I?

The day is almost over, and I don't think there's any point in going back to Belgravia now. I ought to get home and see Laura, who has been sending regular text messages to make sure I'm back okay from Paris, but an email appears on my phone as we're heading back to the hospital lobby. It's from James, my friend and one-time employer:

> Help! I'm at a work party of Erland's at the Travellers! I don't know anyone. Come and have some mulled wine with me and save me if you can . . .

Excellent. That's what I'll do. James will have some advice, I'm sure of it.

I arrive at the Travellers Club on Pall Mall about twenty minutes later, having put on some lip gloss in the cab. I'm not exactly dressed for a Christmas party but never mind; I'm not out to impress anyone. I make my way up to the library at the Travellers, where the room is already crowded with people. This is an old-fashioned gentlemen's club and the ratio of men to women is about ten to one, which I suppose also reflects the fact that tailors like Erland are most often men. I spot James almost at once because he's so tall and also because he's standing on his own, staring up at the plaster frieze that runs around the wall by the ceiling.

I go over and stand beside him, also looking up at the classical figures picked out in white against a coral background. 'Very impressive. Just like the Elgin Marbles but smaller,' I say and James looks down at me.

'Beth!' A smile breaks over his face. 'Hurray, you're here!' He drops a kiss on each of my cheeks. 'What a treat. And yes, that lovely frieze is a copy of the Elgin Marbles. It might be all we have left if the Greeks get their way. How are you, sweetie? Let me get you a drink. Erland's having a whale of a time flirting with half of Savile Row. We can amuse ourselves.'

A moment later I'm holding a cup of hot wine heavily scented with cinnamon, cloves and orange, and telling James the latest developments. It's a relief to get all the happenings in St Petersburg off my chest. He grasps the implications immediately.

'Oh dear me,' he says solemnly. 'Poor Mark. This is bad. It's very bad.'

'I haven't been able to tell him when he's so ill. It's the last thing he needs.'

James nods gravely. 'Absolutely. But he will need to know at some point.'

'Will he? I know it sounds desperate but perhaps I could persuade Dubrovski to keep it quiet.'

'Indefinitely?' James shakes his head. 'I don't see how. Unless you've got extraordinary powers of persuasion.' He looks at me with interest, gazing down through the lenses of his little gold-rimmed spectacles. 'Have you got that kind of hold over Andrei Dubrovski? Does this mean our friend Dominic is history?'

'Of course not,' I say indignantly. Then, after a moment, I sigh. 'Oh, James. It's so complicated.'

'I've no doubt it is. You were convinced Dominic was sleeping with the minxy Anna last time I saw you. Has that been cleared up?'

I nod. 'She was messing with my head, and Dominic's head, and trying to come between us. There is one mystery though – I still have no idea how she knew so much about Dominic and me, and all the details of our relationship. Dominic swore he didn't tell her and I believe him. But I've cleared up something else: Anna drugged me that night in the catacombs and it wasn't Andrei who had sex with me. I'm sure of it.'

'Well, that's a relief,' James says with a smile. 'I'm glad something's been made clearer – it generally happens the other way around where you're concerned.'

'Yes,' I say slowly, 'but Andrei has made it plain he's still interested in me. He wants me to forget Dominic and be with him.'

'A lot of girls would jump at the chance,' James remarks. 'He's handsome and extremely rich.'

'I don't care about that,' I reply. 'I love Dominic and that's all there is to it, you know that.'

James smiles at me. 'I do know that. You could no more be with Andrei Dubrovski than with me. You're a true romantic, aren't you? Love or nothing.'

'Absolutely. Love or nothing!' I smile back at him.

'So where is the divine Dominic?'

'He's working abroad. It's not going to be easy but I'm sure we'll work out how we can be together.'

'You'll find a way,' James says comfortingly. 'You two will always gravitate back to each other, I'm sure of that.'

I sip my mulled wine. It's not quite as straightforward as I've made it sound, but I hope that it soon will be. This time, when Dominic and I are reunited, there will be no way we can be divided.

# CHAPTER SEVEN

I sleep so deeply that night that I don't have a single dream. I wake up to my alarm and it feels as though I fell asleep just moments before. The activities of the last few days are certainly telling on me, that's for sure.

Once I've showered and dressed, I join Laura in the kitchen for breakfast, which we usually eat standing up and leaning against the counter while we swap news. Laura looks particularly cheerful and bright-eyed as she munches on her granola.

'Hey, Miss Impulse! Good to see you. Are you planning to stay in the country today or do you have a quick jaunt to Florence planned? Whizzing to Vienna for the night, perhaps?'

I laugh as I pour out my own granola. 'No, not today. Maybe next week I'll fancy it, we'll see.'

'Well, actually, you're not the only one who can decide to make some travel plans.' Laura nods excitedly to an envelope propped up against the toaster with my name on it. 'Open it.'

I take up the envelope and examine it. That's Laura's handwriting on the front. I rip it open and inside I find a Christmas card.

'Oh, that's lovely, Laura, thanks!' I say, surprised. We don't usually give each other cards.

'Open it!' she insists, impatient.

I open the card and out drops a piece of paper. I pick it up and unfold it. It's a printout from a website, the confirmation of two flights to New York, leaving on the coming Friday and returning on the Monday

'It's the trip we promised ourselves, remember!' Laura is practically jumping up and down with excitement.

'Of course!' I stare at the printout. 'A girls' trip to New York. How wonderful.'

'I decided to take matters into my own hands yesterday. My boss reminded me that I had to take my final couple of days holiday this year or lose it, so I did some instant searching and found these flights. You'll be able to get the time off, won't you?'

'Yes, I'm sure it will be no problem.'

'That's what I thought. So!' Laura smiles broadly at me. 'Are you pleased?'

'I'm totally thrilled,' I say. 'I can't wait.'

I mean it too. It will be brilliant fun to go away with Laura. So why do I feel a tiny bit reluctant to leave London? I put it out of my mind. Who could ask for more than a Christmas trip to New York City?

Caroline is perfectly happy about my taking time off before Christmas.

'To be honest, Beth, I don't expect you'll be doing terribly much before the new year. Mark always said this was a quiet time unless someone decided to buy something truly incredible as a Christmas present. Take this opportunity to have some fun. I expect we'll all be busy again in January.'

As far as I can tell, she's right. Everything in the office has slowed right down. Perhaps people know Mark's sick, or perhaps the art market is just a bit quiet, but with so little else to do, I'm able to get on top of all the pesky admin. At this rate I may consider going home early for Christmas, once we're back from our trip. I wonder how long Mark is going to be in hospital and if he will want me here while he's recuperating. I'll have to ask Caroline about it and discuss what's best to do.

Just then an email flashes into my computer inbox. I see that it's from Andrei, and a swirl of apprehension turns nastily in my stomach. I knew it was only a matter of time before he called on me again. The last thing he said was that there was a job he wanted me to do, and there was no way he was going to let me out of his life, not after what he said on the plane.

I know I've been pretending to myself that I can handle Andrei Dubrovski and shake him off as easily as Dominic seems to think I can, but the truth is that I'm just as entangled with him as ever – more, because of Mark.

I click on the email and open it. It reads:

Beth
    I need you this evening. Come to Albany at seven o'clock for an important meeting.
    A

As usual, his tone infuriates me. No pleases or thank yous or any social niceties. Andrei is incapable of basic politeness, it seems. He still assumes I'm at his beck and call whenever he likes.

*The problem is, I am. He's got me just where he wants me.*

I fire back a response saying I'll be there. It's a good job that I haven't got any other plans.

There's something particularly Christmassy about Piccadilly. Maybe it's the old-fashioned feel to the buildings, the grand old houses that are now shops and galleries. Perhaps it's the bright arcades with their tempting displays of jewels, silver and leather. It's probably because of the landmarks like the Ritz, draped in lavish Christmas decorations and sparkling with lights, the Royal Academy and the pale blue frontage of Fortnum and Mason with its Christmas trees and the glittering window displays full of lavish food and drink. Whatever it is, it's hard to ignore, especially in the frosty winter darkness.

There is Albany House, set back from the main road with its small private car park in front of it. Thousands of people must walk past it every day, not knowing that behind its classical exterior lie dozens of luxurious apartments where poets, politicians and film stars have lived. This is where Andrei has chosen to make his London home, right in the centre of the glamorous heart of Mayfair, inside the establishment itself. There is privacy behind these walls, which is no doubt why he chose it. Without belonging to this place, no one can wander in. Porters guard the main entrance and a camera is focused on the back door that can only be opened with a security card. No doubt Andrei feels safe and anonymous inside this bastion of privilege.

The porter recognises me as I enter and says a cheery 'Evening, ma'am' as I pass the tiny lodge. Not so long ago I came here every day to catalogue Andrei's art collection and arrange its display in his Albany set. It feels like another lifetime.

I go down the Rope Walk to Andrei's staircase, wondering what he wants me to do. I'm apprehensive: not only does he have power over me, but that he knows it too. He's not the kind of man to shy away from getting what he wants by whatever means necessary. I just have to hope that I've got the inner strength to face him down. If I can get away from him, I'll have removed the final obstacle to being with Dominic.

I knock on the front door, banging the great fish-shaped brass knocker. The door is answered at once by Andrei's bodyguard, who beckons me inside. I can hear the murmur of voices from the drawing room and I check my watch. It's not seven o'clock yet. Whatever this important meeting is, it seems to have started.

The bodyguard, as silent as ever, leads me to the drawing room, opens the door and gestures for me to go inside. I step in and see several men sitting on the sofa. Andrei is in an armchair facing them, and he stands up as I come in.

'Ah, Beth. You're here. Good.' He looks to the men.

'Gentlemen, you'll remember Beth from our visit to the monastery when we first saw the Fra Angelico.'

I look more closely at the men and realise that I recognise two of them. One is the abbot of the monastery, wearing a suit and looking quite different out of his robes. The other is one of the brothers I remember from that day. I don't know who the other two are, but one of them is regarding me strangely from dark eyes. I glance over but I don't recognise him.

'Come in, Beth, and sit down. I want you here because of course this matter concerns Mark and therefore you. Mark, sadly, can't be here himself, so Beth is his representative.' Andrei gestures to a chair. I go and sit down, wondering what I'll be expected to do.

Andrei speaks again. 'The first thing to say is that we want all this settled quietly – don't we, Beth?'

I nod.

'There's no point in dragging reputations down, or making allegations of fraud or criminal activity. The abbot here is just as shocked and horrified as I am that the painting has been revealed to be a fake.'

I glance over at the abbot but he doesn't seem particularly shocked or horrified. In fact, he looks quite happy as he nods away in agreement.

'And so we've decided that we will simply do an exchange. The monastery will return my money, and I will return the painting to them to do with as they will – on the condition that they do not attempt to pass it off as a genuine Fra Angelico.'

'I see.' I glance around the men again. The man with

the dark eyes is still regarding me in that curious way. 'That sounds satisfactory. I'm glad you've come to the agreement so easily.'

I'm pleased – this is definitely the best solution. If the painting is quietly returned and no fuss made, then perhaps Mark's reputation will remain unblemished. We might even be able to organise some kind of statement where Mark retracts the authentication that Andrei put out in his name and the Hermitage concurs after the event. I'm feeling quite warm again towards Andrei – he's worked this out very well for us. He does have the kind side I saw in the orphanage. His heart is a good one. I don't really understand why I'm here though. This has all been agreed without me so why did he want me at this meeting? Then Andrei looks over at me again.

'Beth, I'd like you to organise the repayment of the funds.'

'Me?' I'm surprised. I'm an art assistant, not a banker.

Andrei nods slowly. 'Yes. Didn't Mark tell you? He arranges the financing for all my art purchases. He pays through his own accounts and I refund him the money. That's how I would like it to work in reverse as well. The abbot's advisers will sort out the details with you. The money will come to Mark and then to my account.'

'I see.' It seems a rather pointless arrangement to me, but Andrei and Mark must have their reasons. If that's what is always done, it must be what Mark wants.

Andrei stands up, smiling rather coolly. 'Good. I must leave you for a moment. I have a call to make. Beth, perhaps you could give your details to Brother Gregor?'

As he leaves the room, one of the brothers comes over to me but it isn't the man with the staring eyes. That one continues to observe me as I discuss the practicalities with Brother Gregor and swap email addresses so that we can facilitate the payment online. As we are completing things, he comes over and hovers near me, obviously waiting for a chance to speak. When Brother Gregor moves away to talk to the abbot, the other man steps forward.

'Miss, I wanted to talk to you. To see if you have any news.'

'News?' His voice, deep and low, has a strange effect on me. It sounds familiar. 'I don't know what you mean.'

'News of Dominic Stone. He has not been to the monastery for some time.'

My insides clench at the sound of Dominic's name. 'N-n-no,' I manage to stammer out. 'He won't be back. He's no longer working for Mr Dubrovski.'

The monk's face falls. 'Then that means – Miss Anna . . .'

'Anna?' I echo, astonished to hear her name spoken by this monk. When James mentioned Anna last night, I wondered what she was doing since leaving Andrei's employment so suddenly. It still bothers me that I haven't discovered how she knew that Dominic had begun to practise self-flagellation or how she was in possession of the secrets of our life together, but as long as she keeps well away from Dominic and me, I can live with that.

'Will Miss Anna be back?' the monk asks urgently.

I see her beautiful face in front of my mind's eye: the smooth skin and feline green eyes, the bee-stung lips and glossy dark hair. No wonder this monk is disappointed she hasn't been there for him to feast his eyes on: Anna's smouldering sexuality would no doubt cause seismic waves in a house of celibate men.

'I don't know, I'm afraid. I don't think so.' I watch his face set into lines of disappointment and resignation. 'I'm sorry.'

He turns to go back to his chair and I have a sudden flash of memory. It's not the face, I'm sure I've never seen it before. It's that voice. I've heard it . . . but when? Then it comes to me. I hear him talking to me through the darkness. *That's it! This is the monk who took me to Dominic that night. Is he the one who taught Dominic how to beat himself with knotted ropes to rid himself of his base desires?*

I can hardly ask that here in front of everyone but I'm sure that this is the man who led me through the dark monastery that night and reunited me with Dominic. What was his name? I hear Dominic's laughing voice in my memory: '*Did Brother Giovanni freak you out?*' Yes he had, with his hooded face and lantern, like something from a horror film. That monastery was certainly a curious place. It was odd that not only did they have a Fra Angelico to sell to Andrei but his right-hand man and woman, Dominic and Anna, were both staying there too, working on Andrei's big commodities deal.

The meeting seems to be over. I wonder if I can leave or whether I ought to wait for Andrei to come back. Just then my phone beeps to announce an incoming text. I take it out of my pocket and open the message.

Rosa's master would like to see her tonight.

I gasp. Dominic! What does he mean? Is he in London? I quickly fire a text back.

Where?

The answer arrives in seconds.

In the boudoir at eight o'clock.

I check my watch. It's already half past seven. I can get to the boudoir from here in time as long as I can leave quite soon. Another text comes through to me:

Where are you?

Oh God. I don't want to answer that one. If I say I'm in Albany he'll know at once that I'm with Andrei, and I don't want to face that problem quite yet.

Not far off. I can be with you soon.

Just then, Andrei comes back into the room and I tuck my phone away. He begins to talk to the abbot, obviously thanking him and preparing him to leave because the next moment, the bodyguard is showing all the monks to the front door. When we're alone, Andrei turns to me and smiles.

'I'm glad that was resolved without too much trouble. Aren't you?'

'Yes,' I say sincerely. 'Thank you for sorting it out.'

'It's in my interests too. Let me know when you've managed to transfer the money, won't you?'

I nod. I'm dying to get out of there and over to the boudoir but I don't want Andrei to guess at my impatience.

'How is Mark?' He walks over to the drinks cabinet and opens it. He pours out measures of vodka into two crystal glasses and adds ice from a silver ice bucket, and some slices of lemon. He passes one to me even though I haven't asked for it.

'He's doing as well as we can hope,' I reply. 'I don't know when he'll be out of hospital. He's still very weak, but he'll need to begin his course of radiotherapy soon.'

Andrei nods and sips his vodka. He stares at me from under those hooded lids. I can feel myself becoming more anxious. Dominic is in London – I don't know why or when he arrived, but he's definitely here – and my compulsion to be with him is something I don't think I can fight.

'Are you all right, Beth?' Andrei says. 'You seem a little on edge.'

103

'I'm fine. Really.'

'I hope we can put the matter of the Fra Angelico behind us now. I've got some new ideas for our next collaboration. You've done marvellous work here on my London home. I'm very happy with it.' He smiles at me.

I return it though I know my own smile is weak. All I can think about is that Dominic is waiting for me – or for Rosa – just a short distance away. Not being able to go to him is unbearable.

'So . . .' He swirls the vodka in his glass and the ice chinks against it. 'I'd like you to do the same to my Manhattan apartment. My decorators have not long finished refreshing it and I'd like you to bring your eye to it.' He gazes at me, assessing my reaction. 'What do you think? Does the idea of a few weeks in New York appeal to you?'

I try to absorb this news. A few weeks in New York? That's so weird. Before I think better of it, I say, 'I'm going there next week.'

Andrei raises an eyebrow at me. 'Really? What a coincidence.'

'A weekend away with my flatmate,' I say. 'A girl thing.'

He looks amused. 'Shopping and cocktails? I believe that's what you mean by "a girl thing".' He shoots me a sardonic glance. 'I approve. Well, as long as you are there, you must visit my apartment and take a look around. If you want the job, I'd love you to start as soon as you can in the new year. And if you want to attend some auctions on my behalf, you can do that too. I'm prepared to put down a big budget if you find the right pieces. I trust your taste, I'm sure you'll select what I want.'

I stare at him. *Oh my God, how wonderful.* This is a dream job, and it means that he has decided that no matter what happened over the Fra Angelico, he's prepared to keep Mark as his art adviser. I imagine what it might be like: staying in New York, shopping at the auction houses with a virtually unlimited budget and working through Andrei's art collection. If it's anything like his London one, it will be full of treasures. What an amazing opportunity . . .

*Wait. You can't do this.*

I can't stay in Andrei's orbit. Dominic wouldn't be able to stand it but that's not the only reason. Andrei's made it clear that he has intentions towards me, and this job is probably part of his plan to reel me in. I'm not interested in him that way, and no matter how great the job, if I accept it I'll also be accepting his terms and letting him get close to me on a personal level. I'll be implying I want a relationship.

*Great. My perfect job comes with strings attached.*

I open my mouth to refuse but something stops me. I can see Mark on his hospital bed, so weak and ill. I can't risk Andrei taking against me while Mark is still so frail. When he's stronger, in a few weeks' time, then I can finally extricate myself. Until then, I'll have to play a waiting game.

'That sounds incredible,' I say, and I don't have to pretend – that much is true. 'I'll have a look while I'm in New York and we can take it from there. I'll need to talk to Mark, of course, and make sure he's happy for me to take some weeks away from the office.'

Andrei's laser-beam gaze is fixed on me and I feel sure he can read my mind. He's wondering why I'm not leaping at this opportunity and saying yes right away. After regarding me carefully for a moment, he says, 'Why don't we discuss it over dinner? I have a table at the Caprice, if you'd like to join me.'

'Oh . . . I . . . I can't. I have plans.'

'Plans?'

I nod. 'I'm meeting a friend.'

'I see.' Andrei walks over to the fireplace and leans against it. He turns to look at me. 'A friend who arrived this evening from Paris?'

My mouth drops open. I stare at him, speechless. *How the hell do you know that?*

He replies as if he can read my mind. 'I make it my business to know what certain people are doing – where they are and where they're going. I can't afford to take my eye off anyone who is threatening my business. I'm sure you understand that.' He puts his drink down on the chimney shelf and walks towards me. 'I thought I told you that he is no good for you. I mean it, Beth. You can't be involved with us both. I told you you'd have to make that choice and I understood that you'd decided you want to stay with me.' He gives me an icy look. 'You can't serve two masters.'

I have a vivid flashback to Dominic and hear his voice saying, 'Tell Rosa I am a loving master if she is a willing and obedient maid.'

But Dominic is only my master in the bedroom, when we choose to enact that scenario. Out of it, we are equal. Whereas Andrei wants me to obey him in every aspect of my life, and that's something I could never do. Fury rushes through me at his arrogance.

*You bastard, how dare you force me to make this choice? My romantic life has nothing to do with you and you're confusing my role as a professional with something completely different.*

Dominic wants me out of Andrei's life because he wants to protect me. Andrei wants me to drop Dominic so that he can control and manipulate me. *I* want to tell him exactly where he can go, in no uncertain terms. But I can't. Not yet.

'Okay,' I say quietly.

'Okay?' Andrei looks surprised at how easily I've submitted to him. He gives me a sideways look. 'So . . . you'll come for dinner with me?'

'Not tonight,' I reply firmly. 'I have to see him. I need to explain.'

Andrei's face goes cold and hard. 'I don't want you associating with that snake. He's a fucking traitor.'

*No, Andrei, you're the traitor. You're also a massive egotist who can't take rejection in any form, not even when a loyal employee explains he wants the chance to make it on his own. You can't take the fact that I keep turning you down for another man.*

'Let me tell him that,' I say. 'Don't you like that idea?'

He hesitates and then says, 'I do – but I'm surprised you're prepared to dump him without putting up more of a fight.'

I think quickly. 'Dominic's made me no promises. I can't rely on him. Whenever there's any trouble between us, he disappears. Besides that, he's fucked up. I expect Anna told you that. I've tried to reach him and help him, but nothing seems to work. I can't commit to someone so unstable.'

*Oh my God, it sounds so plausible. I had no idea I might feel like that. Do I?*

'All right,' Andrei says, looking pleased. Perhaps he wants to believe me. 'You'd better keep your appointment. But I'm keeping my eye on Dominic. I have no choice now that's he set himself up against me. You can tell him that if you want to.' He glares at me. 'I don't like the thought of you being with him.'

'I have to see him this time.' I return Andrei's gaze, not blinking.

His mouth twists slightly as though in distaste. 'Go on then. Get it over with.'

Once I'm out of Albany House, I begin to run, dodging the Christmas shoppers and dashing across roads. I want to get away from Andrei as fast as I can.

*How is it possible that this has got even more complicated?*

I'm chilled by the idea that Andrei knows that Dominic is in the country. Does his web of control really extend that far? How far is he willing to go to keep tabs on the people who interest him? I feel a stab of fear and wonder if someone is following me, watching me at this very moment. I glance around but I can't see anyone trailing me as I run through the crowds and across Berkeley Square.

All I want is to be with Dominic. My phone buzzes and I pull it out to look at the text:

Rosa is late. She'll be punished.

Dominic wants me too. Or does he want Rosa? Or are we the same person? My skin prickles as I imagine what my master might have in mind for me at the boudoir. All I care about is that Dominic wants Rosa, and I intend him to have her.

'Come in.'

The voice comes softly from the darkness inside the hall of the boudoir. I step into the blackness, panting from my hurried journey. I can't see anything. I hear the slap of leather against the palm of a hand, and I pull in a hot breath.

'You're late. You've made me wait. You know how I feel about that.' Dominic's voice is low and caressing but threaded through with authority.

'Yes, sir.' I'm already throbbing with desire and the tickling excitement of not knowing what might be going to happen to me. I have faith that my master wants me to experience the pleasure of pain and the pain of pleasure, but that, finally, the delights of what he does to me will triumph. I'm not Beth any more. I'm Rosa, the willing, the humble, the submissive maid who will take everything her master wishes for her.

'Kneel on the floor.'

I drop to my knees and let my head fall down, and I close my eyes.

'Take off your coat.'

I obey, sliding it from my shoulders and letting it fall to the floor. I hear footsteps. Dominic is moving away from me. There is the snap and flare of a match lighting and then a candle is lit. It sends flickering shadows all over the room but I keep my head down.

'Now – take off your clothes.'

Keeping my humble kneeling stance as much as I can, I unbutton my shirt and slide my skirt off, wriggling out of it and slipping off my shoes at the same time. I'm in my bra and knickers and a pair of woollen winter tights.

My master approaches me, evidently savouring the sight of me kneeling on the floor in my underwear with soft golden candlelight playing over my skin. He comes down and kneels beside me. He has a pair of scissors in his hand, I can see them glinting in the half-light. He runs the other hand over the back of my neck, brushing my hair out of the way as he smooths his palm over my shoulders and down my spine.

'Beautiful Rosa,' he whispers. 'You're all mine, aren't you?'

I nod.

'Look at your breasts, the way they fill that bra of yours. They're so luscious and gorgeous. I want to see them.' He takes the scissors and presses the point against my upper chest, not enough to hurt but enough to make me gasp with surprise. 'Don't worry, Rosa, I won't hurt you. I want to see your body.' He runs the point of the blades gently down to my breasts, into my cleavage and then up over the mound of my left breast. The tickling point makes an electric trail across my skin. He takes it over the fabric of my bra, circling it round my nipple, which hardens immediately, sticking out under the soft material. 'There it is,' he says softly. 'It's giving you away, Rosa. It shows me that you like this.' Then, deftly, he turns the blades and slices away the cup of my bra, revealing one breast. He drops his mouth and takes my hard nipple into it, sucking hard and nibbling at the sensitive tip. When he releases it, he says, 'That's beautiful, so delicious. I could suck all day on your nipples. They taste like honey.'

My sex is rippling with excitement, twitching beneath me as it swells and grows damp with desire. He takes the scissors again and cuts away the other cup of my bra, giving the other breast the same loving treatment with his tongue and teeth.

'Much better,' he says, pulling away from me and staring at my breasts, the nipples wet with his saliva. 'But there's more to be done. Kneel up, Rosa.'

I obey, aware that I'm wearing my thick black tights. I had no idea when I put them on that I'd be seeing Dominic that day, or I would have worn something sexier. He observes me and I keep my neck bent, my head drooping down and my arms beside me.

'I like your underwear,' he says softly. 'Very suitable for you, Rosa. Nothing too fancy. But perhaps we could make these a little more . . . accessible.'

He takes the blade of the scissors and runs the point over my hips. The sensation is almost unbearable: tickling, tormenting. I want to buck and wriggle underneath that point but I try to stay still – I know that's what he wants. I can't help breathing hard and trembling a little as the blade swoops and dives downwards to my sex, skimming across the top of the mound there. I can't stop a little moan escaping as the sensation makes me throb and contract in tiny, tickling convulsions. Desire is racing through my veins like lava down a hillside, setting everything inside me burning. Dominic runs the point of the blade over my other hip in a long swirling motion.

*Oh God, I had no idea he could make me feel like this with that one sharp point . . .*

Then he snaps the blades apart with a shearing sound, pulls the waistband of my tights away from my skin and begins to cut with a strong, regular motion. He slices downwards from my waist to my thigh, then turns the blades and cuts carefully around my upper thigh. 'Nearly done,' he murmurs, and starts again from the other side, slicing down and then cutting around the circumference of my other leg. The waist and gusset of my tights have now completely disappeared, leaving the legs sliding down towards my knees. 'Not quite finished yet,' he says and I sense him smiling. He takes the remnants he's cut off me and rips two strips from them. He uses first one and then the other to tie my tights on around my thighs so that I have makeshift black garters holding up what are now black woollen stockings.

'Perfect,' he says, observing his handiwork with satisfaction. 'Just as I wanted. But . . .' He takes up the scissors again and points that treacherous tickling blade at my white knickers. 'There's still something that needs my attention.'

I can feel that the white cotton is already wet with my juices, and I'm sure he can see that. He pushes the point of the blade downwards, not hard enough to hurt me but enough so that I can feel its hardness against my soft lips beneath the fabric. God, that semi-sharpness is incredible. I can hardly believe I'm responding like this to the movement of a pair of scissors but I can barely stop myself edging my thighs apart to let him slide the points beneath me. My clit is pressing out against my knickers as though begging for attention. Oh, wow, this is amazing . . .

This time he doesn't cut off what I'm wearing. Instead he plucks the wet fabric from the centre of my knickers and cuts out what's between his fingers, deftly keeping the blade away from my skin. 'Not quite enough, I can't see all your charms,' he remarks, and slices the blade further downwards so that he removes all the fabric that covers my sex. I'm entirely revealed now. 'Very nice,' he murmurs, leaning back to observe me.

I feel incredible. The slicing away has left me in tattered, shredded underwear, my breasts and my sex open to view, my tights left on as thick black stockings tied with ragged ribbons, but it feels like one of the sexiest things I've ever worn. I'm almost shuddering with the power of my arousal.

'Rosa,' he whispers. 'So beautiful. So disobedient. You made me wait. You must learn not to do that.' From behind him, he produces a large hard cushion that stands a ruler's length proud of the floor and pushes it against my thighs. 'Lean over that.'

I do as he says, wrapping my arms around the cushion. He gets up and walks around behind me. 'Push your bottom in the air,' he says. I thrust it upwards.

Those scissors press against my buttocks again, and then they are chopping at the back of my knickers. I feel my buttocks are bare to him. There is not much left of my knickers now: the elastic and some tattered cotton.

'Time for your punishment, Rosa.'

The first touch is soft, something tickling and gentle, swiping over my bottom. I realise it's a long tail of hair being played over my skin. I sigh a little. It's pleasant and soft but I know that means something else must be coming. Sure enough, the tail of hair leaves me, but only for a moment. An instant later, it slaps down on the skin of my bottom with a flicking hiss.

'Oh!' I cry, but more from surprise than pain. It stings but not enough to cause any real hurt. Another blow lands on my rear, flicking across the centre of my buttocks. The biting little stings prickle everywhere, setting my bottom glowing.

'Let me know that it's working, Rosa,' says my master.

I press my bottom upwards and say, 'I deserve my punishment, sir.'

He brings another stinging flick down on my skin and I cry out, 'Ow! Ow, sir, you're hurting your Rosa!'

'Because I love her,' he says in a kind voice. 'But she must learn her lesson.'

Thwack. The tail of hair hits hard, some of the hairs finding hot little places across my sex. It hurts more, but I can't help responding to the bite, arching my back as it hits me. Oh God, it's making me so incredibly aroused that I want to press against the cushion to alleviate the desperate need mounting between my legs and in my swollen clit.

Now he runs the tail of hair back over my bottom, soft and gentle again as it strokes over my reddened behind. It's so sweet and tender as he makes a circular figure of eight across the skin. Then a pause and – flick! – it whacks back down over me.

'Ahh,' I moan, clutching the cushion hard. He lands another and another. I move my bottom as if to avoid the strokes, moaning; it's pain but not torturous pain. It's stimulating me, making my skin hot and affecting my sex like nothing else as it prickles and throbs with excitement and longing.

I take ten of those tormentingly exciting blows, crying out loudly with each one, savouring the soft circular kisses between the tingling thwacks that make me wetter and more needy with each one.

My master likes to hear the effect of my punishment, I know that, so I beg him not to hurt his maid, who only wants to please him, and shriek when the tail whacks me. When he reaches the tenth blow, he says, 'You've taken your punishment well. Perhaps it's time to reward you.'

My master takes the flogger, turns it around and presses the thick leather handle against the entrance to my sex. I sigh and groan as he moves it around in the wetness, running it up towards my clit and then pressing it hard against my opening, as though he's going to fuck me with its hard, textured thickness. I can't help opening my legs to let him access me all the more easily. I want something inside me, now. My hips are already moving as though I'm being fucked and I'm making a low throaty moan of desire.

The handle is taken away. I feel him move closer to me and hear the slide of a zip. *Oh yes, please, Dominic, give it to me now.*

To my delight, I feel the smooth head of his penis at my entrance. He pauses only long enough to be sure that he is correctly positioned and then he pushes hard inside me, filling me up with the whole length of his cock. I'm so ready, so wet and open, that he slides in with ease, thrusting inside in one strong movement. It's all I want and more: my back arches as he hits home, pulls back and slams himself in me again. It's the fierce fucking I want so badly after the stimulation of the flogger. He puts one arm underneath my belly and the other around my breasts so that he can pull me into him even deeper as he fucks very hard, bucking his hips against me with every thrust. Then he drops one hand and his fingers find the hard nub inside my clit and start to play with it. I groan out loud and almost before I know what's happening, I've exploded with the incredible force of my orgasm, my head twisting as I gasp and shudder with the flood of sensation engulfing me.

Dominic gives half a dozen fierce thrusts and then suddenly, to my surprise, he pulls out. I'm panting, still luxuriating in the after-effects of my orgasm as I wonder what he's doing.

'You've come, Rosa,' he says. 'You came so fast, no doubt because of the beating you enjoyed so much. But I think there is still more pleasure for you before I take my own.'

I look over my shoulder and I can see that he's smiling as he looks at me, still prone beneath him, my legs spread apart, my back bare to him.

A moment later I can feel something hard and cold pressing against the lips of my sex. What is it? A dildo? Is he going to fuck me again with something else? In the past Dominic has enjoyed pleasuring me with toys, or ordered me to take extreme stimulation without coming. Is he going to do that again?

'You're very good,' he murmurs. 'This is something new for you, Rosa. But I want you to relax and let it happen. I promise you, you'll enjoy the results.'

He's pressing the short thing into me, rubbing it around. I'm so well lubricated from my orgasm, the thing is sliding about. I can't think how he's going to use it inside me, it feels too short, too small . . .

Then he pulls the stubby cool thing up from my entrance to my rear. I know suddenly what's he's going to do and I gasp. I'm not sure I want that. It's never been something I've desired.

'Let me try, Rosa,' he says coaxingly. 'If you don't like it, you only have to say. Give it a chance . . .'

Shall I? This is so small, so short and seems so harmless.

'If you want to, sir,' I say.

'Thank you.' He sounds sincerely grateful as he takes the well-greased little plug and presses it against the entrance of my rear. *Oh God, I'm not sure . . . I don't know . . .*

Then he pushes it gently. 'Press out against it, you'll find it easier,' he murmurs so I push slightly out, fearful that I might be doing the wrong thing. 'Yes, that's it. You're so lovely, I can't tell you what this sight is doing for me.'

It's cold and smooth and I feel it pass more easily than I had imagined just into the entrance. It feels huge, as though I'm bulging round it, but it doesn't hurt at all.

'That's it. It's there. Now, my sweet, you'll feel this all the more, I promise.'

His cock is at my entrance again and he pushes it in, not slamming it into my hungry sex as he did before, but entering me with exquisite slowness and I immediately understand why. The small plug he has inserted in me has narrowed my channel, making me tighter as his cock presses up against the obstacle within me.

'Ohhhh.' I can't help letting out a long groan as he inches forward, stretching me deliciously, filling me up as I've never been filled before.

'Yes, that's right,' he murmurs throatily, 'you like this, don't you?'

'Yes,' I moan. 'Oh God . . .'

His penis has gone into my very depths, his balls are pressed against me, his thighs hard against my bottom. He starts to move in and out, only withdrawing a few inches and then sliding forward again in easy, rhythmic thrusts, but the sensation is incredible. It's as though he's filled me entirely. His cock feels three times bigger as it thrusts into my core.

'You're fucking me,' I gasp. 'Oh I don't know, I can't . . .'

Each forward thrust seems to press the breath out of me, as the head of his penis hits the top of my vagina with a delicious pleasure that's close to pain. I can't help gasping and moaning as he begins to gather speed again. My stomach is melting with liquid lust and my clitoris is alive again, quivering beneath me as it's pressed against the cushion. It seems to be affected too by the tightness in my bottom, as though it's being tickled from behind as well as in front.

Dominic's panting now, almost growling as his cock plunges into me. The next moment he has grasped me round the waist with his huge hands, pulled me off the cushion and turned me over on the floor so that I lie in front of him, my breasts thrusting up from my tattered bra, my stockinged legs open to him. He looks down at my open sex: in the candlelight, his eyes are burning with desire and his face is set in an expression of lust. His penis stands proudly erect, wet with my juices. Then he's on me, his penis taking possession of me again, his weight heavy and delicious on top of me as his mouth devours my shoulders and neck and then finds my lips.

As we kiss feverishly and passionately, he thrusts deep into me, his hips moving with a delectable motion, pushing his cock into my tight passage. We're both moaning as we kiss and then I feel everything boiling up inside me, deeper and more intense than before. A fierce orgasm is coming to claim me and I'm helpless before it as it plucks me up into the tornado, whirling me around as a fusillade of fireworks go off inside me. As I'm surrendering to the intensity, Dominic pulls me even tighter against him and rocks with the force of his own climax, pouring it out inside me as we come together.

Afterwards, once we've got our breath and recovered ourselves and Dominic has removed the little silver plug that caused so much sensation, we laugh about the fact that I don't have much in the way of under-wear left.

'Take something from the bedroom,' offers Dominic.

'You mean some of the leather or the crotchless silk?' I ask, and we giggle again.

Dominic's collection of underwear for me isn't exactly designed for practicality but after a shower, I find some silky knickers and a bra and put those on. My tights will do as long as the makeshift garters stay in place. Dominic opens a bottle of wine and we drink glasses of chilled Chablis in the sitting room.

'So what are you doing in London?' I ask. 'I thought you were going to Montenegro.'

'There was a delay of a day or so before I could see this guy, so I decided on a flying visit to you.' He kisses me. 'Or rather – to Rosa.' He smiles wickedly at me.

I'm glad that Rosa exists; she's been the way we've been able to come back together but I feel a slight prickle of anxiety that she may be a permanent fixture. Could I cope with that? I know I'll do anything to be with Dominic but I can't pretend that in the end, I want him to be making love to me – not to a fictitious character. But I won't press it now – these are early days and I can feel our relationship healing after the recent schism. If Rosa helps, then that's fine with me.

'I have to tell you something,' I say hesitantly.

'Mmm?' He looks over at me.

I don't know if I should say it, but I've decided that honesty is going to be everything between me and Dominic, and I have to tell him the truth. 'This evening . . . I was with Andrei.'

It's like shutters come down. His face closes off from me and his eyes go cold. 'I see.'

'No, wait, listen to me. I have to explain why I'm still working for him. It's because of Mark.'

Dominic cocks his head towards me and waits to hear more.

121

'The Fra Angelico turned out to be a fake, and Andrei wanted to blame Mark for it. I couldn't let that happen, Dominic. Mark is so sick at the moment, God knows what it would do to him if his reputation is destroyed.'

'It's a fake?' Dominic frowns. 'But Andrei paid millions. No wonder he's pissed off.'

I nod. 'It's his own fault, he wanted it and wouldn't wait. But he needs a scapegoat, and Mark was going to be it. I appealed to his better nature and he agreed to protect Mark – on one condition.'

A stormy look fills Dominic's eyes. 'Let me guess. You're part of the package.' He gets to his feet and begins to pace around the room. God, he looks handsome when he's angry. 'Damn Dubrovski, he's ruthless. He doesn't care what it takes for him to get what he wants.'

'Calm down, he's not going to get me. Not like that. But I do have to carry on working for him, just for a while. Just till Mark's stronger. I had to tell you. I want everything to be completely open between us now. No more secrets.'

Dominic's jaw is set and his lips are tight. I can tell he's battling his fury against Andrei.

'Please,' I say gently, 'you must believe me – I'm not going to let anything happen – and I think Andrei is too proud to force the issue. He wants me to come to him of my own accord. Well, he'll be waiting till Hell freezes over.'

That seems to break through Dominic's own mini-freeze and he smiles reluctantly.

'You see?' I say triumphantly. 'I knew you could smile!'

His smile broadens. 'Okay, okay.' He sits down next to me on the sofa. 'It kills me that you're still going to be around Dubrovski but if you have to, then . . . well, you have to.'

'Thanks,' I say softly. 'I know you don't want to say that. I appreciate that you trust me. By the way, you need to stay on your guard as well.'

'Really?' He looks at me questioningly.

'Yes. Andrei knew you'd arrived here in London. He let it slip when I said I was meeting a friend.'

Dominic looks grim-faced again. 'That doesn't surprise me, not one bit,' he says. 'I told you what he's like – he's pathological when it comes to what he thinks is his honour. It's just old-fashioned pig-headed pride, but he considers it some kind of manly quality to get obsessed with his enemies. He'll have people tracking me, no question.'

'He doesn't mean you any harm, does he?' I ask, suddenly worried.

He shakes his head. 'Not physical harm, no. At least, not at the moment. But he wants to monitor my movements, no doubt see if I approach any of the contacts I've made through his business. He suspects I will want to poach investors for my own company. I'm sure he's getting his lawyers ready to sue me if I try anything that breaks the terms of my old contract with him.'

'And will you? Poach anyone?'

He fixes me with a look. 'I don't go after them. But if they come to me – well, that's another matter.'

'Oh God, Dominic, you've got to be careful.' I'm suddenly fearful. I don't want him to cross Andrei and risk any reprisals.

'I'm not afraid,' he says with a laugh. 'I do the right thing. I won't try and approach them. But I'm also not going to turn away genuine prospects for my business. I'm going to make a success of this. It's what I've been waiting for.'

'I know, I know . . .'

He turns to look me straight in the eye, his dark brown gaze sincere. 'These weeks are vital to me; you know that. It's why we can't be together right now. I have to do this. But as soon as I've got to where I need to be, then I'll come back to you – if that's what you want.'

'Of course it is,' I whisper. 'I can't be happy without you.'

He puts out his hand and strokes my cheek softly. 'I'm so glad we're back together.'

'Are we?' I ask, putting my hand over his so I can hold it to my face. 'Back together?'

He nods, smiling. 'I don't think we can help it.'

'No more secrets,' I say.

He nods and bends towards me for another kiss. 'Absolutely. No more secrets.'

# CHAPTER EIGHT

Dominic sends me home that night in a chauffeur-driven car. The driver drops me back at our flat some time after 11 p.m. I'm utterly exhausted after everything that's happened this week and I'm looking forward to a lazy weekend. Luckily, Laura is in exactly the same frame of mind, and we spend a fun couple of days in the cosy flat, making our plans for the trip to New York at the end of next week. We find a decent midtown hotel and start searching for good bars and places to eat.

'We can do all our Christmas shopping as well!' announces Laura.

'We don't want to bring too much stuff back,' I say, always cautious. 'And we don't want to spend the entire time wondering what to buy for other people. This is our girly trip away, remember!'

We'll compromise, we decide, with an hour or two in Bloomingdale's to get some gifts. The rest of the time we'll be pleasing ourselves and will do any panic shopping in the last few days before Christmas, once we're back in London.

'Did you tell Dominic about our trip?' asks Laura. I've told her that I saw Dominic last night and that it looks as though it's all back on.

'Yes, but I explained that it's a girls-only weekend so he didn't get too jealous.'

'Are you going to see him over Christmas?'

I shake my head. 'I don't think so. He's going to be travelling over the holidays – schmoozing businessmen at various parties and getting them when they're in a festive mood. I don't know when I'll see him again.'

'I'm sure you'll meet up afterwards,' Laura says consolingly. 'It's brilliant that you guys are back together.'

I can't help beaming at her. 'I know. It's fantastic.'

She laughs at my expression. 'You're such a barometer – when you're happy with Dominic, you're upright and perky, and when you're not, you wilt and go sad. You're definitely in perky mode. This bodes well for our trip!'

Laura's right, I am happy – and not just because I'm feeling so sexually sated by Dominic. I'm full of hopes for the future and looking forward to the New York trip. But when I get back to work on Monday, it's to find that Caroline is more solemn-faced than ever.

'Mark's had a setback over the weekend,' she says when I arrive. 'He's caught an infection and it's absolutely floored him.

'Oh no,' I say in dismay. 'Poor Mark!'

'He's being pumped full of antibiotics at the moment. He's not well at all.'

'I was hoping to visit him today.'

Caroline shakes her head. 'I'm afraid not. He's not up to it. I'll let you know when he can face visitors.'

126

I feel awful that I'm going to be going away on a jolly jaunt when my boss is so ill but Caroline gives that idea short shrift.

'Don't be silly, Mark would be delighted that you're going to have fun. Besides, I know he takes trips to New York all the time. I'm sure that he'd consider it an advantage that you're going to get to know the city.'

That's a comfort and I do my best to concentrate on my work so that I can clear my desk in time for the trip away. The problem is that I have a new distraction: Dominic. Now that I have his new details, and now that having our correspondence spied on isn't the issue it was when he worked for Andrei, the emails start arriving, one every hour or so, telling me where he is and where he's planning to go. I enjoy the feeling of being so connected to him. Ever since we've met, Dominic has been prone to vanishing on me, and I realise that I'd half expected to hear nothing at all from him once we were apart. But now I get emails from the car on the way to the airport, from the VIP departure lounge, from the first-class cabin, just messages of a few words letting me know where he is and where he intends to go next.

Then I realise: Dominic is making sure I know his plans. Perhaps he's being followed by one of Andrei's men, and wants to ensure that his whereabouts are on record.

The thought is a chilling one – but I already know that Andrei is tracking Dominic's movements. Why would he suddenly have stopped doing that? I can't help feeling afraid but I remember Dominic laughing at the idea that he might let Andrei's actions affect him.

*He's doing nothing wrong*, I remind myself. *Andrei can't do anything against him.*

But I remember the warning James gave me when I first became involved with Dubrovski, telling me that Andrei had come to his fortune in murky, perhaps lawless ways, and that he thought I should be very careful before associating with him.

Images of Andrei flash in front of me: he's elegant in his tailored suits, driving his smoke-grey Bentley convertible. He's sophisticated in his tastes, loving his art collection and his beautiful apartments, and enjoying the finer things he can easily afford.

But once he was a bullet-headed orphan fighting his way to the top in the sleazy backstreets of Moscow. Boys like that get tough fast and they learn to take their opponents out without a shred of feeling because, unless they act first, they'll be the ones left for dead in an alley.

No one would want to cross Andrei, I'm sure of that. And now the man I love has set himself up as his rival.

I want to be strong, as strong as Dominic, but I can't help being afraid.

The next few days pass quickly as I prepare for the trip to New York. Andrei emails me the details of his apartment and says that his housekeeper will be expecting me to drop by at any time. I look up the address online and see that his apartment is in a luxurious block right on Central Park. I might not know New York, but I can guess that this is an extremely prestigious address. Maybe I'll take Laura to see it and we can ooh and aah together at a glimpse of Manhattan life that we'd never normally see.

Mark is still too ill to receive visitors but Caroline tells me that the doctors are confident they're getting on top of the infection. It's been a setback but not something we should worry too much about. That's a huge relief.

'You go to New York and enjoy yourself,' Caroline says with a smile as she watches me finishing up the last bits and pieces before I head off on the Thursday. 'You can't do anything here.'

'Thanks, Caroline. Will you give Mark my love?'

'Of course. Now off you go! You can tell me all about it on Tuesday.'

I leave the office that evening feeling excited. We're actually going tomorrow! It's going to be fun, I just know it. If only Mark were better, then life would be wonderful.

*Except . . .*

A disloyal little voice sounds in my head. I try to shush it but it pipes up before I can make it be quiet.

*You'd prefer to be going to New York with Dominic.*

Stop it! I'm going to have a fantastic time with Laura.

*Yes, but with Dominic there would be romance and kisses and . . . sex. Lots of lovely, mind-blowing sex . . .*

Sex isn't everything, I scold myself. Friendship is pretty important too, remember? I tell myself that I owe Laura some time. She's single and I've not exactly been the perfect flatmate over the last few months with Dominic – and Andrei – taking up so much of my time. This is payback. And I'm looking forward to sipping Cosmopolitans in some fancy bar – I just won't expect the evening to end in multiple orgasms, that's all.

I shiver as I remember the last, extraordinary orgasm I had with Dominic. With that little silver plug he's taken me along another path I could never have imagined going down. I try to remember what I was like at the beginning of this extraordinary year: I was so inexperienced, thinking that my small-town boyfriend was the centre of the universe, and seriously considering settling down with him. Thank God for Hannah and her enormous tits! If she hadn't tempted him into bed, we might never have broken up and I could be having boring sex with Adam for the rest of my life.

As I take the Underground home, I wonder where Dominic is at this moment. He emailed me this morning to say that his meetings in Montenegro had gone very well, but that he's taken an unexpected trip to Klosters, the expensive skiing resort where millionaires like to gather for Christmas. He'll be staying in a friend's chalet while he socialises on the slopes and makes those all-important contacts, the ones who might be interested in putting some serious money into his investment fund.

It's going to be full on. Skiing, après-ski, après-après-ski. Hard work, honey, but you know me, I'm the self-sacrificing type (or am I?). I'll keep in touch. Enjoy New York, have fun with Laura. Take care.

D x x

I send back a reply full of excitement about our New York plans and telling him to enjoy himself skiing. It's only later, as I'm letting myself into the flat, that I have a sudden pang of guilt. I haven't told Dominic that I'm going to visit Andrei's apartment while I'm in New York, or that Andrei's offered me this new commission for next year. I'm cross with myself – what happened to no more secrets? I've promised that I'm going to be open and honest with Dominic now. There's no point in keeping things to myself, it only leads to misunderstandings.

But there's no real harm in it – after all, I'm not going to see Andrei. It's just a look around his apartment to keep him happy. And if I'm honest, I'd like to see it, get a feel for the art he has there and work out what I might do with it, even though I've no intention of taking the job. And I'll tell Dominic in my next email. Definitely.

Laura and I are both hyper with excitement that evening, checking our luggage over and over again, making sure we have passports and money, maps and guides, and all the bits and pieces we can't travel without, from phone chargers to lip salve. We're so keyed up that we open a celebratory bottle of wine and drink it very fast with our supper. So we open another and end up a bit drunk, chatting away until we realise with horror that it's nearly midnight and we're supposed to be up at four for the taxi that's taking us to the airport. We tidy up and turn in, but I can't get to sleep.

It's weird but I'm so excited to be travelling like any other ordinary person. I've enjoyed my experience of the luxurious world of the very wealthy but it's indelibly linked in my mind to ownership. I've only been given access to that world because I've worked for Andrei and I can only enjoy it on his terms. It's not mine, or anything close to mine, so really, it's no more meaningful than a fairground ride. Whereas my ticket to New York, and the hotel and everything else, has been paid for with money I've earned. I'm proud of that and I'm going to enjoy this trip a million times more because of it.

I don't know what time I go to sleep but it feels like about five minutes before my alarm goes off. I drag my eyes open and groan, then force myself out of bed and into the shower. I meet Laura as I come out and she looks red-eyed and tired too.

'We shouldn't have had that wine last night,' she says, heading into the bathroom.

'Tell me about it! Taxi's due in fifteen minutes.' I think I'm going to feel awful, but as soon as I'm dressed in jeans, a sloppy T-shirt and a sharp dark green blazer and biker boots, I feel good again. A drink of water helps clear my head and just as Laura is bringing her bag into the hall we hear the beep from the taxi outside the flat.

'Let's go, sister!' she says, her eyes bright.

'You betcha!' I smile back. This is fun already. I can't wait for the adventure to begin.

We make the airport in excellent time because the roads out of London are deserted at this time of the morning. We're excited and desperate for coffee by the time we arrive but we decide to check in first so that we can go through security and settle down in the departure area for a bit. We're going to have a good hour or so to wait – plenty of time to have breakfast and browse in duty-free.

At the check-in desk we hand over our passports and cases. The woman behind the desk checks everything over, taps things into her computer and scans our passports. Then she looks up and smiles at us. 'Good news, ladies. You've been upgraded.'

'What?' Laura exclaims.

'Yes. Congratulations. You're flying first class to JFK.'

'Oh wow!' Laura gives a little jump of pleasure and excitement.

'Why?' I say with a frown.

The woman looks at me, evidently surprised by my reaction. 'I don't know, I'm afraid. It's just what it says on the computer here. You're now first-class passengers. You wait for your flight in the first-class lounge.'

'What's wrong with you?' asks Laura as we make

our way to the VIP lounge. 'Aren't you excited that we're upgraded? I've never travelled first class before!'

'Of course I am,' I say as heartily as I can, not wanting to spoil her pleasure. But the truth is, I'm a little upset. I can sense someone's hand in this, and I feel as though my private trip has been invaded. I was proud that we were doing this alone. Now we've been given a little bonus that we've not earned or paid for.

*Unless it's just your lucky day . . .*

*Yeah, right!*

The first-class lounge is nice, though. We take full advantage of the delicious food and steaming coffee on offer, then curl up on the sofas with a range of magazines to while away the time till our flight is called. When it does, we're ushered through carpeted corridors and on to the plane before anyone else, turning left as we go on board. In first class, the luxury is in stark contrast to the cramped conditions in economy: vast comfortable seats that can be turned into beds at any time, a packet of expensive-brand toiletries plus slippers, masks and even a pair of silk pyjamas in case we want to change into something comfortable. And that's before we've begun playing with our personal entertainment systems or ordering whatever we want from the menus.

'I could *live* on here!' Laura says ecstatically. 'I can't believe we've been so lucky.'

The pleasure on her face softens my hostility towards whoever decided to do this for us. Maybe it's not such a bad gift. The problem is that I suspect Andrei is behind it and that makes it hard for me to enjoy it. He's got a way of making me accept things from him that I don't really want: nights in hotels, expensive dresses, jewels – and now this.

*Relax,* I tell myself as the plane begins to taxi down the runway. *There's nothing you can do about it. And in New York, you'll be far away from Andrei. Just enjoy.*

# CHAPTER NINE

When we arrive at JFK it's only mid-morning, and we get another burst of energy as we head off the plane, through passport control and out into America. It feels simultaneously familiar from all the movies and shows I've watched that are set here, and foreign, with the strange accents and different feel to the place. I've never felt so British. Laura and I have planned to get a yellow cab into Manhattan but as we exit the arrivals lounge, I'm startled to see my name being held up on a card by a black man in a dark suit and peaked cap.

'Look, Beth!' Laura nudges me at the same moment. 'That's your name!'

'Miss Villiers?' The man smiles at me. 'How are you? I'm here to take you and your friend to your hotel.'

'What?' I say, suspicious again. 'Who booked you?'

'I've no idea, ma'am,' he says politely. 'I just do what my boss tells me.'

'Beth,' hisses Laura, 'this is probably part of the first-class service!'

I'm not so sure. I stare at the driver. 'What's your company? Does the airline book you?'

'All sorts of people book us, ma'am, I can assure you we're completely reputable. Now, would you ladies like to come this way? The limo is waiting.'

'A limo!' Laura exclaims, her eyes bright.

I hesitate. This is probably fine. It's probably part of the service. Where's the harm? 'Okay,' I say reluctantly. He takes our luggage and we follow as he leads us out to where a long square-nosed limousine is waiting. We slide into leather seats, the driver loads our luggage and then we're off, heading out onto a motorway and towards the famous Manhattan skyline. I try to put my negative feelings to one side and just enjoy it as Laura chatters away about our plans for the rest of the day. I must be one ungrateful woman if I can't enjoy being treated to the finer things in life – but I can't help wishing that whoever it is would just butt out of it and let me get on with things in my own way.

It takes about an hour to get to Manhattan and crossing the bridge onto the island itself is a thrilling moment. The sky is a cool unblemished blue and filled with icy sunshine. The temperature is very cold but that only adds to the wintry, Christmassy glamour of the city. As the limo proceeds up the famous grid-patterned roads, we gaze out, drinking in the sights of the busy city, pointing out landmarks we recognise, and thrilling to the numbered names of the streets. We've chosen a modest hotel in midtown, one that's close enough to the action that we can walk just about anywhere, but which is still in a reasonable price bracket. The photos online showed a pleasant, rather old-fashioned place, and we've booked a small twin room, which is all we need.

I'm surprised when we come to a halt on East 57th Street in front of a very glamorous hotel, an elegant building that soars up into the sky. A doorman comes over and opens the car door but I'm leaning forward and knocking on the glass partition between us and the driver. He lowers it.

'Where on earth is this?' I demand. 'This isn't our hotel!'

'This is the Four Seasons, ma'am,' replies the driver. 'This is where I've been told to bring you. I understand you have reservations here.'

'Well, we don't!' I exclaim. 'Our hotel is on Lexington Avenue. Please take us there at once.'

The doorman is standing there baffled, obviously waiting for us to get out. Laura is half in and half out, listening to the conversation with anxiety in her eyes.

'Do I understand, ma'am, that you don't want to stay at the Four Seasons?' The driver shoots me a quizzical look over his shoulder. I can tell he thinks that this is just plain weird.

'That's right. We're at the Washington on Lexington Avenue.'

'Beth . . .' Laura is looking at me as the driver shakes his head in disbelief.

'Laura, we didn't book the Four Seasons and while it looks amazing we can't pretend that this is part of the first-class flight. I don't think they go that far.

Someone is being way too generous and I don't like it. I want to go to the hotel we chose together.'

I can see from Laura's face that she knows this is the right thing to do, no matter how enticing the luxury being dangled in front of us. She sits back in her seat. 'Okay. Let's go to the Washington.'

'Thank you, you can close the door now!' I say to the doorman, and he obeys, evidently confused and having understood very little of what's just gone on. I have a feeling that there aren't many people who react angrily to being brought to the Four Seasons.

The driver sighs and heads off into the busy Manhattan traffic and, fifteen minutes later, he draws up in front of a much smaller, more modest red-brick hotel.

'Here you are, ma'am,' he says, 'just like you wanted. This is the Washington.'

'It looks fantastic,' Laura says stoically, though I can tell she's yearning a little for the glamour of the other hotel.

'It's just what we need – and what we can afford,' I say firmly. 'Thank you, driver, you can drop us here.'

A few minutes later, we're standing at the reception desk in the traditional-looking lobby. It's not exactly the last word in New York chic but it's very cosy with its patterned rugs and brass light fittings. The man behind the desk is neatly turned out with gelled-down hair and elegant hands. He's checking our reservations.

'Oh,' he says, looking at his screen with a frown. 'That's most unusual. Hold on a second while I check with my manager.'

Laura and I exchange glances.

'What now?' she murmurs. 'Another upgrade?'

'But no one knows we're here,' I say. 'I didn't tell anyone we were staying in this hotel. Did you?'

She shakes her head.

The man returns with his manager, who has a neatly trimmed moustache and pale blue eyes. He smiles at us.

'Good morning, ladies, how are you? There's been a change to your reservation.'

I groan internally. Here we go again.

'I'm afraid it's been cancelled.'

'What?' I exclaim.

'Cancelled?' echoes Laura, her face falling in dismay.

The manager nods gravely. 'That's right. Cancelled.'

'Please uncancel it,' I say, trying to sound as imperious as I can. 'We didn't give any instructions to cancel, I've got my confirmation printout right here. We need our room!'

'We can't do that, I'm afraid, the room has already been rebooked and we have no other availability. It's a busy time of year. I'm sure you understand.'

'But . . .' I can hardly believe my ears. How has this happened? 'Where are we going to stay?'

The manager makes a beckoning gesture to a man standing by the door. 'That's all been arranged, so I understand. This car has been sent for you.'

The man comes up to us and takes up our luggage. 'If you'd like to follow me, ladies.'

Laura and I exchange helpless looks. We don't have any choice now. The Washington can't give us a room even if it wants to. Outside, another limo is waiting for us. We climb inside this one, which is very similar to the last. Our new driver loads our luggage and then we're off again. This time we seem to be heading away from midtown again, back the way we came. Then we're in a different part of the city, away from the grid and into a more loosely gathered set of streets.

'This is the Village,' Laura says, staring out of the window. 'I came here when I last visited. Definitely one of the coolest parts of town, much more arty and boho than the area around Central Park.'

'I suppose that's good,' I say, watching the sights outside as they glide past the window. I'm still feeling cross that our plans have been interfered with like this. But why on earth would Andrei have booked us into the Four Seasons, cancelled our reservations at the Washington and then arranged another hotel? I can't make it out.

'I know you're not happy about all this,' Laura says tentatively. 'But this is your Russian guy being generous again, isn't it?'

I feel bad. From Laura's perspective, a glamorous hotel and limos are amazing things to be enjoyed. She has no idea how Andrei has tried to control me and how much I resent him interfering in my life, even when the things he does look like wonderful, generous presents. Well, I've tried to reject this one but Andrei's out-thought me somehow.

'Sorry,' I say to her with a smile. 'You must think I'm a sour old killjoy. I just wanted to get away from

Andrei's generosity for a while and it seems that he isn't going to let me.'

'Maybe it's not him,' Laura suggests. 'Maybe it's Mark. An early Christmas present, or something.'

'I suppose that's possible. Caroline might have made the changes.' I frown. 'In fact, I might have told her we were staying at the Washington now I think about it.'

'There you are then.' Laura's face clears. 'It must be Mark. That's good. We can enjoy it with a good conscience now, can't we?'

I nod. I'm not convinced but I don't want to spoil Laura's fun.

The driver stops in front of a fashionable-looking hotel with a steep flight of steps into an amazing lobby.

'The Soho Grand,' he announces.

'Wow!' sighs Laura, her eyes shining. 'I've heard about this place, I've always wanted to come here. It's supposed to be amazing!'

'Looks like we don't have any choice,' I say sardonic-ally, as porters and doormen rush up to help us out and into the hotel lobby. I guess that we don't look like high-end guests as the receptionist is friendly but cool until she types our names into her system with her perfectly manicured nails. Her eyes widen with quickly concealed surprise as she gazes at her screen and then she turns to us with a bright smile.

'Ladies, we're so excited that you're going to be join-ing us for your stay. You're going to love the Loft North, it's our most amazing suite.'

'*Suite*,' breathes Laura, her face alight with excitement.

*Suite,* I think crossly. Not just a room. A goddamned suite. A loft. That doesn't sound like Mark's style to me. It sounds much more like a man with limitless resources who always expects the best.

*Well, whaddya know?*

The hotel is incredible. Everywhere there is colour and stylish good taste that mixes contemporary and vintage sensibilities, from the lobby with its turquoise leather seats to the Victorian-style industrial wrought iron staircase. We can't stop gazing about us, drinking in the gorgeous surroundings and the fashionable people who are everywhere, sitting chatting on sofas, drinking in the bars, reading in the library area. This is so cool.

We're ushered to a lift by a very polite young man, who takes us up the many flights to the top of the hotel. Then he unlocks the door of the loft and shows us in. We walk in, open-mouthed as we gaze about it.

'Oh my God,' breathes Laura. 'This is like my dream apartment come to life.'

She's right. There's very little of the hotel room about this place. It looks like somewhere you'd want to live. It's modern and yet completely stylishly timeless with its mixture of surfaces and textures: wood, concrete, marble, leather, suede and velvet. The sitting room is perfectly judged, with comfortable-looking sofas and armchairs covered with cashmere throws and luxurious cushions, and a desk set up with a Mac computer and iPad. On the shelves and tables there are ornaments and books, while on the walls are beautifully framed black-and-white shots of New York life in the fifties.

'Over here is your fully stocked bar,' the young man says, showing us a concrete bar with leather stools in front of an array of bottles. 'Let me show you the bedrooms.' He leads us to the master bedroom, a huge space decorated in tones of taupe and stone with a contrasting pony-skin ottoman. Its bathroom has a luxurious deep free-standing slipper bath as well as a huge shower.

'I think this had better be yours,' says Laura, giving me a sideways look.

'I won't fight you on that,' I say with a smile. I've decided to relax and enjoy this amazing place. For one thing, I don't have a choice, and for another, I don't want to spoil the atmosphere by being a grouch. *And it is incredible, there's no denying that . . .*

We're led back through to the suite to the second bedroom, which is only marginally smaller than the first and has its own bathroom as well. Back in the sitting room, our guide says, 'You've got a plasma television, of course, with surround sound and a selection of films. You have a full-time concierge service with instant response, so ask for anything you want at any time. The iPad over there is loaded with information about the area, where to go and what to see. And of course, the terrace is there for you as well.' He gestures to what is possibly the best thing about the room – the enormous private terrace with its extraordinary view over lower Manhattan all the way to the Empire State. 'We can have heaters lit outside for you if you're feeling the cold.' He smiles. 'Is that everything, ladies? Any questions or shall I leave you to settle in?'

'That's great, thank you,' I say, and remember we're supposed to tip in New York. I pull a five-dollar bill out of my purse and hand it to him. 'We'll ask if there's anything else.'

'Thank you,' he says, pocketing the money with a smile and a bow. 'Enjoy your stay with us.'

As soon as he's gone, Laura and I stare at each other, unable to believe what's just happened. We're in one of the best rooms in New York. We clutch each other's hands and start jumping up and down, shrieking and laughing with disbelief.

'There's only one problem,' Laura says, when we've calmed down enough to talk.

'Yes?' What could possibly be wrong with this place?

'I love this room so much, I don't want to go out. We're not going to see any of New York at all!'

It's lucky we made some plans because without them we might not have stirred from our luxurious apartment, but we have a timetable of things we want to see and do while we're in this amazing city.

After settling into our suite and trying out all the amenities, including ordering a delicious lunch of crab salad and smoked salmon, we head out on foot, determined to see all we can before it gets dark. It's cold outside but we're well wrapped up and full of excitement. We take the subway uptown and make our first scheduled stop at the Metropolitan Museum of Art, and while away a few hours looking at some of the masterpieces there. Then we venture into Central Park, where it's already getting dark, and buy hot chocolate and salty pretzels from a stall. We wander around talking about all the things we want to do while we're here. I'm aware of a weight off my shoulders for the first time in ages. I feel carefree here, and it's great to be with Laura, just two friends together. Romantic bliss is wonderful, but this is just plain fun.

My only worry is that Andrei is obviously throwing around a lot of cash to give us first-class flights, limos and that stunning hotel room. It's exactly the kind of extravagant gesture that would appeal to him. Mark would never choose a hotel like the Grand, and he certainly wouldn't book the penthouse suite. And the way Andrei second-guessed that I'd insist on leaving the Four Seasons has his cunning hallmark on it. I don't like the idea of that one bit – he's pulling me ever deeper into his debt with these expensive gifts and, worse than that, I don't like the fact that he knows exactly where we are. Even while we're wandering through the galleries of the Met, or strolling through Central Park as darkness falls and the lights begin to glitter, I can't help wondering if someone is watching us. Every now and then I glance over my shoulder to see if we're being observed, but I spot no one. Eventually my paranoia begins to wear off. There's no sign that we're being followed and I tell myself that no one could possibly have tailed us on the subway or round the museum. It's in my imagination.

Back at the hotel, we enjoy long baths before getting dressed to go out. We've been up for hours and it's the middle of the night our time, but we're still fizzing with excitement. The iPad supplies us with plenty of suggestions for dinner and the concierge books us a table at the place we choose.

Before we go out that evening in our glamorous dresses and high heels, I check my email inbox. There's one from Dominic.

Hey gorgeous girl, did you get to New York okay? Are you enjoying yourself? Tell me everything. Can't wait to see you when you're back.

D x

I hesitate for a moment before I go to type a reply. Do I tell him what Andrei has done? Won't it infuriate him? What's the point in upsetting him?

*No more secrets,* I remind myself.

*Yes, but I'm going to tell him. I don't want to ruin his day by making him furious. It'll be better when I explain everything face to face.*

I type back:

Hi sweetie

Yes, we got here fine with a couple of interesting adventures. We're having a fab time but can't write more now, we're going out for dinner. Shopping tomorrow, skating at Madison Square Gardens, seeing Frick collection. All amazing.

Can't wait to see you too

B x x

I stare at my message, reading it back. Should I tell him about our upgrades?

Laura comes in, looking wonderful in a tight black silky dress with flowing sleeves and dark gold glittering shoes. 'Come on, Beth, we'll be late. Our reservation is in ten minutes.'

'Coming, coming.' I hesitate for a second and then press send.

# CHAPTER TEN

Over the next two days, we have an unforgettable time in New York. We see so much, visiting the literary sights that mean so much to Laura, and the artistic ones that appeal to me. We both enjoy doing the touristy things as well, like going to the top of the Empire State. I adore the Frick collection and the stunning modern works at MOMA, and just soaking up the atmosphere in the glamorous Village. There's also the added thrill of Christmas that gives a special sparkle to all our shopping: on one afternoon we see about twenty Santas walking around Fifth Avenue and we can't resist a horse-drawn carriage ride around a frosty New York driven by Father Christmas himself.

We have a marvellous time, either enjoying the luxury of our loft suite and the way our every need is answered almost before we're aware of it, or seeing the sights of Manhattan. Even though I love being with Laura and all the giggles we have, I can't help missing Dominic. When Laura and I snuggle up in our carriage with a rug over our knees, I wish suddenly and fervently that he was here to wrap his arms around me and kiss me tenderly as we're pulled through Central Park, the bells on the reins jingling and our

Father Christmas calling out 'Ho, ho, ho!' in just the best fairy-tale way.

I get another message from Dominic that I pick up on the Mac in our suite, but it only asks if I'm having a good time and tells me that he's broken his personal best on the black run, so I just give him the highlights. After all, I'm home on Monday evening and once all this excitement is over, I can tell him about the weird things that have happened.

On Monday morning, when we're tired but still not wanting to go back home even though our flight is in the evening, I get an email. As soon as I see it, my heart starts to pound and my palms dampen. I hadn't realised how much Andrei has been on my mind throughout this weekend until I see his name in black print on the screen.

Beth.
My housekeeper tells me that you still haven't been to my apartment. Are you intending to go? Please let me know.
A

It's the intrusion of cold, hard reality. I've been lost in a pleasant world of enjoying myself with Laura. I've always known that at home my problems still await me but I've let myself forget them for a while. This email reminds me that they can't really be banished.

I call Laura, who's been out on our terrace taking

photos of our incredible view. She comes in, her nose glowing from the frosty air outside.

'Oh, Beth, I can't believe this is our last day. I don't want to go home!'

'Me neither – it's been amazing. But, listen, would you mind if we make some last-minute changes to the day? I know we need to be on our way to the airport at seven and we had some plans but I've had an email from Andrei – I need to go to his place. It won't take long, and he won't be there. Would that be okay?'

Laura sits down on the arm of my chair and looks at the screen. 'Are you kidding? I bet his apartment will be amazing, I'd love to see it.'

I smile at her. 'Great. I'll let his housekeeper know that we'll drop in today.'

Andrei's apartment is on the edge of Central Park in a splendid building that looks like a Victorian Gothic castle, ornate with carving and embellishment. We approach it hardly believing that we're going to be allowed into somewhere so grand, but when we tell the doorman that we're here to visit Mr Dubrovski's apartment and he's checked our names, we're ushered in through the carved arched doorway and then through to a huge, impressive hallway where a porter in gold-trimmed livery waits for us.

'Mr Dubrovski's housekeeper is expecting us,' I say loftily, trying to sound as though I'm the kind of person who ought to be waved through these hallowed portals but probably sounding completely stupid. Laura hovers at my elbow, her eyes wide as though waiting for us to be told to sling our hooks, in which case she'd probably be straight out the door.

The porter checks a list he has somewhere under the lip of the desk and nods. 'Yes, you're expected. Please go up to the eighteenth floor.'

The lift is extraordinary, nestled behind two sliding wrought-iron gates and containing a red velvet seat below a big gilt-framed mirror. I press the large black button and the lift rises smoothly to the eighteenth floor. We emerge into a thickly carpeted corridor and right in front of us is a huge mahogany door with golden numbers on it reading 755.

'That's it,' I say to Laura.

'Okay.' Her eyes are huge and she looks quite scared. This is the most unpredictable part of our trip so far.

'Come on. Let's get it over with.' I stride forward and knock on the door. A moment later it's opened by a smartly dressed woman in her forties with a sharp dark bob. She says nothing but looks enquiringly at us.

'My name is Beth Villiers,' I say tentatively. 'Mr Dubrovski said I should come.'

Her face softens immediately and she stands back to let us in. 'Yes, of course,' she says in a surprisingly friendly voice. 'I got your message. Come in.'

I walk inside, Laura close behind me. At once we see the extreme luxury of the place: everything is shiny, polished, expensive and in perfect taste, from the floor of white and green checked marble to the polished ebony lampstands. Like Andrei's apartment in Albany, this place is done in a strong neo-classical style but it's noticeable that there are no pictures on any of the walls.

*I guess this is where I come in.*

'I'll show you around,' says the housekeeper, leading us into a beautifully decorated room with a stunning view over the park: as far as we can see from the broad windows, there is the spread of the park edged with beautiful buildings. In the sitting room itself a polished grand piano sits by the window, and comfortable sofas face each other over padded ottomans loaded with beautiful art books.

'This is the informal sitting room,' explains the housekeeper and she proceeds to lead us through a dozen more rooms including a long wooden-floored room hung with huge crystal chandeliers, which she calls the ballroom.

'Incredible,' breathes Laura as we follow the housekeeper from room to room. 'This is amazing. Imagine what it must be worth!'

I don't say anything – this doesn't surprise me, but then, I know Andrei. Even as we climb a staircase to another floor with six luxurious bedrooms, the master bedroom with a sunken marble bath, I feel as though this is exactly what I would expect him to own. It's incredible and expensive but there's something missing: a real heart and a sense of someone with passions and interests who actually lives here. I know that's what he wants me to add to his home with my choice of art. I remember how cool the Albany apartment seemed until the paintings were up. The beautiful Fragonard portrait I bought for his bathroom made the room come alive. That's what this place needs.

We return to the lower floor and the housekeeper takes us back to the first room we entered – the cosy small sitting room with its view of Central Park.

'Can I get you some coffee?' asks the housekeeper. 'Tea?'

I check my watch. We only have a few hours before we need to be back at the hotel to pack and catch our taxi to the airport. 'I'm not sure . . .' I say.

'Yes please, I'd love some coffee,' pipes up Laura. As the housekeeper goes out, she turns to me with an impish smile and nudges me playfully. 'Come on! How often are we going to get to hang out in a place like this? It's our last few hours in New York. Let's live it up a little.'

'Okay,' I say, reluctant to tell her that I don't feel right in this place. It makes me think of all the many ways Andrei wants to control me. I only feel able to give myself, surrender myself, to someone who loves and cherishes me. Without that, I couldn't dream of submitting myself. Just being in this apartment makes me aware of how my relationship with Andrei isn't like that at all.

We sit in that magnificent apartment that makes us feel as though we're floating over the park. The housekeeper brings us coffee and hazelnut biscuits and then leaves us to enjoy them. Laura chatters on and I listen, but I'm eager to be off.

'Are you all right?' enquires Laura, nibbling a biscuit. 'You're awfully quiet.'

'Yes . . . but I want to get back to the hotel,' I say.

'You're right,' Laura says. She drains her coffee cup and puts it back on the saucer. 'This is a home but it feels a million times colder and less welcoming than our lovely loft. Let's go back and enjoy it while we can.'

The housekeeper walks us to the door to let us out. 'I believe we'll be seeing some more of you very soon, Miss Villiers,' she says as she opens the huge polished doors on to the corridor.

'Perhaps,' I reply.

'And you're leaving today?' she asks. 'This evening?'

'That's right. We're going to the airport in a few hours,' I say. I want to warm to this outwardly friendly woman but somehow I can't. I feel reluctant to say too much.

'Have a wonderful trip home.' She smiles at Laura. 'And you too, miss.'

'Thank you. We will!' Laura gives her a broad, open smile. I envy her the ability to trust anyone who's in the employment of Andrei Dubrovski.

'Goodbye!' I say, trying to hide my impatience to be on our way. 'Come on, Laura, we've got to get going.'

In the taxi on the way downtown I breathe a huge sigh of relief. I didn't feel right in that apartment at all. The whole time we were there, I felt under observation. While Laura is gushing about the

155

beautiful apartment and how lucky I'll be to work there, all I can think is how happy I am to be out of it, and how little I ever want to go back.

It's sad to return to our loft apartment. We've had a wonderful time there and it feels like home even though we've been there such a short time. Laura has booked a last massage in our suite and while she's being pummelled and smoothed, I take the opportunity to log into my email and catch up. I've been sending my parents updates about the trip and I want to upload some pictures and send them.

As soon as I log in, I see a message to me marked urgent. I click on it at once to open it. It's from Caroline.

Dear Beth

I hope this reaches you in time! Good news – Mark is out of hospital. He made a great recovery in the last day or so and the doctors thought he'd be more comfortable back at home. He's so much brighter, you wouldn't recognise him. I told him you were in New York having a little holiday and he was very excited. I know you've probably already made plans but just in case you read this in time, Mark wants to know if you can stay on in New York for a few days. He has some meetings he'd like you attend, and a sale that's coming up at Christie's. He'll pay for your new return ticket and a hotel room for however many nights you need. I can sort it all out from this end.

Let me know what you intend to do – and see you
soon!
Best regards,
Caroline

I read the message three times before I absorb the
contents properly. It's hard to take it in and it's only
when Laura comes in and reads it over my shoulder
that I understand.

'Oh – you lucky thing!' Laura exclaims. 'You're
going to stay on here!'

'But that means you'll be going home on your own,'
I say with dismay. I was looking forward to our flight
back together.

'Yes.' She looks a little downcast. 'That's not so
great, but don't worry, I've been completely jet-
lagged since we got here so I'll probably sleep all
the way anyway.' She gives me an envious look.
'Does that mean you're going to stay here in the
loft?'

I laugh. 'I don't think Mark's budget will stretch to
that. I don't know much the loft costs but I should
think it's several thousand a night. Besides, Caroline's
told me to find another hotel room.' I don't tell her
that from Caroline's email, it's pretty clear that Mark
didn't pay for the loft.

Laura goes quiet. 'I hadn't really thought about
that,' she says after a minute, obviously a bit awed by
what we've been given. 'I'll never forget this, I really
won't. Don't worry that we're not going home together,

157

I've already had this incredible experience because of you. Stay on and enjoy yourself.'

'It won't be so much fun if I'm on my own – and working,' I point out.

'It's still New York,' she says with a grin.

I can't argue with that.

Things move up a gear as Laura gets ready for the ride back to the airport and I look for another hotel room. I wonder about staying on in the Grand, where I've had a marvellous time, but I also feel like going to a totally new place. Andrei booked this, and as long as I'm here he'll be able to keep tabs on me. I send an email to Caroline asking for her advice and she replies saying that she'll book the hotel where Mark usually stays and send me through the details when it's done, along with an itinerary of what Mark would like me to do.

It's horrible saying goodbye to Laura as she climbs into the car that's taking her to the airport. We hug each other hard.

'See you back in London,' Laura says. 'It's been amazing.'

'I'll be back before the end of the week,' I promise.

'You'd better,' she grins.

'I've got to be home for Christmas, haven't I?' I smile at her. 'Have a good trip home.'

I can't help my eyes prickling as the car drives off into the busy New York traffic, taking Laura away from me. I suddenly feel incredibly lonely.

'Come on,' I tell myself, 'you're strong. You can do this. Now, let's get moving.'

I check out of the Grand and take a taxi to the address that Caroline's given me. It's in a leafy, residential part of the city dominated by those large houses they call brownstones. The place I'm staying looks like a private house except for the flagpole protruding from the front and the six twinkling Christmas trees on the pediment above the front door.

I go up the steps and push open the heavy polished wooden front door, smiling to myself as I go in. This place is so Mark: it's like an elegant gentlemen's club done in very good taste with excellent paintings adorning the walls. The aesthetic is modern country house, and I can understand why Mark would feel right at home here.

The receptionist is friendly but businesslike. 'Miss Villiers? Welcome. The bellboy will take you up to your room. Enjoy your stay with us. Please let us know if there's anything we can do. Mr Palliser is a very good friend of ours so we're anxious to make your stay as pleasant as possible.'

As I'm shown into another hotel room and tip another bellboy for bringing up my luggage, it occurs to me that I've been in more hotels in the last few months than I have in my entire life, and not just any hotels – some of the best in the world, in St Petersburg, Paris and New York.

But, as I look around my comfortable new room, I

can't help wishing that Dominic was here to share it with me.

I start work for Mark the next morning. I'm very glad of Caroline's detailed itinerary and the maps she supplies because as soon as I'm off the tourist trail, New York becomes a lot more complicated. Now I'm looking for art galleries in expensive but obscure parts of town or off the beaten track, locating offices inside vast skyscrapers in midtown or heading uptown or even into Brooklyn to find dealers in their lairs. Once there, I introduce myself and talk about Mark's latest finds, show his catalogue and examine others, taking notes on current exhibitions and interesting finds. I flag any sales that are coming up and the gossip about any big buyers who are displaying a yen for a particular artist or style. I'm constantly scrawling memos to myself or typing up reports to email to Mark so that he knows every detail of what's going on. Within a day or so, I begin to feel quite the New Yorker, stepping out confidently to hail cabs, or dashing down into the subway, battling through the Christmas crowds, clutching a take-out coffee and a bagel. I get used to eating alone but while breakfast and lunch I can do on the run, I order room service from the hotel in the evenings and eat in my room. It's not much fun but I can't face going to the dining room on my own, and at least in my room I can watch television or read, which gives me a little company.

I can also check my emails. Laura writes to tell me

she's safely back and that she went first class all the way. I wonder what Andrei makes of that, and I've only been in my new hotel for a night when the first message comes through:

Beth,
Why didn't you take your return flight? Where are you?
A.

I stare at it, feeling pleased that I've managed to escape out from under Andrei's observation. I suppose that as long as I was at the Soho Grand, he knew where to find me. Now I've slipped out of view and he doesn't like that at all.

I don't reply. Instead, I send a message to Dominic.

Hi sweetie
Guess what, Mark's asked me to stay on in New York for a bit and work, how about that!! It's amazing here, I'm really enjoying it but I'm working hard. No more shopping and cocktails for me, but Laura and I had a brilliant time together. I'll be home at the end of the week and then heading back to my parents for Christmas. Where are you? What are you doing? When can we see each other? I miss you. I LONG for you in every way.
All my love
Beth

The next day, there's another message from Andrei.

Beth,
    Tell me where you are immediately.
    A.

I laugh softly to myself. *Ha, ha, Mr Control. You don't like this much, do you? Well, I'm not your possession and you don't own me.* But I don't want to enrage the tiger too much, in case he loses control and decides to let out his claws. I send back a brief reply.

Andrei,
    I'm staying in New York for now.
    B

I like that: as terse and direct as his own messages. There's a reply from Dominic that's all too short as well.

Gorgeous girl,
    Exciting that you're still in New York, where are you staying? Still firming up my Christmas plans. I'll let you know. We'll meet as soon as I'm free.
    D x x

I know he's busy but I still can't help wishing he'd write me a little more in his messages. I send back another email telling him what I've been up to and where I am but he doesn't reply immediately. Out on the black runs again, no doubt.

The upside is that my work is fascinating. I love what I'm learning about the international art market and how Mark works with his business rivals so that they can all make a good living in this curious world. The hours slide by almost with my noticing them and when I find myself sitting in a Christie's auction, raising my paddle to bid for a Chagall, I practically have to pinch myself. The Chagall goes to a Chinese phone bidder in the end, but even so, I'm thrilled to have been there among all the other dealers. I have a coffee with the head of twentieth-century art afterwards and then return to my hotel for lunch before my afternoon appointment, which is in a part of town I haven't been to before, uptown on the West Side.

I come out of the hotel and notice that the weather has definitely changed. The lucid blue skies have disappeared to be replaced with heavy low white-grey cloud that sucks all the light out of the day and seems heavy with snow. The temperature has dropped further and my feet feel numb in my shoes within a few moments of walking. I can't really wear jeans and biker boots to my business appointments so I'm reduced to wearing the one pair of thin shoes I brought with me when I thought I was coming on a weekend jaunt, not a business trip. There hasn't been time to buy anything else. Luckily the jacket I brought keeps me toasty on top but it doesn't cover my thighs and my skirt is not particularly warm. Well, it's only a few blocks till I get to the subway. I thrust my hands further down into my pockets, shove my chin down into my turned-up collar and walk faster to get my blood circulating.

Nevertheless, by the time I get to the subway station, I'm shivering and I head down into its warm atmosphere with relief. Down in the station, I look for the platform that will take me uptown to the right area. I've often found it confusing working out where I am and where I'm going, despite the simple grid system. Once I came out of the subway and didn't realise I was facing the wrong way, so I started walking the mirror image of my route, heading in exactly the opposite direction. It took a while before I realised my mistake. I want to take a train that will stop up in the early hundreds, which I've read is the northern edge of the Upper West Side. I've looked at the map and while the address is not in the area I've become familiar with, it doesn't seem too far away.

A train comes rumbling into the station and I think it's the one I want, so I get on and sit down. I reach for my map and guidebook and instantly curse mentally to myself. I can see them right now on the little table in my room where I put them down at lunchtime and didn't pick them up again. All my information is tucked inside my guidebook. I don't even have the address of the dealer I'm supposed to be visiting.

I take out my phone and do a search on my email to find the details that Caroline sent me and I'm relieved to see that her email is there, along with the itinerary attachments. Good. When I get out at the other end I should be able to find where I need to go.

After a while I look up, becoming vaguely aware that we haven't stopped at a station for a while now. In fact, I can see that we're passing through stations without a pause, hurrying on uptown. *What's going on? Why aren't we stopping?*

My stomach swoops downwards as I realise that I must have taken an express train by mistake, one that races up towards the north missing out all the midtown stops. I feel a dart of fear – where will it stop? I imagine it flying up the length of the island, through a tunnel under the river and out into the upper boroughs of New York, depositing me in some strange faraway place.

*I'm going to miss my appointment!* I think, panicked. The train rattles on and I try to keep calm. It's perfectly simple. I can just catch a train back. There's no need to worry, it's going to be fine. The carriage is quite empty now, just scattered about with solemn-faced, silent New Yorkers. I hope I don't look frightened. Horror stories of helpless tourists attacked and mugged start to flit through my mind.

*Don't be so silly. Just keep calm and you'll be fine.*

At last the train comes to a stop. I pick up my bag and get off, trying to give the impression that this is exactly where I meant to come. On impulse I put my ticket in the barrier and head out of the station. Once I'm above ground I'll be able to access my emails and load a map so that I can see where I am.

Outside, it's dark and now that I'm away from the well-lit centre of town, the sparkle and glitter of

Manhattan is almost completely gone. I have no idea where I am, except that the streets are in the high 100s. I try to click on the attachments that Caroline sent so that I can view them. It might be quicker to walk to wherever this dealer is. While they're loading, I try to open my map app, so that I can get some directions and locate my position.

I wait for ages, clicking and reclicking. *Shit! Why can't I access anything?* I'm obviously out of range. I take out my phone battery and try rebooting it, but with the same result. I can't get Internet access.

*Shit, shit, shit!*

I look around and see a man lingering nearby. He's standing between me and the subway entrance, his back against a wall and his hands in his pockets. While he isn't exactly looking in my direction, I can't help feeling that he's aware of me, maybe even watching me. And here I am, standing alone, fiddling with an expensive phone. What if he's about to mug me?

There has to be a café or a bar nearby, I think, maybe one with Wi-Fi. I make an instant decision, turn away and start walking in the direction I think will take me towards downtown. I feel better as soon as I'm moving, but it's bitterly cold now that I'm out of the station. I shiver and start walking as fast as I can, keeping my eyes open for a place I can get out of the cold, but I seem to be in a very residential district, walking down block after block of apartment buildings. There are shops, but none of them look like the kind of places I can walk into and warm up or find an Internet connection. Each time I see another, I decide to press on. It's so cold my hands are numb and I can hardly press the buttons on my phone, which is still constantly loading but never delivering. My cheeks feel leathery under the biting wind and my feet have almost no sensation of the path as I walk along it.

Then I realise that the man I tried to avoid is walking behind me. I see him out of the corner of my eye and know with a nasty swirl of fear that he is following me. I recognise his hunched shape, the hands in the pockets.

*Oh God, is he going to attack me?*

I pick up my pace but my freezing feet refuse to go much faster. They are so numb that I stumble as I walk.

*Damn this phone!*

I daren't take it out of my pocket now in case this guy wants to mug me for it. I need to get into a shop, any shop. But now I've decided that, I can't see anything likely as I stumble along in the darkness. I tell myself to go up to a front door, any door, and knock or ring the bell. Surely someone will help me. But somehow I can't find the courage to approach a stranger like that. I'll hold out for a shop, I tell myself.

He's coming closer to me. I'm frightened now. I'm lost in the darkness of a strange city, I'm freezing cold and I'm about to be attacked. I can hear his footsteps getting nearer. He's gaining on me.

*I won't let this happen. I won't let him hurt me.*

I spin round to face him. I can't make out his features in the darkness and I try to speak bravely but only hear a quavering voice come out of my mouth: 'What do you want? Is it my phone? Do you want that?'

He stops when he sees that I have. His eyes glitter in the darkness but he says nothing.

'Well? Why are you following me?'

Still the man says nothing but simply gestures to the road. A huge black car is pulling up at the side of the kerb right next to me. The back door opens and a voice says roughly, 'Beth, get in at once.'

It's Andrei Dubrovski.

# CHAPTER ELEVEN

I'm so incredibly relieved to see him and to be out of the biting cold, but it comes out as anger.

'What are you doing here?' I shout as soon as I'm in the car. Andrei leans across me and pulls the door shut. 'Why are you following me? Did you have that man tailing me all the way? Don't you have any idea how frightened I was?'

Andrei stares at me from burning blue eyes. 'You should be grateful. You clearly had no idea where you were, and your clothes are completely unsuitable for this weather. Yes, that man is working for me.'

'But . . .' I shake my head in disbelief. 'How on earth did you know where I am?'

He gazes at me as the car glides smoothly into the road and heads south. 'You've been staging quite a disappearing act, haven't you?'

'What are you talking about?' I glare at him. 'Because I don't tell you where I am, I've disappeared?'

'Correct.' I noticed that his gloved hands are clenched. 'You refused my generous offer of the Four Seasons for you and your friend. Then you also gave up your reservations at the Washington and left. It was only when you appeared at my apartment that I picked up your trail again but then you refused to tell my housekeeper your plans – and didn't take your flight home. I've been extremely concerned.'

I look at him, noting the stubborn thrust of his lower lip and his cold eyes even while thoughts are whirling around my head.

*I refused the Four Seasons and ... disappeared? Then who booked the Soho Grand? If it wasn't Andrei then ...*

'But how did you find me after that?'

'You were playing silly games with me when you refused to tell me your whereabouts,' he says tersely. 'I guessed you must have stayed at Mark's request so I spoke to his sister. She kindly gave me your itinerary. I put a man on your trail to ensure your safety and I decided to meet you after your appointment tonight. Apparently, you've been dining by yourself in your room. I thought that seemed rather sad.'

'How sweet of you!' I say sarcastically. I'm furious that he thinks I'm so weak and helpless that I need a big man to take care of me. If I hadn't been freaked out by the man following me, I would have sorted out my situation without any trouble. It was annoying, but getting lost was not the end of the world. 'Does it make you feel like the strong guy to rescue me from the situation you helped to engineer?'

'You're being very childish,' he replies. 'I don't understand why you won't accept what I'm willing to give. Why turn down the Four Seasons? Where did you go?'

I don't reply to that. I need to think about the

little twist that events have taken. Instead I say, 'Where are we going? I have an appointment. I'm already late.'

'Not any more. I cancelled it.'

'What?' Fury rushes up inside me. 'How dare you? That's my job! How dare you interfere?'

'I'm your employer too. I've explained to that dealer that you'll be seeing him tomorrow morning instead. We're going back to your hotel to collect your things and then you'll be staying in my apartment.'

'What? No! Anyway, I'm going home tomorrow. My flight is in the evening.'

'Not necessarily,' Andrei says carelessly.

This is getting weird. 'What do you mean?'

'You don't need to fly home on a commercial flight that gets you in at some ungodly hour in the morning. We can fly back together.' He smiles at me for the first time, a chilly smile. 'This is the perfect opportunity for us to spend some time together. I believe this city is considered very romantic. I would like to show some of those aspects to you.' He leans towards me and despite everything, I can't help feeling the pull of his physical magnetism. 'Beth, let me do this. You keep pushing me away. Believe me, we would both enjoy ourselves a great deal more if you stopped doing that.'

I'm holding my breath, my eyes wide. He has so much power because he isn't afraid to do exactly as he likes. I don't know how I'm going to be able to resist his extraordinary will. I feel helpless like a toy or a possession, and I don't like it at all. No relationship should be like this.

'Now, we're going to get your things and then I'm taking you out for dinner.' He leans back in his seat. 'And that's the end of the matter.'

There's not much I can do. I need to get back to midtown anyway, and it's freezing outside. I can't pretend this isn't better than struggling back to the hotel by myself. All right, let Andrei think he's got his own way. I'll go out for dinner with him, but I'm getting on that flight tomorrow no matter what he thinks.

The traffic in central Manhattan is crazy and the streets are thronged with people doing their Christmas shopping or seeing a show or going to parties. The atmosphere is festive and the air is full of Christmas songs as they pour out of shops or from carol singers standing on street corners. I wish Dominic were here. I feel myself yearning for him. I want to ask him something as well, something that really can't wait any longer.

We finally arrive at my hotel.

'Go and pack. Get them to bring out all your luggage,' orders Andrei. 'I'll wait here.'

I give him a defiant look as I climb out of the car but I do as he says. Will I have to stay in that cold, soulless apartment of his? Well, it's okay by me as long as it's only for one night, and there's a lock on the bedroom door. If Andrei thinks that tonight is his lucky night, he's in for a re-think in the very near future.

Fifteen minutes later, I emerge from the hotel, a porter following behind with my luggage. The car door opens and Andrei beckons me into the comfortable interior, tipping the porter with a fifty before we go.

'Good.' He looks at me with a satisfied expression, a smile playing over those stubborn lips. He's in a happier mood now that he's got his way. I can tell he thinks everything is going smoothly.

*I'll only go so far along this path,* I think but I say nothing. There's no point in antagonising him this early in the evening.

When we reach the splendid Victorian Gothic apartment building on the edge of Central Park, Andrei is practically humming, and he seems very pleased with himself. The car passes under the ornate archway into the private courtyard and we go in. I keep silent the whole way. After all, I can be pretty stubborn myself when I want to.

As we ride up in the lift, Andrei says to me: 'Renata will show you to your room when we arrive. You'll find a dress and shoes laid out for you to wear this evening. You have thirty minutes to get ready, then I'll expect you in the ballroom. Is that clear?'

I open my mouth to protest and then I think better of it. I might be bristling at all this but I still need Andrei on side. If he wants to act out the role of my benefactor, then let him. But I haven't asked for any of it. I don't owe him. He needs to understand that a bargain is only a bargain if two people agree to it.

The housekeeper is waiting at the open door to the apartment as we arrive, and she greets us both politely.

'Good evening, Renata. Please take Miss Villiers to the white bedroom, as we discussed,' Andrei says. A butler appears from the shadows of the hall and helps Andrei take off his coat. He turns to me. 'The ballroom. In thirty minutes. Don't make me wait.'

'Surely that's a woman's prerogative,' I return tartly, and smile sweetly at him.

He stares at me, a tiny frown between his eyebrows. He's not sure if I'm teasing him or not. 'Well . . . not long.'

'This way, please, miss,' says the housekeeper, and I follow her up the thickly carpeted staircase to the upper floor. The white bedroom occupies a corner position, its huge arched windows overlooking the sparkling vista of Manhattan with the park dark and inky directly below. As its name suggested, everything in the room is white, every chair, cushion and picture frame, everything, including a baby grand piano with a white lizardskin stool. I glance at it, thinking it's rather wasted on me as I can only manage to play 'Chopsticks', no matter how gorgeous the piano is. This is the second piano I've seen in this apartment. I wonder if Andrei plays.

'I'll be back to fetch you in half an hour,' says Renata politely. 'Your bathroom is through that door. Your dress is hanging in the closet. Please call me on the telephone by your bed if you require anything at all.'

'Thank you,' I say, and she goes out, leaving me alone.

I look around the luxurious room and at the magnificent view. Then I go to the bathroom to take a shower.

\* \* \*

The dress that Andrei's provided for me is very beautiful and in exactly my size. It's red, which seems to be a colour he likes on me: a fitted silk sheath split up the back, and demure with tiny cap sleeves but still enticing at the low neck. My arms are bare and on my feet I wear very high scarlet heels. Looking at myself in the mirror as I twist to see the back view, I have to admit it's sexy. There's just time to brush out my fair hair and twist it up into a chignon, and do my make-up. Then there's a knock at the door and Renata is there.

'Good, you're ready,' she says with a smile. 'Mr Dubrovski hates to be kept waiting. You look very nice.'

'Thank you,' I say. Dressed in red and leaving the safety of my pure white bedroom, I feel like a sacrificial victim being taken to appease an angry god. *But I'm no victim. I'm going to make sure of that.*

Renata leads me to the ballroom, the long gallery hung with mirrors and chandeliers that Laura and I visited just a few days ago. None of the chandeliers are lit – instead candles burn in large gold candelabra placed at intervals on small tables along the room. On another table by the window I see a bottle of champagne chilling in an ice bucket beside two slender crystal glasses. There's no sign of Andrei.

*Typical! After all that nonsense he's the one making me wait!*

I walk across the polished wood floor, careful in my very high heels, towards the window. The view is simply irresistible. Along the avenues, traffic crawls, the head- and brake lights looking like festive chains of gold and red. Everything below sparkles and glitters, and the sky has cleared a little to a dark navy.

'You look beautiful.' I turn to see Andrei walking across the ballroom towards me. He looks extremely handsome in a dinner suit, white dress shirt fastened with jet studs, and a black silk bow tie. His shoes are polished to mirrors and I can smell the fresh lemony scent of his cologne. 'That colour is perfect on you.'

'Thank you,' I say with a smile. 'For letting me borrow this dress.' I put a very slight stress on the word borrow so that he can be quite sure how I feel about it.

He smiles at me with a knowing look in his blue eyes. They've softened tonight, the ice in them disappearing and making him look almost human again. When Andrei chooses to use his charm, it's certainly considerable. He has presence and charisma in that well-cut dinner suit and it's hard to ignore the rippling power in his broad shoulders and large hands, or the craggy attraction of his features and those striking eyes.

'I have something else for you. A gift.' He walks past me to the table where the champagne is chilling and picks up a slim black box that I hadn't noticed before now.

I walk towards him tentatively. *What now?*

He doesn't give it to me but opens the box himself and shows me the contents. I gasp. Lying on a bed of ruched white satin is a necklace of huge grey pearls, each one perfect.

'This is not for you to return,' he says firmly. 'Turn around.'

I turn. The dress is cut very low behind and I realise that I'm displaying the expanse of my back to him. I give a very slight shiver at the thought. Then the necklace is lowered down in front of me, the pearls landing gentle and cool across my collar bone and Andrei pulls them round to fasten at the base of my neck. 'There,' he says as he releases it. 'Let me see.'

I turn around. He looks at my neckline with a smile lifting the corners of his mouth. 'Very good. Take a look yourself.'

I go to one of the great gilt mirrors that line the room and look at the necklace. It is truly beautiful, the pearls like smoky orbs against my skin. They gleam in the candlelight. 'I love it,' I whisper. I turn back to look at Andrei, who is taking the foil off the bottle of champagne. 'But of course I can't accept a gift like this, it's far too expensive.'

Andrei shoots me an impatient look as he tears off the wire holding in the cork. 'I wish you wouldn't keep mentioning what everything costs. I didn't expect you to be quite so vulgar about it.'

'It puts me under an obligation,' I say firmly. 'You know that as well as I do. If I could afford to give you the same sort of gifts then it would be vulgar to discuss the cost. But as I can't, it's not vulgar, it's honest.'

'Whatever it is, please shut up about it because I'm not interested.' Andrei deftly extracts the cork of the bottle with a satisfactory pop and pours out the champagne into the two glasses. 'The necklace is divine on you, it's how I want you to look. Now come here.'

I go back to him and he hands me a flute of champagne. 'To our new collaboration,' he says, touching the rim of his glass to mine with a tiny chime.

'Our . . . collaboration,' I say, and we both sip the fizzing liquid, our eyes still locked on one another.

'Now.' Andrei puts down his glass and smiles at me. 'We're in a ballroom so there's one thing we must do.' On cue, a waltz begins to play through a hidden sound system, as crystal clear as if a chamber orchestra were in the room with us. He holds out his hands to me. 'Miss Villiers – may I have this dance?'

I stare at him then put down my champagne. 'Yes,' I say slowly. 'You may.'

He takes me in his arms and pulls me close against his chest. One hand lands on the small of my back, the other hand grasps mine and holds it tightly. I'm aware of the warmth of his body coming from below his shirt and the pressure of his thighs on mine as he begins to lead me into a waltz. I thank goodness my father taught me the basic waltz years ago, so that I know how to move backwards and to the side as my partner turns and moves me. Andrei is an excellent dancer, I can tell that. I hardly need to think about what I'm doing; he makes sure that I move effortlessly with him. I catch glimpses of us in the mirrors as we pass, a couple in their elegant evening clothes moving gracefully to the music. My pearls glimmer at my neck and my skin shines white in the candlelight. This is like a perfect dream, and I can feel myself becoming lost in it. Outside the city seems lit up just for us as the music pours into the room, lifting up my spirit and making me feel like I'm flying as Andrei waltzes me around the beautiful floor.

Suddenly his mouth is close to my ear. 'All this could be yours,' he murmurs in a low voice. 'I want you to share it with me. This could be our life. It could be beautiful. You're lonely and lost, Beth, and so am I. I want a family, someone to breathe life into my world, to give me true joy. You're that person; I've known it for so long. Your love would be worth having, your grace and beauty would illuminate my world. Beth . . . please . . . I want you to think about it tonight.'

I start to pull away from him but his grip is iron strong.

'Don't say anything now. Don't spoil this moment. You want to resist me, I know that. Your resistance is what makes me certain you are the right person for me. Think about it. We will talk later.'

I say nothing as he turns me around the room, confused by what he is saying. I want to say no right now, so that he's under no illusions, but this is all so dreamlike I can hardly believe what I've just heard. The music comes to an end, and I stare at him, breathless. He raises my hand to his lips and kisses it.

'Thank you, that was beautiful. And now, our car awaits.'

In the hall, the housekeeper brings out a gorgeous black cashmere coat and helps me into it. I slip my phone into the pocket while she puts a wrap around my shoulders for good measure, and Andrei's butler brings out his coat and gloves. Then we descend in the lift to the waiting car. We are driven for no more than ten minutes before we arrive at the restaurant, a place of thick linen, silver, crystal and the buzz of sophisticated conversation. All eyes follow us as we pass, and I hear the murmur of Andrei's name. Of course, he must be famous in this city.

We're taken to a very grand table and given every courtesy and attentive service. Andrei orders for us, and he keeps up a flow of talk as we wait for our food, telling me about the vision he has for the apartment in terms of art. He wants modern masterpieces, he tells me. And he wants some big names too. If a Picasso or Van Gogh comes up, he's seriously interested. I listen in a daze, replying when necessary. The food comes and it's exquisite: incredible classical French cuisine with each plate like a work of art itself. I don't feel that hungry until I taste it, then my appetite explodes into life. The flavours are so intense that I feel as though I'm living on another level when I eat.

It's when we've finished our main courses that Andrei stops talking for a while and stares at the table-cloth, tapping it with one fingertip. I watch him, a wreath of anxiety curling in my stomach. I get the impression that a crunch moment is approaching. I've been lured into the trap – will the door now spring shut? How on earth will I get out?'

'So, Beth,' Andrei says. He takes a gulp of the ruby red wine in his glass and I realise with a dart of surprise that he's nervous. 'You heard what I said to you in the ball-room. I want you to know that I'm utterly serious. I believe it is necessary to my future happiness to have you. I want you to create my homes and bring my family into existence. I want you to be an integral part of my life.'

'Well, this is all very romantic,' I say, trying to laugh and make light of what he's saying. 'They should take a cue from you and rewrite the marriage vows! Do you, Beth, agree to be an integral part of my life?'

His hand stops moving and his eyes spark as he looks at me. 'Don't joke about this, Beth. It's very important. I've never been more serious.'

I stare back at him. My hands are shaking lightly and I hide them under the tablecloth. 'You know I can't do this,' I say, trying to make my voice as firm as possible. 'I appreciate what you've said to me – I'm flattered – but I'm not the right person for you, Andrei. You deserve someone who loves you.'

He flicks his gaze back down to the tablecloth and his jaw clenches. He starts tapping again. 'You say this because you're still infatuated with that snake, Stone. But you're wrong. You would love me if you gave me the chance. You saw me at the orphanage. You know I have a warm heart, I'm a good man. You can love me. You will.'

'You can't force it, Andrei,' I say gently, suddenly full of pity for him. 'You can't make someone love you, or buy their love. It isn't possible.'

He stares up at me and I've never seen his eyes more flinty or determined. 'It is possible,' he rasps out. 'I intend to make it possible. I will make life with me your only option.'

'What do you mean?' I can't help the sound of fear in my voice. I know he's ruthless. What lengths will he go to in order to make me do what he wants?

'First you have to know that Dominic Stone is going to be utterly destroyed. I know what he's up to and I intend to attack him in every way open to me. He will feel the might of my lawyers, the power of my network and, if necessary, the strength of my fists if he doesn't comply.'

I stare at him, feeling truly afraid of him for the first time in my life. *The strength of my fists? That sounds very, very bad.*

'What makes you think I'll want to be with you if you're going to do this?' I ask, trying to remain calm and rational.

'If you agree to my suggestion, I am prepared to offer Stone an amnesty. You can tell him that he has until the end of the year to return to his employment with me, all grievances forgotten and some very favourable terms. After that, his chance will be lost forever.'

'Tempting,' I say sarcastically. 'After this, I'm sure he'll be desperate to work with you again.'

He glowers at me. 'You don't know what's good for you, Beth. You don't know how to make yourself happy. I do. That's why I'm prepared to take Dominic back in return for you. And that's why I'm prepared to continue protecting Mark.'

I go very still. A cold clammy feeling races over my skin. 'What?'

'You heard me. If you're by my side, I will protect Mark for the rest of his life. If not, if you remain stubborn, then I'm prepared not only to ruin Mark's professional reputation, but to sue him for malpractice, and I promise you: I won't stop until he's lost everything. I'm prepared to see him in prison.' Andrei fixes me with that cold blue stare and says in a quiet voice, 'Are you, Beth?'

I gasp. This is unbelievable. One minute he's reminding me how kind he is to orphans, and the next he wants to blackmail me into becoming his partner by threatening me with the destruction of everything that Mark has built up over the years. He would ruin my kind, loyal friend without a second thought.

'That would kill Mark,' I say in a whisper through lips that almost refuse to move. 'You know it would. It's a death sentence.'

Andrei smiles at me, the cold smile of the shark. 'Then be with me and everyone will benefit – Mark, me, and most of all, you, Beth. I wish you could see it. You'll have everything in the world, anything you wish for will be yours.'

'Except true love,' I say in a cracked voice. 'You forgot that, Andrei.' I manage to get to my feet, throwing my napkin on to the table. 'Excuse me, please. I'm going to the ladies' room.'

He nods curtly and I don't linger. Instead, I push away from the table and walk through the dining room as quickly as I can on my spindly heels. A waiter gestures me in the direction of the restrooms and I push through the doors until I find myself in the plush quietness of the ladies' room. I run to the mirror and stare at my frightened eyes and pale face.

'I can't believe he would do this,' I say to myself, the horror evident in my expression. 'Would he really? Would he? Oh my God!' Am I really trapped? Can I condemn Mark to disgrace, ruin and probably death? Can I have Dominic thrown to the mercy of Andrei's hired thugs and crooks? What if Andrei has him killed?

'No!' I whisper. 'No.'

Tears rush up into my eyes as the stress of this day begins to tell on me. I'm exhausted and this feels like I'm in a living nightmare. How did I get into this situation? Is it really true that the more I resist Andrei, the more convinced he'll be that I'm the perfect woman for him? How the hell am I going to get out of that? I try to control my emotions but I can't. I begin to sob and the minute it's started I can't stop. I pick up a fresh towel and press it to my face, weeping hard.

I cry for a minute or more when I suddenly feel a hand on my shoulder and hear a gentle voice.

'Hey – are you okay? Stupid question, you're obviously not. Can I help you?'

I look up, still sobbing and sniffing, and see a pair of friendly brown eyes in a smooth, pretty face. It's a woman in her mid-thirties, elegant and very good-looking, with straight and glossy dark hair. She's looking at me with pity and concern.

'I'm sorry,' I say, choked.

'Don't be, you don't have to be sorry,' she says in her soft musical voice. 'What's the problem?'

'I'm with a man,' I say, feeling relief in just sharing some of what's oppressing me. 'He's putting pressure on me to be with him when I love someone else. He knows I don't feel that way so he's using emotional blackmail to force me into it.'

The woman looks appalled. 'That's dreadful!' she cries. 'What a bully! What does the other man think about this?'

'He doesn't know yet.'

'Then you should tell him right away!'

'I don't know where he is!' I wail, overcome again with the hopelessness of my situation. 'I miss him. I really need him. But it's more complicated than I can explain. Oh God, I don't know what to do.'

The woman looks at me with determined eyes and takes my hand. 'You mustn't let this man bully you. He's probably all talk, bullies are. Walk away and don't look back!'

I shake my head and sniff, the sobs subsiding. 'You don't understand. He's capable of anything.'

'Then you mustn't go back to him,' the woman says in a spirited voice. 'He sounds thoroughly dangerous.'

Now I'm calmer, I realise what's been bothering me about this woman since she started talking and say almost wonderingly, 'You're British!'

'That's right,' she says, smiling, 'and so are you. We Brits have to stick together. Listen, I'm not letting you go back to that man. You're coming with me. I was just leaving anyway. You can come back to my place, it's not far from here.'

'But all my stuff is at this man's apartment. He has everything – my clothes, my work things . . .' I look helplessly at her. Besides, if I leave Andrei high and dry, who's to say he won't be so incensed, he'll decide to carry out his threats?

'Don't you worry about that,' the woman says firmly. 'We'll send my brother round to get your things. He's gone out to meet his girlfriend. As soon as he's back, I'll tell him to get this guy to return everything or we'll call the police. I think you'll find he's not as tough as he seems.' She smiles at me. 'I'm serious. You mustn't go back to him. Give in to a bully and you'll be submitting to him and his ways for life. Do you want that?'

I shake my head.

'No,' she says. 'You jolly well don't! Now, let's go. We'll get your coat from the cloakroom and I'll go and explain to this man that you're coming with me. You wait in a taxi outside and I'll join you there. No arguments!'

I feel too tired to argue. I want to tell her that her plan is too dangerous but the way she says it makes it sound so wonderfully simple. Perhaps I should just let this woman take control.

'That's decided,' she says. 'Now, let's go. You need to get away from here as soon as possible. Tell me what table you were at and what this man looks like – I'll go and speak to him right now.'

# CHAPTER TWELVE

*What am I doing? Isn't this just going to inflame Andrei – make him carry out his threats?*

I'm sitting in the back of a taxi that's waiting with its engine running outside the restaurant. I can guess that Andrei's car is somewhere nearby waiting for him to summon it. I shiver and wrap myself a little more tightly in the black cashmere coat.

*This is madness! I've nothing. Even the clothes I'm standing up in aren't mine!*

I hear the tap of heels on the pavement and then the taxi door opens and my new friend gets in beside me. She calls an address to the driver and we're off.

'What did he say?' I ask.

She slides a look in my direction from under curling black lashes. 'You didn't tell me that your friend is Andrei Dubrovski.'

'Oh . . . yes . . . I should have said.' I'd forgotten that Andrei is well known in this city.

'He's a fairly intimidating character – I've heard plenty about him. So there was a slight change of plan. I told him you'd been taken ill in the ladies' room and I was going to look after you. I said I'd bring you home when you were feeling better.'

'Did he believe that?'

She laughs. 'I'm not sure. But he wanted to, so he did. He asked me to bring you to his apartment and gave me his card. I said you should be with a woman for now, and that shut him up. But he doesn't have my name or address, so you're safe for now.'

'Not for long,' I say in a dull voice.

I'll have to go back to him, I know that. I'm beginning to realise that Andrei has got me surrounded. I have no choice now. I'm going to have to explain this all to Dominic somehow. My heart feels like it's breaking. Just when we've found our way back to each other, we're going to be separated again, and this time forever.

'You'll feel better in the morning,' she says confidently. 'There's a way out of this, don't you worry.'

Just then my phone buzzes with a text. I pull it out and look at it.

Rosa, where are you? Your master needs you.

I gasp. *Dominic!* What does this mean? Where is he? I don't reply at once – my brain is whirling with the possibility that he might be in New York. What shall I do? I desperately want to tell him everything that's happened, but I suddenly wonder if that's wise. I know that Dominic will laugh in the face of Andrei's offer. He's more likely to decide to kick the shit out of his old boss – and that might sign Mark's death warrant. I stare at my phone, trying to work out what to do.

Rosa, have you decided to serve someone else? Is that it? I'm told you left with a man tonight and took your luggage. Have I lost my Rosa?

*Oh my God, is he in New York?* I breathe in sharply, quivering with excitement. I want to call him this moment, but I can't with my new friend in the taxi with me.

'Are you okay?' she says, watching me. 'That's not him, is it? He's not threatening you, is he?'

'No, no,' I say quickly. 'It's my other friend.' I text him quickly.

Sir, Rosa adores you and wants to serve only you. She offers you her humble apologies and longs for you to join her.

The reply is fired back:

Where are you, Rosa? Are you safe?

I tap out another message:

Yes, but I don't know where I am. I will let you know when I do, very soon.

The phone buzzes almost immediately:

All right. I will wait to hear from you.

I click off the text, feeling a little more hopeful. Dominic must be here in New York City. Oh God, I hope it's true! I long for him with every cell of my being. If I can only see and feel him again, surely everything will be all right.

Just then my friend's phone chimes and she takes a look at it. 'Oh good,' she says after a moment, 'it's my brother. He's on his way, probably with his girlfriend. We can send him round to Dubrovski's place for your things.' She looks out of the window. 'And here we are, at home.'

The taxi pulls up outside a tall brownstone house and we climb out. She pays the fare and then leads me up the worn stone steps. 'Home sweet home!' she says, and unlocks the white painted front door.

At once we're in the cosy hallway of a chic but lived-in home. It's stylish with clean modern furniture and bright with books and pictures. The polished wood floors have the occasional discarded pair of shoes or newspaper on them, and the chairs look sat in. It's a relief to be in a proper home at last after all the hotels and Andrei's soulless apartment.

'Come through,' my friend says, hanging her coat on an antique stand. 'Throw your things anywhere. Take those shoes off if you like, there's a pair of slippers by the stairs. I'll get you a jumper, you're going to freeze in that dress, pretty though it is.'

As she leads me into the sitting room, she says, 'And by the way, my name is Georgina – you can call me Georgie. What's yours?'

'Beth,' I say, feeling a million times better to be somewhere normal.

'Beth?' She frowns. 'That's odd.' Then she remembers herself. 'Would you like something? Coffee, tea? Something stronger? I've got wine or whisky if you're feeling really in shock!'

'Tea would be lovely, thank you,' I say gratefully.

'Yes, good old British tea. I bring it over from home whenever I can. They just can't make it here.'

I'm glad to have those high heels off and a pair of soft woollen fur-lined slippers on. Georgina picks up a jumper from the back of the chair and passes it to me. While she disappears off to get the tea, I slip on the jumper and luxuriate in its cosy depths. I wait for her to come back, padding around the room and scanning the shelves, looking at photographs and the spines of her books.

This evening is not at all what I expected. I thought it would be a room-service supper in the hotel and an early night, preparing for my homeward flight and making a list of any last Christmas presents. Now I'm in a stranger's house somewhere in New York, wearing an evening dress and without my luggage. I pick up some of the photographs on the shelves. They show Georgie with her friends, on the ski slopes, on the beach, larking around, or looking smart at balls, garden parties and weddings. A faded colour photograph shows two adults and two children standing on the veranda of a large villa somewhere exotic and hot. I take that one up to examine it more closely. The children are a boy and a girl, the girl just a little older, both dark-haired and dark-eyed. The girl is Georgie, I'm sure of that, despite the difference between the child with short hair and gangly limbs and the elegant woman in the kitchen. The boy must be her younger brother: he has eyes like hers and the same dark colouring. Both are tanned. Behind them are their parents, the man in a formal suit, the woman in a flowery sundress and hat. I put the photograph back on the shelf and walk over to the fireplace where there are more pictures in silver frames.

Georgie comes in with a mug of steaming tea, which she puts on the coffee table. 'Here you are,' she says cheerfully. 'Sit down and make yourself comfortable.'

'Thank you,' I say. 'I'm just looking at your photographs, I hope you don't mind.'

'Of course not.'

I gesture at the photograph of the two children with their parents and say, 'Is that you?'

Georgie sees where I'm pointing and nods. 'Yes, me and my brother and my parents. They're both dead now.'

'Oh – I'm sorry.' I think that she seems very young to be an orphan.

'Yes, it is rather rotten but that's how it is. My father worked far too hard and my mother drank too much – she was a diplomatic wife and was bored out of her skull by all the endless parties she had to attend, especially as we lived abroad and she missed her home desperately. Eventually the cocktails became her only consolation.' A wistful expression passes over Georgie's face. 'And they killed her in the end. She was only fifty.'

'That's so sad,' I say softly.

Georgie smiles. 'Yes. I still miss her. It's turned me into a bit of a health freak, if I'm honest. But that's no bad thing – perhaps we can sometimes learn from our parents' mistakes.'

I wonder if she has a partner or a husband to comfort her now that she's lost her parents, but there's no sign of anyone else living here and it seems rude to ask. I think of the other child standing on the veranda in the photograph. 'And does your brother live in New York too?'

She sighs with a wistful smile. 'I wish he did. But he's far too high-powered to stay in any one place for long. I adore him but keeping track of him is not easy – he has a habit of vanishing for months at a time. I didn't even know he was going to be in town until today, I wasn't expecting him till Christmas.'

Just then the doorbell sounds and Georgie says, 'That must be him. I won't be a second.'

She goes out and I turn back to the mantelpiece. My eye is caught by a large photograph that isn't framed but has been propped behind some of the others. I reach over to extract it. Voices come floating in from the hall.

'Hi, darling! So where is she?'

The answer comes back in deep male tones. 'She can't make it, I'm afraid. It's just me.'

At the same moment as I pull the photograph out, the voice pierces me like an arrow. I realise that I'm staring at a picture of Georgie and Dominic, their heads close together, big smiles across their faces; their similar, olive-skinned, dark-eyed faces. And I know beyond all doubt that the voice I've just heard is his.

I gasp, dizzy with realisation, and turn around. There in the doorway is Georgie. She is saying, 'Beth, this is my brother, Dominic' as she turns to gesture to the man behind her, and I'm frozen with disbelief as Dominic stands there, tall, handsome, and the sight I've longed for most in the whole world. He's staring back at me in astonishment and then a huge smile bursts over his face.

'Beth!' he exclaims and strides towards me, his arms open. I rush forward and lose myself in them as he wraps me in his embrace. I'm half laughing and half crying but flooded with joy and relief to be with him. His body is warm and delicious against mine and I never want him to let me go, ever again.

'You have an infinite capacity to surprise me,' he says tenderly, dropping a kiss on my head. 'Just when I think I've lost you, fate brings you back to me.' He pulls back so he can gaze down into my face. 'But what on earth are you doing here?'

'Wait a second!' It's Georgie, who's standing with her hands on her hips, looking completely bewildered. 'Are you telling me this is *Beth*? Your Beth, who you were going to meet tonight?'

Dominic turns to smile at her, his eyes sparkling. 'The very same. She wasn't at her hotel when I got there – serves me right for thinking a surprise would be a good idea. How did you find her?'

Georgie looks worried and says, 'Dom, can I have a word please?' as she beckons him out into the hall.

He's reluctant to let me go, I can feel that, but he says, 'Sure.' He follows her out. I stand in the sitting room, elated and excited, but I can hear what they're saying out there.

'Dom, this girl is involved with Andrei Dubrovski!' Georgie is hissing. 'I found her weeping in a restaurant bathroom because he's trying to make her commit to him! Do you know how incredibly dangerous this is? Your history with him is hardly sweetness and light – he's not going to take kindly to you stealing his girlfriend!'

'I'm not stealing anything or anyone,' Dominic returns calmly. 'Beth and I have been together since before she met Andrei.'

'What? How?'

'It's a long story. I'll tell you all about it one day.'

'But Dubrovski has Beth's stuff. I was going to send you round to get it, but I don't think that's such a good idea now.'

'He thinks he can have her if he wants. Beth isn't going to let that happen and neither am I. Now – let's go back and involve her, I don't like talking about her like this.'

They come back into the room, Georgie looking embarrassed and anxious, while Dominic appears strong and happy. He comes right over and puts his arm around me.

'It sounds like some crazy stuff has been happening. Is Andrei up to his old tricks?'

I nod, feeling like the terrible weight that's been oppressing me is lifting from my shoulders. 'He's worse than ever.'

'I want to hear all about it.' He smiles down at me, his dark brown eyes warm and loving. 'But first, let's sit down and catch up a little. I was going to surprise you tonight but, as usual, your surprise is bigger and better. Georgie, how about some tea for me? I've missed the way you make it.' He turns his smile on her.

Georgie shakes her head at him and sighs, as though he's a hopeless case, but she can't resist his charm. 'Okay, Dom. Tea on its way.'

As soon as we're alone Dominic pulls me to him. 'Oh God, it's good to have you back,' he says throatily, and then he kisses me, his lips tender at first but quickly becoming passionate as my mouth opens under his. When at last we part reluctantly, he says, 'Thank God you're all right. I've been pretty damn worried since I arrived at the hotel to hear you'd left.'

'Andrei's been tailing me,' I explain as Dominic leads me over to the sofa and we sit down together, our hands clasped, 'and he's putting on pressure like never before. He's making threats, against you and Mark, and he's made it clear he wants me to be with him.'

Dominic's eyes sparkle dangerously and he says in a low voice, 'Does he, now? Well, he's going to have to learn that he can't get what he wants with bully-boy tactics or threats. Bring it on, I say. If he wants a fight, he can have one.'

I put my other hand on his knee and say fearfully, 'Please, Dominic, you don't know what he's like . . . the things he's said . . . I couldn't bear it if he hurt you.'

'On the contrary,' Dominic replies, 'I know exactly what he's like. That's why he's being like this. He wants to shut me down because I know all his weaknesses. I was prepared to deal honourably with him and keep the secrets he entrusted me with when I worked for him. But he's made it plain how he wants to proceed, and that's fine with me. He's going to regret taking me on.'

'What are you going to do?' I'm frightened at the prospect of Dominic facing down someone of Andrei's power and might, but Dominic seems stronger and more confident than ever.

'I have an idea or two,' he says mysteriously. 'But let's not talk about him now. Wait until we get to my place.'

'Your place?' I echo, puzzled.

Dominic nods. 'Things are changing, Beth. The work I've done over the last few weeks is paying off. I have some big investors coming on board with me and my company is about to become a major player in the mining and commodities world. I'm setting up an office here in New York as well as in London. Dubrovski isn't going to like it when he hears who my new partners are – mostly because they're people he's wooed and failed to win in the past.' He pulls me tight to him. 'My assistant here has leased me an apartment until I can find something I want to buy in the new year.'

I stare at Dominic. He's his own boss now and it suits him. I realise that he's been hungry for this ever since I've known him and now he's like a panther that's been asleep but is stretching its limbs and rippling its muscles, preparing to exert its power in the hunt.

Georgie comes back into the room carrying two more cups of tea, puts them on the table and sits down in the armchair. She looks a little happier now.

'I can't get over it,' she says, shaking her head and looking from me to Dominic. 'When you told me your name was Beth, I thought it was strange because Dom was going off to meet a Beth, but it never occurred to me it might be the same one!'

'It is weird,' I agree, smiling at her, my hand still tightly in Dominic's. I shoot him a look. 'He's never even told me he has a sister!'

Dominic frowns and says vaguely, 'Haven't I?'

'No, you haven't!'

Georgie hands him a cup of steaming tea. 'That doesn't surprise me in the least, I'm afraid, Beth. I had no idea you existed either, until today.' She gives her brother a gently rebuking look. 'You've really got to learn to share a little more, Dom.'

'I'll try,' he says with a smile, taking the cup. 'Thanks for the tea.'

'You've got to make him change his ways, Beth,' Georgie says to me as she sits down.

I smile at her. I'm loving seeing Dominic in this family environment. I feel more connected to him than ever now I'm accepted by his sister. *She just assumes we're together like a normal boyfriend and girlfriend.* The thought fills me with happy warmth.

'By the way, Georgie,' says Dominic, 'I'm afraid it's going to be a slightly shorter visit than planned. I'm taking Beth away.'

'I thought you were going to say that,' Georgie says but without rancour. 'Well, it's a treat to see you, no matter how fleeting the visit.'

'I'll be around a lot more in the future,' Dominic says. 'I'll be working here for about half the year.'

'Oh good,' Georgie says brightly, looking happier. 'I've missed my baby brother, I want to see more of you!' She turns to me. 'And what about you, Beth, where do you live?'

'London,' I say, suddenly feeling bleak as I realise that for at least six months of the year I'm going to be without Dominic. Then I feel his hand tighten around mine.

'For now,' he says softly, and a burst of happiness radiates through me as he smiles down at me.

Half an hour later we are zooming through the streets of New York in a steel-grey sports car.

'Your sister was very kind; she was going to let me stay at her house. I hope she doesn't think I'm rude.'

'I'm sure she doesn't,' Dominic says, his eyes on the road.

I pause and then say, 'You know, you've never told me much about yourself. Not about Georgie, and not about your parents either. I was sorry to hear that they've both passed away.'

There's a silence while Dominic stares at the road ahead and then he says softly, 'You know I've always found it hard to open up about things like that. But I'm glad you've meet Georgie, I really am. And I will share more with you, I promise.'

I'm so glad to hear that, but I don't want to push it any more, not right now, so I say, 'It would have been nice to stay a bit longer with Georgie and get to know her.'

'Mmm.' Dominic shoots me a meaningful glance. 'And I hope you understand, but I can't do all the things I want to do to you in the spare room of my sister's house. It isn't really my style.'

I feel a shiver of delicious anticipation. Tonight promises to end in a way I couldn't possibly have imagined when I was sobbing in the ladies' room earlier.

Dominic drives us expertly through the Manhattan traffic, and takes us suddenly off the road and down into an underground car park. He brings the car to a stop and looks at me, his face shrouded in shadow. 'Here we are,' he says softly.

My heart begins to race, thudding hard in my chest as the adrenalin of excitement begins to course through me. He opens the door, gets out, comes around to my side and opens my door. He puts out a hand and I take it. As he helps me out of the low-slung seat, he gives a sudden pull so that I fly up and into his arms. He holds me tight, running one hand down my back and over my behind. I'm staring into his eyes, seeing the desire that's burning there, and then he drops his mouth to mine and kisses me. I surrender to him completely, opening my mouth and letting his tongue take possession of me. He tastes glorious. I want to drink him down, absorb him into my very being, become one with him. I tilt my head back and sink into his arms. He's pulling me to him and I feel the hard curve of the car's roof against my back. He has one knee between my thighs, pushing my legs gently apart so that he can press in against me. I feel the hard bulge at his groin and sigh with the delight at the evidence of his lust.

'I want you right here,' he says in a low voice. 'But . . .' He looks up towards the CCTV camera that's focused on us. 'I don't particularly want the guards getting their rocks off over us. Let's go upstairs.'

I have to swallow hard to try and regain my equilibrium. I was ready to let him fuck me right there, up against the car, or down on the oily floor of the car park. Instead he takes my hand and leads me over to the lift. Its doors slide open a moment later and we're in the mirrored interior. I glance up, aware of the dark eye of the security camera.

'Fuck them,' Dominic says. 'I want to kiss you.'

As the lift soars upwards, he pulls me to him and kisses me hard, his tongue feverish in my mouth and mine in his. We're insatiable for one another, my fingers in his hair, pulling his head to me, his arms tight around me, one hand at my neck stroking sensitive places under my ear and at my throat. I want to moan and beg, ask him to take me right now no matter who's watching, but instead I revel in the passion of our kiss. I know I'll get what I want before too long.

Then the lift stops and the doors open. I blink, bewildered, as though I've just woken from an intense

201

dream. 'Come on,' murmurs Dominic, taking my hand. He takes me down the hall to the door of an apartment which he opens with a code tapped onto a pad by the door.

Inside, we are in a large apartment with a panoramic view of the city through its floor-to-ceiling windows. It's bare and unlived-in, with only a minimum of furniture.

'Rented,' Dominic says as he closes the door behind us. 'I won't be here long but it will do for now.'

I turn to him and let my coat fall open, standing before him in my red cocktail dress and high heels. His gaze rakes over me appreciatively.

'You look stunning,' he says. Then he notices the pearls at my neck. 'Is that new?'

I reach up and unclasp the necklace. I drop it into the pocket of my coat and then let the coat fall to the floor. 'Borrowed finery,' I reply. 'I think it all disappears at midnight.'

He glances at his watch. 'It's almost midnight now.'

'That's why it's got to go,' I say. I reach for the zip at the side of the dress and pull it down. Then, with a shimmy, I let the red silk slide down my body until it's in a pool at my feet. I step out of it and stand before him in my bra and knickers. I let his gaze travel over me and then kick off the heels. 'There,' I say. 'Now the spell is broken.'

'You're free of the enchantment,' he says, staring at me intently.

'I always was,' I return. 'He never managed to put me in the tower, no matter how much he wanted to.'

Dominic takes a step towards me. 'Beth . . .'

My heart thrills to hear it. 'Beth?' I say gently. 'Not . . . Rosa?'

He smiles at me, a delicious lopsided smile that makes my stomach spin with delight at the sight. 'I adore Rosa – she's so sweet, so giving, so . . . submissive. It gives me great pleasure to help Rosa learn to be obedient and show her what she is capable of. I hope I'll have that opportunity many times in the future.' He takes another step towards me, his nearness sending my senses into a flat spin. 'She's also done something very important. She's brought me back to you, Beth.' Now he's so close I can feel the warmth radiating off him, catch the gorgeous scent of him. It makes me giddy and liquid with desire in my depths. 'Rosa is my playmate – but Beth . . . you are my love.'

I draw in a sharp breath. It's wonderful, amazing to hear him say it. *He loves me!* I knew it somehow but to hear it is enrapturing.

'I love you,' I whisper back.

He puts out a hand and runs it gently over my shoulder and down across my chest, his fingertips making a burning trail over the mounds of my breast that begin to rise and fall with the increased pace of my breath. His touch is setting me alight but there's something different about this. I'm not Rosa tonight, and this man is not my master. We aren't going to play at punishment, the kind designed to awaken my senses and send me into a frenzy of desire. Instead, with every touch of his hand I feel tenderness, as though he's marvelling at the softness of my skin and the delicious feel of my breasts in the same way that I marvel at his beauty. He takes my hand and leads me through a doorway and into the next-door room, a smaller darker place without the floor-to-ceiling windows of the other one. It's barely furnished, with only a bed, a chest of drawers and a lamp that glows against the wall, emitting a low golden light that leaves the room bathed in shadows.

As we reach the bed, Dominic turns and takes me in his arms, pressing me to him and kissing me with infinite slowness and intensity. We are both lost in each other, absorbed by the movements of our lips and tongues, obsessed with tasting one another and letting the roiling excitement in our loins and bellies begin to build. I realise how much I love this moment, as the thrill of anticipation and mounting desire creates such a pleasurable sensation of soon-to-be-assuaged need. As our bodies respond, mine to his strong hard masculinity and his to the soft, yielding treasures of my breasts and the delectable heart of my sex, we both know that we each have the capability to give and receive the most intense delight. We can surrender to voluptuous pleasure, wallow in our lust for each other, do anything we want, because we're of the same mind, the same desire – and, best of all, the same heart. Our pleasure in each other is so sweet because there's no one else in the world we want to do these things with. When we're together, and his body is joined to mine, moving inside me, our lips melded, then we don't need anyone or anything else. Our whole world is ourselves and the joy of our union.

And tonight, I remind myself, I'm not Rosa.

I reach out and begin to unbutton his shirt, something Rosa would never do unless ordered. Dominic watches me as my fingers work downwards. His chest is rising and falling a little faster as I reach the end and slide the crisp cotton back over his muscled arms. I leave the shirt on his lower arms so that he is pinned lightly inside it, his arms behind him, then I run my hands over his chest and the soft covering of hair between his nipples. I tilt my head forward and put my mouth over one nipple, taking the small red bud into my mouth and rolling my tongue round it. I pull it gently between my teeth while I pinch the other between my thumb and forefinger, twisting it lightly. Dominic groans a little. He likes this, I can tell. After I've stimulated his nipples to hard points, my mouth leaves them and moves up his chest to his arm, where I breathe in his scent and nip lightly at his skin, my hands smoothing around his stomach and back, my nails dragging over the surface. I can sense his desire in the way he's watching me as I pay homage to his body with my lips and tongue and fingertips, revelling in the feel of him and the sensations I know I'm creating in him. I stand on my tiptoes to kiss his neck, biting with the lightest of touches, licking him, tasting him as I work towards his mouth. He's desperate for our kiss, I can sense that, but he's still pinned inside the shirt that I haven't yet allowed him to take off.

I press against him, letting my breasts move against his bare chest, the fabric of my bra stimulating my own nipples as I brush it over his skin. Finally I tip my head to his and touch his lips very lightly with mine, pulling away before he can have the kiss he longs for. I return to move my lips across his, this time letting the tip of my tongue run over them. He opens his mouth slightly, his breath coming faster but I won't let him speed things up this time. I want to revel in this exquisite anticipation, the way what I'm doing is revving us both up. I let my tongue move with more force, dipping it between his lips just long enough to make him think that he can have it completely before darting away again to leave my lips nudging and kissing that full pirate's mouth that I love so much. Then, at last, I can't wait any longer: I crave the dark, deep possession of his mouth. I press into his mouth, taking it for myself, drinking in his intoxicating taste and he responds powerfully, taking what he can from me. I pull his shirt off so that his hands are free and at once he has cupped my face with them, as though he wants me as close as it's possible to be.

I don't know how long we kiss for, but our senses are roused almost beyond bearing by the darting play of our tongues and mouths. I've never luxuriated so long in a kiss before, or realised how desire grows stronger and harder the longer two mouths are entwined. I feel as though I'm soaring through sparkling space as our kiss grows deeper and all encompassing.

Then, I realise that he has lifted me up and I instinct-ively wrap my legs around him so that he can easily carry me to the low bed. He sinks slowly to his knees, our mouths still joined, and lowers me onto the bed. He pulls away from our kiss and lets me recline so that I'm lying on my back and he's kneeling over me, gazing down at my body with darkly burning eyes. I reach up to run my fingertips over his chest, tracing the outline of his defined muscles, dragging a trail down to the curls of dark hair above his waistline. They lead down to where I know treasure awaits me. I stare into his eyes as my fingers meet to unbuckle his belt, and then undo the buttons on his trousers, aware of the heat radiating out from within. I can see the great bulge beneath the fabric but I'm careful not to touch it – not yet. I want to take all these delights slowly. This is not a night for games or for rushed pleasures, where we gallop breathlessly, eager for the end of the course. This is a night for slow, sensual lovemaking, just for us, for Dominic and Beth, whose bodies work so beautifully together.

He stares back at me, panting lightly, as I push down his trousers to reveal his boxers beneath. Now I can see his gorgeous length, so strong and hard, full of desire for me. I reach inside the shorts and release it, so that it stands out proud and eager. Dominic lets out a low sigh as I touch it but I let it go at once, instead feasting my eyes on it. He's so beautiful, and the sight makes me pulse between my legs, the throbbing tickle telling me that my sex is already yearning to feel that iron length pressing into its blood-hot, wet depths.

*But not yet . . . not yet.*

I want to give him pleasure first. I want to kiss and lick his erection, take it in my mouth and love it. He's still kneeling before me, so I lift myself up and hold him by the hips so that I can run my tongue up his length, from the nest of his balls to the smooth head. He groans as my tongue glides over the tip of his penis, drawing a figure of eight around the tiny hole on the top before spiralling over it and pressing down. Then I'm lapping the sensitive skin, bathing it with my mouth, and then taking my lips, grazing teeth and darting tongue back down the hot taut skin to the base. I do this twice more, lingering as long as I can over each stage of the journey up and down his cock.

I know he can barely stand it but it's testing him in the most enjoyable manner. I can hear him breathing hard as he watches me suck him, anointing him with my mouth. His fingertips play in my hair and across my head, exerting tiny pressures when I touch a sensitive spot or move somewhere new. He groans a little when my teeth touch him, just softly enough to draw a gasp from him.

'Oh God, Beth,' he murmurs. 'I can't take much more. Holy hell, what you do to me . . .'

I let go of his penis and lie slowly back down. He knows at once what to do, moving around and lying next to me so that his penis is close to my mouth and his face is at my sex, his tongue and teeth already nibbling at my thighs. I sigh with delight. I'm so hungry for him, my mouth for his cock and my clitoris for the touch of his tongue, and I want those things both at once. He knows and understands, and wants those things just as much as I do. His cock presses at my lips as he inhales my scent and darts his tongue to tickle and play at my entrance. He seems to relish licking the juices that rush to meet him, lapping slowly at my lips and running his tongue up the burningly sensitive bud at the top that's longing for him to stroke the tip of his tongue over it. As I take as much of his length as I can in my mouth, sucking him hard, he buries his face in me, his tongue bringing me unbearably delicious sensations that are turning my limbs to liquid.

As we work with our mouths to bring each other such delicious pleasure, I feel the excitement building, my sex throbbing under the little pulsing waves that ripple outwards every time his tongue presses down and tickles so unbearably on my clit. It wants to be stroked and petted, driven relentlessly and rhythmically to a climax, and as Dominic licks and laps, it begins to open out like a flower, delivering delectable sensations that grow in strength.

But I don't want to come yet. Not yet. We've only just begun.

I pull away from Dominic's erection and he understands at once. He turns his body to bring his face to mine. His lips are wet with my juices as he claims my mouth, pressing his tongue deep into me, delivering the taste of my sex that he's been enjoying so thoroughly. I kiss him eagerly, aroused by the flavours of our lovemaking. Now neither of us can wait any longer, our bodies refuse to resist the imperative for them to join together. I couldn't stop myself taking him in even if I wanted to delay a little longer and he is breathing hard with the need to be inside me. I feel it – the hot battering ram of his penis pressing against my entrance, the natural lubrication that's flooding me easing his way as he takes it home.

'Oh God,' I cry out, opening to him as wide as I can to take that girth into me.

'Do you want this?' he asks. 'Is this what you want?'

'I want it.'

'It's yours, all of it . . . all of me . . . it's all yours.' He thrusts hard inside me. My back arches, my head tilts back. One hand grasps his bottom and squeezes hard, as if to press him further and deeper. I rake the other hand across his back, digging my nails into his skin with the force of the sensations he's giving me, as though I need to urge him on to ever more powerful fucking.

He's only too happy to obey. My encouraging hands and my urgent mouth make him find a fierce rhythm, taking his cock far within me and back, returning again and again, each thrust charging the erotic force within to greater levels. I don't know how long I can hold out before I have to surrender to this elemental need to come. I ride each piercing thrust, rocking myself against him so that I take the maximum pleasure from his body grinding into mine, and each time I climb a little higher, a little closer to my peak.

'Oh Christ, Beth,' he says. 'Are you going to come now? Come for me, please, I want to see you—'

His words trigger the shudder that means I'm going over the edge. I can't fight it. It's coming. And then I convulse, my body offering itself up to him in great, shaking waves. I can see nothing and I only know that I'm possessed by all-engulfing pleasure that judders to the end of every limb. I think I'm crying out, perhaps I'm shrieking, I have no idea, but when I return to a kind of awareness, I'm still moving under the last, luxurious waves of my orgasm. I realise that Dominic is not there yet, and I open myself to the second pleasure of being fucked hard in slippery, post-orgasmic openness. I could lie here all night, enjoying the delicious movements of his cock inside me, but I know it won't be that long. He's getting closer, his thrusting more rapid, my orgasm has powered an irresistible lust in him and he has to come himself. I feel his penis swelling inside me, his movements slow and grow stronger as he thrusts harder and harder to bring on the climax he needs so much. I open my eyes, willing him to taste the pleasure I've enjoyed, and watch as he stiffens, his back arches and his orgasm pours out in delicious jets.

'Oh Beth,' he groans as it comes.

I hug him tight, revelling in the sweetness of his climax and the love I can hear in his voice.

# CHAPTER THIRTEEN

We wake at the same time, as wintery sunshine pours through the windows of the apartment. We're lying in one another's arms on the slippery satin sheets of his bed and we don't speak for a while as we luxuriate in our closeness, my head pressed against Dominic's solid chest, listening to the rhythmic thump of his heart. I think to myself idly that even though satin sheets are supposed to be so wonderful, I prefer crisp cotton every time. Cotton can be cool or warm, depending on what you want, and you never risk sliding off it onto the floor ... While these thoughts spin lazily around my mind, Dominic is stroking my hair and occasionally rubbing my earlobe gently between his thumb and finger.

'You need to tell me all about Andrei,' he says at last. 'I have to know how things are between the two of you.'

I start to tell him everything that's happened since I saw him in Paris; how Andrei appeared to have accepted the situation with the painting and how he'd worked out a compromise agreement with the abbot.

'Oh, that reminds me,' I say, 'I think your friend Brother Giovanni was there.'

Dominic looks at me quizzically. 'Really?'

I nod. 'I didn't recognise him, of course, because it was dark when I met him, but I did recognise his voice. And he came up to me to ask after you.'

Dominic's face darkens a little. 'Did he now?' He frowns. 'Brother Giovanni had a powerful influence over me while I was at the monastery. He seemed to sense my inner turmoil and he provided a willing and compassionate ear. He was so understanding, so eager to help me.' He hugs me a little tighter and I thrill to the touch of his warm skin against mine. 'It was Brother Giovanni who explained to me some of the tenets of his order, how the Dominicans believe that you can purify yourself with punishment.'

I tilt my head so that I can stare into his eyes. 'I guess that made a kind of sense for you,' I say softly.

He nods his head. 'It seemed so incredibly relevant to me. I was still coming to terms with what happened to us, how I took you too far across the boundary of what you could stand when I took you to the dungeon. Punishment of others had brought me and them such pleasure – until I submitted you to a punishment you didn't want. It made sense to me that punishing myself might purge me both of the guilt I felt, and of the desire to do it again. I've been the master for so long – dominating myself was going to be my biggest challenge. Brother Giovanni explained it, he helped me every step of the way. He taught me to use the knotted rope to scourge myself and for a while it helped, it really did. I thought I could beat my desires out of myself. Or, at least, my desire to hurt you.'

'And did you?' I whisper. 'Beat it out of yourself?'

He pauses for a while before he answers and I can see the struggle in those beautiful brown eyes. 'No,' he says at last. 'Not entirely. But my attempt to taught me a lot of things. It taught me that I was going to have to lose my fear of love, and accept that love was going to dominate me. But also that it was stronger than my urges and if I had to, I could channel it into different routes.'

'Rosa?' I ask gently.

He smiles at me. 'Rosa is inspired, my love. She is the gentle, submissive soul I need sometimes. Chastising her gives me a deep thrill. Watching her shudder and climax under my ministrations is extraordinarily pleasing. But she only exists in the bedroom and I've learned that my alter ego doesn't always need to be present. There are other ways to live and different ways to love.'

I sigh happily and snuggle in tighter to his chest. So the dark thrills of my life with Dominic will go on – when he and I choose to enter our play world of erotic games. I'm so happy: within myself I have the capacity to surrender to pleasure, to take my body further along the road to submission and pleasure than I'd ever imagined. I know that we're only at the start of the journey that will take us to many and varied delights, and that Dominic will be my stern, loving, protecting, disciplining guide. I shiver with the thrill of what awaits the master and his humble Rosa.

And outside that world, there is Beth and Dominic – lovers who support and nurture one another in equal measure.

If it weren't for Andrei, everything would at last be perfect . . .

The thought enters my mind, bringing with it a bitter feeling of fear and anger. 'Dominic,' I say, sitting up, 'Andrei has said he wants to destroy you. He's given you until the new year to accept his offer to return to him or he'll crush you and your business. He even hinted at violence if you didn't comply.'

Dominic looks scornful. 'He's a thug. He won't frighten me that way. If he thinks I'm going back to him, he must be unhinged. I'll never work for Andrei – or anyone else, for that matter – ever again. I'm in charge now and that's the way it's going to stay.'

I knew that would be his response. I can't help admiring his utter conviction and his fearless attitude to his old boss, even though I'm scared for him. I know he won't change his mind though, even for me.

'But there's something else,' I say. 'Last night he finally came clean about what he wants from me.'

Dominic shifts and looks at me questioningly. 'Yes?'

'It's . . .' I hesitate. I hardly know how to say it and I can't help being apprehensive about Dominic's reaction. It's not going to be good, I'm sure of that. 'He told me in so many words that he wants me to be his life partner and have his children.'

Dominic goes still. 'What?' he says in an icy voice. 'Does he mean marriage?'

'I think so,' I say, wretched. 'That's what he implied. That I could share his life and create his family for him.'

He laughs but it's a cold, harsh sound without any joy in it. 'Why the hell does he think you're going to marry him?

'He says it's going to be the best thing for me, even if I don't know it.'

I see a look a little like fear spark in his eyes. 'You don't want to, do you?'

'Of course I don't!' I declare. 'I love you, you know that! Even if I didn't, I don't love Andrei and I never will. I could never marry him.'

'So why does he think you will?'

Sadness sweeps through me as I remember exactly what Andrei said. 'He's trying to blackmail me. He says he'll destroy Mark if I don't. He'll argue that Mark authenticated the painting and use it to sue him, and he'll make the sure the world knows about it.'

Dominic frowns, thinking hard. Then he says, 'That's exactly the kind of scurrilous behaviour I'd expect from Dubrovski. But something doesn't make sense about all this.' He looks down at me. 'You say the abbot was happy to take the picture back and return the money?'

I nod. 'He seemed perfectly fine about it.'

'And there's an end to it,' mutters Dominic.

'I thought it was odd that you and Anna were working in the same monastery as the painting was discovered,' I say. 'You must have been there a while, to get to know Brother Giovanni.'

Dominic nods. 'Yes. We used it as a base while we were working on the big deal. Andrei had a comms room set up and we stayed there on and off for quite a few weeks.'

'And then he bought the Fra Angelico.' I remember something else. 'Did Brother Giovanni get on well with Anna? He asked after her too.'

'Did he?' Dominic thinks for a second. 'I don't remember him ever having anything to do with her. They all kept clear of Anna. Maybe they could sense something dangerous in her.'

'Something infernal,' I say with a smile. I try to imagine the effect that the beautiful, highly sexed Anna might have in a monastery. 'He wanted to know when she'd be back. He seemed disappointed when I said that she wouldn't.'

There's a pause while Dominic absorbs this, then he says slowly, 'So Andrei intends to destroy Mark if you don't do as he asks. I see. Clever of him. Most people's weak spot is the people they love. And it's all because of this picture.'

I nod. 'That's right.'

Dominic sits up abruptly. 'Is your flight leaving tonight?'

'Yes.'

'I'm coming back to London with you. I want to follow something up, something that might explain what Andrei's game is. In fact, we'll leave as soon as we've collected your things from Andrei.'

'So I'm just going to leave him?' I say, half excited and half afraid. 'Despite his threats?'

'What's the alternative?' asks Dominic, his dark eyes searching mine. 'Can you go back to him and tell him that you're prepared to marry him?'

'No, of course not!'

'There's your answer. Of course you're going to leave him.'

'But you . . . and Mark . . .'

'I can look after myself. In fact I'm looking forward to a final showdown with Dubrovski. He's earned what's coming to him. As for Mark – I don't think Andrei will play his trump card quite yet. Once he's done that, you'll have no reason to ever go back to him. And besides, something tells me that this is not as straightforward as it seems.'

I sit up as well, my blood tingling with excitement. 'So we're going to go to Andrei's for my things?'

'Absolutely.' Dominic takes my hand, slides it under the sheets and presses it against the erection that's hard and hot against my leg. 'Just as soon as we've taken care of this . . .'

An hour later the grey sports car speeds us through the streets of Manhattan to the Victorian mansion that I left last night.

The guard radios up to the apartment before he allows us in, and when he does, he says to me, 'Just you to go inside, miss. The gentleman must wait outside.'

Dominic nods. 'Okay.' But once we've driven into the courtyard he says, 'Just let them try and stop me.'

I put my hand on his leg. 'Wait, think about it. I don't want to see you men squaring up to each other over my suitcase. Let me go up. If I'm not back within ten minutes, come and find me.'

He looks at me and then says reluctantly, 'Okay. I see your point. But ten minutes only – then I'm coming up.'

'All right.'

I ride the lift up to Andrei's floor and knock on the door of the apartment. Renata answers it, her face stony.

'Hello, miss.' She stands back to let me in. 'I have your bags packed. They're in here.'

'Thank you, Renata.' I step into the hall. There is my case waiting for me.

'Is that everything?'

'Yes. I don't need anything else. I'll be on my way.' I step forward and grab the handle.

'Beth.' I hear the voice as Andrei steps out of the shadows and into the light of the hall. He looks awful, his face tired and drawn and his eyes dull. 'Where have you been? I've been worried about you. Who was that strange woman you left with?'

I look up at him slowly. I hate seeing the agony in his eyes. Even after everything that's happened, I don't want to hurt him. 'She was just someone who helped me when I needed it. The things you said last night devastated me. I couldn't stay with you after that.'

Renata has left us together. Andrei takes a step towards me. 'But why? I only made you the offer of my life and my heart. Did that mean you had to run away as though I wanted to hurt you?'

'You have hurt me!' I burst out. 'You've threatened people dear to me! You've tried to blackmail me into a relationship with you! Don't you realise that I love someone else? You've made it impossible for me to be with you at all. I can't work for you any more, you must see that.'

His face contorts for a moment, his blue eyes fierce. 'What do you mean?'

'I mean that this is goodbye, Andrei.' I put my hand in the pocket of my coat and pull out the thick strand of pearls. Stepping forward, I hold it out. Automatically he puts out his hand and I drop the pearls into his broad palm. They sit there, a pile of glimmering grey spheres. 'I'll send back the clothes later,' I say softly. Then I turn to go.

'Beth!' His voice is cracked with despair.

I turn back slowly. 'I don't think we have anything left to say. I'm sorry it's ending like this.'

'Don't go, please.'

'I don't have a choice. You gave me an ultimatum and I've made my decision.'

'I was serious, Beth. If you walk out that door, I'll carry out everything I said.' His voice has a warning note.

'You mean you'll carry out your threats to hurt the people I love?' I shake my head. 'I thought you were bigger and better than that, Andrei.'

At that moment the lift doors open and Dominic

steps into the hallway. I can see him through the open front door. 'Beth – are you there? Are you okay?'

'I'm fine,' I call quickly. 'Get back in the lift, Dominic, I'm just coming.'

Andrei's face turns hard and cruel and his eyes flash. 'What the hell is he doing here? Were you with him last night?'

'That's none of your business,' I retort. I pick up my case and head for the door.

Andrei is pushing past me in an instant. 'Is that you, Stone? How dare you show up here? Get the fuck off my property or I'll have you thrown off!'

Dominic faces him full on, his shoulders set, his whole body tense and ready. His eyes burn with fury. 'Don't try and pull your tough-guy act with me, Andrei, it won't work. I know you, remember? But you seem to have forgotten the years I worked my arse off for you, making you millions in the process. You seem to think you're the only one owed loyalty around here – but what about what you owe me?'

Andrei almost snorts with contempt as he says, 'I owe *you*?' His lip curls nastily. 'You've got your priorities wrong, my friend.'

'Your friend?' Dominic gives him a look that is simultaneously scornful and amused. 'Hardly. Friends don't behave the way you have, Andrei. We could have been equal contenders on the playing field, both competing fairly with respect for each other, but that's not your style, is it? You prefer bully-boy tactics, don't you? Like a kid who underneath his bluster and his aggression is actually just afraid the world will find out what he really is – just another loudmouth who secretly thinks he isn't good enough.'

Andrei almost snarls and I see his hands clench into fists. Dominic faces him with a flashing, hostile gaze, then he says quietly, 'And you think you can bully Beth, too, don't you? Well, guess what – the villain never gets the girl. Or didn't you know that?'

'Keep out of it, Stone, I'm warning you,' growls Andrei. He's on the edge of losing it, I can tell. 'Let Beth make her own decision.'

'I will,' Dominic says with a half smile. 'I won't blackmail her into being with me – she'll be with me because that's what she wants.'

'You lowlife fucking scumbag,' says Andrei in a tone of fury, and I can tell he's about to explode and do something stupid. I don't want this to turn physical and I know Dominic won't back down if it does.

I stride past Andrei and put my hand on Dominic's arm. 'Not here,' I say quickly. 'Let's go, Dominic. I don't want this trouble now.'

Dominic is locked onto Andrei's stare and they are facing each other, the air thick with antagonism. I put my case in the lift and grab Dominic's hand. 'Come on, let's go.'

'All right,' he says and turns to follow me. 'Beating up the opposition isn't really my style.'

'You'll regret this, Beth!' Andrei calls after me. 'You're forcing my hand, you know that!'

Dominic and I stand together in the lift as the doors slide to a close. My last glimpse is of Andrei's scowling face and icy blue eyes.

'Christ,' Dominic says softly. 'I've never wanted to rip someone apart with my bare hands like that before in my life.'

'You hid it well. I could tell Andrei was about to lose control and lash out, but you seemed very calm.'

'All I had to do was remind myself that I never want to sink to his level.'

'I think I've lit the fuse,' I say, my voice shaky now that the confrontation is over. 'I don't think there's any way to stop the explosion now.'

'You wait,' Dominic says, pulling me into his arms. 'He's not stupid. He knows that it's all he has left over you. He won't squander it, you'll see.' Then he kisses me passionately, as though for a moment he feared he'd lost me again.

We drive back to Georgie's place. She looks relieved to see us, and welcomes us in to have lunch with her. I change out of my cocktail dress and into clothes more suitable for the journey home.

'Could you please have these sent to Dubrovski?' I ask, putting down a pile of neatly folded clothes: the dress, shoes and the black cashmere coat.

'Of course.' Georgie looks casually glamorous in slim jeans and a baggy taupe knitted jumper that sets off the dark mahogany of her glossy dark hair. 'Is everything okay?'

Dominic and I exchange looks.

'Yes.' I try to sound more confident than I really feel.

Georgie sighs. 'I can tell that you aren't going to tell me the whole story but I hope you two know what you're doing. I don't like the thought of you mixed up with that gangster.'

Dominic shoots me an amused look. 'My sister can never really imagine me as anything other than eight years old,' he murmurs. 'She still doesn't believe I can cross a road on my own.'

'Of course I do!' Georgie protests. 'But Dubrovski is dangerous, we all know that. I never liked you working for him in the first place.'

I look over at her, enjoying the way she looks so like Dominic. I'm glad he has his big sister to worry about him. I can't wait to learn more about him and to flesh out the picture of his life and his family.

Georgie appeals to me. 'Beth, you'll talk sense into him, won't you?'

'I'll do what I can,' I say with a smile.

'Do you really have to go back to London?' she says to Dominic. 'I thought you were going to spend Christmas here with me. The cousins have invited us out to the Fairfield estate, it's going to be amazing.'

'I have to go back,' Dominic says. 'I need to get a certain situation sorted.' He gives me a look that makes me tingle all over. 'But I might be back for Christmas. I'll let you know.'

I feel obscurely disappointed, even though I know that I'll be at home with my family. Why shouldn't Dominic be here with his? I try to damp down my sadness as Georgie grumbles, 'Well, you're leaving it very late, that's all. I can't tell Florence whether to expect you or not.'

'She won't mind,' Dominic says carelessly. 'One more won't make any difference, considering it's her butler, six maids and four chefs who do all the work anyway.'

Georgie laughs despite herself. 'Just tell me as soon as you can.'

'I will.' Dominic pushes away his empty plate. 'Come on, Beth. Let's get to the airport.'

A different car is waiting for us outside, a sleek black car with a black-suited driver to chauffeur us to JFK. I don't ask Dominic what's happened to his little grey sports number. I have a feeling that things have changed – he's an important man now, with people to sort things out for him. He's already mentioned at least two assistants and is busy firing off messages as we head away from Manhattan.

I look back towards the spectacular skyline with its iconic buildings silhouetted against the pale blue afternoon sky, the winter sun already low. When I arrived a week ago, I had no idea of what awaited me here. I certainly would never have guessed that I'd be arriving with Laura, but leaving with Dominic.

I turn back to face the oncoming road. I just hope that I haven't flicked the switch that will set off a disaster for Mark, me and for Dominic.

*I guess I'll find out all too soon.*

# CHAPTER FOURTEEN

The journey back is deliciously restful, especially as we're in first class again.

'This was so great on the way out,' I say without thinking. 'Laura totally loved it.' Then I remember that it was Dubrovski who provided all the extra largesse on our trip and I bite my tongue.

'I'm glad you liked it,' Dominic says with a grin. 'Think of it as an early Christmas present.'

I stare at him. 'It was you!'

He nods.

'The first-class flight? I thought it was Andrei.' I think back over what happened.

'I had a feeling you did – when you didn't mention the Soho Grand even though I knew you'd arrived there.'

'That was you too? But not the Four Seasons – that definitely was Andrei. He was furious when we didn't take the rooms.'

Dominic looks bemused. 'The Four Seasons?' he echoes. 'I don't know about that.'

I explain how we were taken there from the airport but that I refused to go in. I tell him that I wouldn't have taken the Soho Grand either, except that he'd been clever enough to cancel our reservations at the Washington.

Dominic laughs. 'So you were at the centre of a tug of love – one party wanting to gift you the Four Seasons and the other the Soho Grand!'

'I'm glad you won out,' I say softly, taking his hand.

'Me too. The thought of paying for an empty loft doesn't excite me all that much.' His eyes glimmer with amusement and he squeezes my hand back. 'But the idea of Andrei paying for two empty rooms at the Four Seasons – now that I *do* like.'

Being together for the seven-hour flight is bliss. We can't keep our hands off each other, constantly re-assuring ourselves with a stroke of the hand, a quick stolen kiss or my head dropped on his shoulder while we watch a film together. I never want this to end because I know that real life is going to intrude on us all too soon and separate us again.

'I don't want to be apart from you,' I say as the captain announces that the plane is preparing for its descent.

'I feel the same,' Dominic says. 'But I've got things I have to do. Believe me, it's all for you, to help sort out this sorry mess. I don't believe that Andrei is going to stop until he's destroyed me and made you regret turning him down. So I'm going to have to take him on – and win.'

'Can you do that?' Worry fills me at the very idea.

'Do you need to ask?' He smiles at me and I feel my confidence come back. I know that Dominic has the strength and the guts to take Dubrovski on. It's what happens if he doesn't succeed that frightens me.

It's late by the time we arrive in England. A car is waiting to speed us into London and it takes us to Dominic's apartment in Mayfair.

'Dear old Randolph Gardens,' I say, looking up at the Art Deco facade as it glimmers in the darkness, illuminated by some lit windows and the street lights outside. 'I'll always be happy thinking of this place.'

Dominic takes my hand. 'It'll always be special but I'm thinking of moving on.'

'Really?' I say, dismayed. I'm so fond of his apartment with its view across to my father's godmother's flat where I was staying when we first met, and of course on the floor above is the boudoir, the little apartment that Dominic acquired to be a delightful playroom for us. 'Where will you go? You're not leaving London, are you?'

'London will always be important to me,' he says gently. 'But I'll be travelling a lot. I need to decide where I'm going to put down roots. My sister is in New York and I'll be working there a lot. It makes sense to be close to family.'

'Yes, I suppose so,' I say, feeling wretched. Dominic's parents are no longer around. Of course he'll want to be close to Georgie as she's all he has left, along with the cousins she mentioned.

Dominic smiles at me and kisses me tenderly. 'Don't worry. We'll be together. I intend to make sure of it.'

He leans forward and directs the driver to take me home.

'I'll be in touch,' he says, with a last kiss. 'But I'll also be sorting things out so don't worry if I go quiet.'

'Don't leave it too long,' I say fervently.

'I won't.'

He gets out and waves farewell as he closes the door behind him. I hate watching as he walks up the steps of the building without me, knowing that we'll be apart tonight. I long to spend the night, and every night, in his arms, breathing in his musky scent, delighting in the joy of being close to his body.

Once we reach home though, I'm happy to be back in my own place. Laura is fast asleep and I realise it's getting on for two in the morning. I collapse into bed and am asleep almost at once.

Laura's thrilled to see me home and keen to hear all about my adventures. I tell her some of it, but I hold back on mentioning Andrei appearing out of the blue. The story of meeting Georgie and the fact that she turned out to be Dominic's sister is enough to keep Laura riveted, and she couldn't be happier that I met up with Dominic. We spend the weekend getting ready for going home for Christmas the following week, going into central London to brave the crowds and do the last of our Christmas shopping. I call my mother, who is delighted to hear from me at long last.

'When are you coming back?' she asks. 'Christmas can't start until you're here.'

'I'm not sure. It's Christmas Eve on Friday, isn't it? I'll be home by then for sure but I need to see Mark first and make sure my work is done before I go.'

'Of course you do. I hope that poor man is recovering. Now let me know when to expect you, won't you?'

'I will. See you soon, Mum.'

'See you soon, sweetheart.'

I put the phone down, thinking that although my dream would be to be with Dominic, I'm very lucky to have my home to go to this Christmas.

On the Monday I finally get back to work, almost a week later than I expected when I left for New York. The city really feels Christmassy now, with a frantic air that proclaims there are only a few days left now for the shopping and the food and all the preparations. Mark's glossy black front door is sporting a huge wreath which looks cheerful enough but I'm apprehensive as I knock on it. Andrei's had a few days now to chew over what happened in New York, and despite Dominic's confidence that he won't do his worst, I'm worried that perhaps I'll find that Mark's had bad news.

Caroline answers, looking pinker in the face than ever but very glad to see me. 'Did you have a marvellous time?' she asks as she leads me downstairs to a conservatory I've not seen used before.

'Yes, amazing. I hope Mark got all my notes. I managed to do nearly all of what he asked.'

'He was very pleased. Considering it was your first time in New York as well. Now, he's in this room because it's lovely and warm and it was easy to get a bed in here . . .' Caroline takes me through into the sultry air of the conservatory and I can already see that Mark is lying on a daybed, his thin limbs on top of the blanket. He turns his head to look at me as I come in.

'Beth!' he greets me but the sound is obscure and not easy to decipher.

'His tongue is still very swollen,' confides Caroline in a low voice, 'but you'll understand him well enough when you get used to it.'

'Hello, Mark,' I say cheerfully, going up to kiss his thin cheek. 'It's so wonderful to see you back at home.'

'Sit down, sit down!' Mark says in his new thickened voice. 'Tell me all about New York. I want all the gossip.'

I set off, regaling him with stories of my adventures, making them as amusing and interesting as possible while the maid brings us coffee. Mark listens happily, laughing at the right places, his eyes bright. I soon get used to the sounds he makes and understand when he asks after certain friends or artworks. I don't tell him about my encounter with Andrei but when he asks me if there's anything else he needs to know, I hesitate just long enough for him to guess that something's up.

'What is it, Beth?' Anxiety crosses his face and he tries to haul himself up to a better sitting position. 'Tell me.'

I feel terrible. I don't want to ruin the cheerful atmosphere or cause Mark any anxiety that might threaten his recovery but I have to let him know.

'It's about the Fra Angelico,' I say reluctantly. 'It's been confirmed by the Hermitage that their experts consider it to be a fake. It's only about two hundred years old according to analysis of the canvas and the paint. I'm so sorry, Mark – it's not a real masterpiece after all.'

Mark gapes at me and then falls back against his pillows with a sigh. 'I feared as much,' he says with a voice not much more than a muffled whisper. 'I wanted it to be the real thing because Andrei did. But I thought it was so unlikely that a picture like that, in a public place, would have gone unnoticed.' He groans. Caroline shifts uncomfortably beside me, obviously concerned for her brother. She puts out her hand and strokes his gently. 'What does Andrei say about it?'

'He wasn't happy at first,' I tell him. 'But he's come to an agreement with the monastery to have the money repaid. He's happy to keep the whole thing quiet.'

'Well, that's one good thing, I suppose.' Mark manages a weak smile and fixes me with his small blue eyes. 'You'll probably have to deal with some of that – Andrei pays for all his art through me.'

'I know. I expect the paperwork will be waiting for me in the office.'

There's a pause while Mark considers what I've told him. He looks mournful. Then he turns to me again. 'You know I didn't want my name given out as the authenticator of the painting but that was done anyway. I wasn't happy at all.'

I reach out and put my hand on his arm. 'I know! I know that. It seems so unfair.'

'Hmm.' Mark sighs. 'I wonder if this will mark a natural end for my relationship with Dubrovski. It's worked well for both of us for so long but I have a feeling that this will have changed all that.' He looks suddenly very tired.

'I think that's enough for now, Beth,' Caroline says. 'Mark had better rest. He hasn't talked so much in days.'

'Yes, of course.' I get up.

'They're saving my radiotherapy until after Christmas,' Mark announces, suddenly cheerful again. 'Isn't that nice of them?'

I touch his arm again. 'Very nice. But you need it, you know, to get better.'

'Perhaps.' Mark's eyelids flicker and close and he exhales gently.

'See you later, Mark,' I say, and go quickly and quietly out of the conservatory and up to the office.


I'm glad that the burden of telling Mark about the painting is off my conscience but I'm more afraid than ever of what Andrei might do. I have some emails from his office about the details of funnelling the monastery money back to Andrei but nothing from Andrei himself. Perhaps he's still in New York, in that palatial but chilly apartment of his. He will have had the parcel of clothes back now. He'll know for sure that I'm not coming back – and soon I'll formally turn down his offer of working at his apartment next year. It's just not possible now.

Later that day I get an email from Dominic:

I have to leave the country for a short while. I'll be back before Christmas. I'll let you know when I'm home. Stay strong and don't worry. Can't wait to see you.

D x x

I can't help feeling melancholy when I read it. Somehow I know that life with Dominic is always going to be like this. He'll always be on the move, doing something, meeting someone, sorting something out or cutting a big deal. What I hate is being left behind – if I could be with him, I wouldn't mind at all.

Another more cheerful message comes through a bit later.

Hi Beth

It's our Christmas party tomorrow night and Dominic's supposed to be joining us. I understand that you two are an item again so please do come along if you'd like to. It would be lovely to see you and have your help toasting a bright new future for us all. Details attached, just rsvp my assistant Grace.

Best wishes

Tom Finlay

I read it over a couple of times and look at the attachment. The party is at a smart hotel in Piccadilly. It sounds fun, but I have no idea if Dominic will be there or not. He might still be abroad, doing whatever his secret mission is. On impulse I email Tom's assistant saying I'd love to come and asking if I can bring a friend. When she says yes, I send Laura an email telling her that tomorrow night is party night. She emails back:

> Whee! I'll get the glad rags out. Sounds fun. See you later!
> Lx

The next day there's still no word from Dominic and I'm beginning to feel the familiar sense of being taken for granted. It makes me all the more determined to go out and enjoy myself that evening, so I take a party dress and shoes into work with me and get changed at Mark's house.

I look in the mirror at my plain black dress and for a moment I'm wistful for the sexy scarlet number I had in New York, along with the shoes and the beautiful pearls, but I put them out of my mind.

*They came at too high a price, remember?*

I say goodbye to Caroline and Mark, and hail a cab outside his house to take me up to Piccadilly; I'm meeting Laura in a pub near the hotel where the Finlay party is being held. She's waiting for me when I walk through the door, standing by the bar and looking very pretty in a short green sparkly dress and high heels.

'Thank goodness you're here!' she says. 'People are certainly getting into the party spirit. I've had to fight off three blokes already.'

'I'm not surprised, you look fantastic,' I say.

'Thanks, sweetie. So do you – although you're off the market now, of course! I got you a drink.'

'Thank you.' I take the glass that Laura passes me and sip the white wine.

'So what's this party in aid of?' she asks.

'It's Dominic's business partner,' I reply. 'I think this is a courtesy invitation to reflect the fact that they've set up this new venture.'

'Great, any excuse for a party is fine by me. Will Dominic be coming?'

'I don't think so,' I say regretfully. 'I think he's away.'

She looks at me with a trace of pity. I know she thinks that Dominic is perfect apart from his little disappearing acts.

'It's business,' I say a touch defensively. 'And once this is dealt with, we'll be able to spend a lot more time together.' I sound a lot more convinced than I feel on this particular point.

'Good,' she says. 'I only want you to be happy, you know that. Now shall we get along to this party?'

Finlay Venture Capital has a private room at the back of a smart hotel on Albemarle Street. We're shown in and I'm a little taken aback at how few people are there. Then I remember the small offices on Tanner Square. I have a feeling that the company isn't all that huge and they've probably invited me just to help swell the numbers.

'Beth, how fantastic to see you!' Tom Finlay strides

across the room towards me, smiling, his brown eyes friendly behind the dark-rimmed glasses. He's a short, stocky man but he's got a vibrancy that makes him seem energetic and friendly. I like his dark brown beard and his cheery smile. 'Is Dominic not with you?'

'Not tonight,' I say. 'He's out of town. Again.'

'You won't be jumping on any trains to Paris to track him down, will you?' Tom laughs at his own joke. 'I was very excited to have a little part to play in your romance. Dominic obviously doesn't mind that I told you where X marked the spot.'

'No – I think he was pleased in the end.' I smile. 'By the way, this is my friend, Laura.'

'Hi, Laura.' Tom leans in and kisses her cheek politely. 'A pleasure to have you with us. Do you work with Beth?'

'Oh no,' Laura says with a laugh, and I think how attractive she's looking tonight, with her light brown hair curling down her back and her face given just enough party sparkle on her lids and lips. 'She's in the very glamorous world of art. I'm just a boring management consultant.'

'Try being a venture capitalist!' exclaims Tom. 'People fall asleep on my shoulder while I'm still getting the words out! They're comatose on the floor when I explain what I do. Now – you haven't got a drink. Let's go and find you a Moscow Mule, they're great here.'

We accompany Tom over to the bar and get ourselves a cocktail each. He and Laura are soon talking away like old friends, while I get into a long discussion with Grace, the company assistant, about whether it's better to live in north or south London. Once I've finished talking to Grace, I get caught up in another group who are chatting about their favourite Christmas television programmes and I'm on my third Moscow Mule before I manage to get away and try to find Laura again.

She's still with Tom but they've ended up sitting next to one another on a leather sofa, deep in discussion, both looking a little flushed after several drinks.

*So that's the way the wind is blowing.* I'm pleased for Laura, it's been a while since she's had a relationship and she is clearly hitting it off with Tom. I just hope it's not one of those one-night wonders, if something does happen. It would do wonders for Laura's confidence to have something more lasting.

It makes me a little wistful though. I've got plenty of romance of my own – or I would do, if my partner would stop vanishing.

I step out into the hall and check my phone. There's nothing there – no message, no text. I quickly tap out a message.

Where are you? I'm missing you so badly! Please tell me when you'll be home. I can't wait to see you. B x

I press send and then loiter in the hotel hall. In a nearby room, another more raucous Christmas party is going on, with loud music, singing and some energetically drunken dancing. Back in the Finlay party, the interminable conversations are continuing and Laura and Tom are still in deep discussion on the sofa. Even from here I can see that they are now flirting heavily, all the signals are there. I don't want to go back in there where I don't know anyone and can't face another long talk about nothing while sipping yet another drink.

I decide I'll take a walk around the block. Some fresh air will clear my head from the fuzziness induced by the three Moscow Mules, and by the time I come back, Laura might be ready to go home. I collect my coat from the cloakroom and head out.

It's cold outside but the air is full of celebration. There are obviously parties going on everywhere, and the pavements are scattered with people in skimpy clothing having cigarettes in the chilly night air. I wander down Albemarle Street and then take a turning into Dover Street, past a pub thronged with revellers and along the pavement. Opposite is me is a row of handsome Georgian houses, their windows blazing with the light of ornate chandeliers, and I can see people moving about in the upstairs rooms. There's a big party going on. I stop and stare for a moment and I realise that it's a private club, one of those glitzy places that count actors, models and minor royals among their members. As I watch a black cab pulls out, and a woman gets out. My eyes are drawn to her at once – she's beautiful with her sharp cheekbones and slanting eyes. She also has a marvellous body, her perfect legs shown off to the best advantage by a short tight black dress. As she turns to pay the driver I see her properly for the first time and it's all I can do to stifle a shout.

*It's Anna! Oh my God, what is she doing here?*

I watch her sashay up to the doorman and I hear her distinctive low voice with its rolling Russian accent. 'I'm here for the Barclay party.'

The doorman says, 'Second floor, ma'am.'

Anna stalks inside, her hips swinging as she goes up the steps.

I stare after her, hardly able to believe my eyes. I haven't seen her since the day in Albany when she invited me to join her and Andrei in bed. Not long after that he sacked her, because, he said, she was in the habit of slipping him various drugs.

I don't know what impulse makes me do it, but the next moment I'm walking across the road towards the club, an imperious look on my face. I'm glad that I'm wearing my best heels as I stride over, pausing long enough by the doorman to say, 'The Barclay party?'

'Second floor, ma'am,' he says with a nod, and I walk past him and up the steps.

Inside I see that I haven't cleared the hurdle quite yet: there's a reception desk where names are being ticked off a guest list.

*Oh God, this is it. Humiliation.*

I begin to walk towards the desk, wondering what I'm going to say, when there's a sudden commotion behind me. I turn to see a familiar face coming through the door accompanied by a crowd of people pressing close to her. For a second I wonder if it's a friend of mine before I realise that the reason the sculpted features and long blonde hair are so familiar is because they belong to a very famous Oscar-winning actress.

Immediately all the attention turns to the new arrival, excitement rippling around the room. I take advantage of the diversion and turn quietly for the stairs, stopping to hand in my coat to the cloakroom attendant whose mouth is hanging open as she stares at the big star just a few feet away. The next moment I'm climbing the grand staircase on my way to the Barclay party.

To my relief there's no one taking names on the door, just a couple of waiters standing with trays of drinks for the arrivals. I pick up a glass of champagne as I pass by and walk into the room. Clutching my drink and looking into the middle distance, I manage to make my way through the crowd without being challenged and soon I start to relax as I realise that most people are concentrating only on the group they are with and no one is that interested in confronting me. I try to spot Anna without attracting any attention.

*Why am I here? What will I say to her when I find her?*

I'm beginning to regret this crazy impulse, and I'm about to put my drink down and leave when I see her. She's in a corner talking animatedly to two men in suits who seem completely entranced by her – but that's no surprise considering her vivacity and that

241

feline beauty. I watch, trying not to stare too openly, and see her pull a phone out of her clutch bag and check it. The next moment she makes her excuses to the men she is talking to and heads out of the room via another door at the back. I put my glass down on a table and follow her, threading my way through the crowd until I reach the door. I step through it and discover myself in a quiet reading room, and look around just in time to see Anna disappearing out at the other end. I hurry after her and emerge from the reading room into a carpeted corridor, where Anna is standing with her back to me, talking into her telephone.

'Yes,' she is saying, 'I'm at the Dover Street Club. You know the one – I'm at the Barclay party. Yes, I will see you, I've already agreed to that. Whether I'll tell you what you want to know, that's another matter altogether. All right. I'll meet you in the top-floor bar in twenty minutes.'

As she ends her call, I slip back into the reading room and run lightly back to the party. I find a spot by the window and watch her re-enter the room and go back to the men in the corner.

*So now I know that she's meeting someone here. I don't have a clue who that might be – so why do I feel so afraid?*

I already know that I'm going to be in the top-floor bar when Anna has her rendezvous so I go and wait in the ladies where I can be out of sight until the time comes.

I check my phone. There's a text from Laura.

Where are you? Have you gone home?

I text back:

No, went out for a walk. Sorry, should have said. Are you all right?

Her reply comes back quickly:

In a taxi with Tom. He's taking me home. He lives in East London.

I smile. So they've definitely found a spark then. Maybe it's better that I'm not there to cramp Laura's style. I send back a message:

Take care and have fun. I'll be home later. Not far behind.

Then I check my watch. It's nearly time for Anna's meeting in the bar. I emerge from the ladies and head upstairs to the top floor.

I find the bar easily enough and sit down at a low table in a shadowy corner. A waiter comes up and asks for my order, so I ask for a lime and soda.

A few minutes before the time for the meeting is due, I see a man walking across the room towards the bar, where he takes a seat on one of the high stools. My heart sinks and depression floods my body. I suspected all along from the moment I saw Anna that once again she was going to be trouble for me, and I lean back into the darkness so that Dominic won't see me from where he is, ordering a beer at the bar and waiting for Anna.

She arrives only a moment later, smiling seductively as she walks towards him with the grace and elegance of a model. She sits down on the stool next to Dominic and I can see her face plainly, although I only have a view of Dominic's back. They are talking with ease and I hear her laugh and the sound of his voice as it floats over to me. I'm seized with a desire to get up and walk over there, demand to know why they are meeting and what they are saying. What reason does Dominic have to see Anna? Her obsession with him has caused a lot of difficulties for us. I feel fury boiling up inside me, a mixture of jealousy and betrayal. Why would he see her without telling me?

Then another voice speaks up, telling me to calm down. Dominic told me he wanted to sort out the mess with Andrei. Surely seeing Anna must be part of that. If I spring out of the shadows now, I could spoil whatever it is Dominic is doing.

*Do you trust him?*

I remember that I never did find out how Anna knew the secrets of my relationship with Dominic. He utterly denied telling her but he was the only person apart from me who knew the details – and she knew everything from what happened in the dungeon at The Asylum to the marks of the scourge on Dominic's back. I've tried to forget about the confusion I felt and the fact it's never been resolved but seeing Anna is bringing it all back.

*So do you trust him or not?*

I look into my heart. I think of everything we've been through. I remember Dominic's eyes gazing down into mine, the pain I've seen there, the tenderness, the love. He doesn't need to pretend any of those things with me. I've always believed that he truly feels them. I know he loves me.

*I do trust him.*

So prove it, I tell myself.

I hear their laughter reach me again. I get up very quietly and without being noticed, I put some money down for my drink and slip out of the room. I walk quickly down the stairs to the cloakroom, get my coat and hurry outside to try my luck hailing a taxi home.

# CHAPTER FIFTEEN

Laura emerges from her room the next morning looking distinctly the worse for wear. Her eyes are bloodshot and her hair is all over the place.

'Thank God it's almost Christmas and hardly anyone is in the office,' she groans. 'I won't be able to do much today. I feel like shit!'

'Did you have a nice time with Tom?' I ask a little smugly as I eat my cereal. I don't have a hangover at all.

She shoots me a look and smiles. 'Mmm!'

'He saw you home, did he?'

She laughs. 'He very kindly saw me right to the door, and inside.'

'Really.' I raise my eyebrows meaningfully. 'And did he stay long? I expect he wanted to make sure you were really, really safe. I mean, tucked up in bed and all cosy.'

'Not quite in bed,' she says, 'but let's say we did sit for a while on the sofa and . . . talk.'

I laugh. 'Was it fun?'

'*Really* good fun.' Laura looks a lot brighter, despite the hangover.

'Are you going to see him again?'

'I think so. I'll see if he sends me a message today.'
She goes to get a drink of water, pouring out a glassful
from the bottle in the fridge. 'I just hope I can make it
through, that's all.'

'Last day tomorrow,' I say. 'Then we go home on
Christmas Eve.'

'Yep.' Laura gulps down her water. 'And I can't wait.'

On the way to work I send Dominic a message.

Hey
Did you get my message last night? Are you back in
town? I really want to see you! I'm going home for
Christmas soon. Please tell me where you are. Lots
of love, B x x

When I emerge from the Underground at Victoria,
my phone starts flashing to indicate a new message. It's
from Dominic.

Sorry for the late reply. Good news, I'm in London.
I've got things to tell you. Can I see you later? D x

I feel a rush of joy. I did the right thing. I trusted him
and he came through. I'm sure he's going to tell me
something to do with Anna. I message back telling him
to meet me after work. I can't wait to see him.

I spend an hour chatting with Mark as he lies on his
bed in the conservatory. Although it's freezing outside,

the conservatory is toasty warm, but Mark is wrapped up in several layers of blankets and still can't seem to shake the chill he feels.

I try to distract him with talk but I'm anxious about the way he seems so weak and frail. It's hard to imagine him being able to withstand radiotherapy. He looks as though downing an aspirin might be too much.

'You must go home and have a wonderful Christmas,' he says to me, his tongue still distorting his words. 'I'll be so much better in the new year. We'll cut our ties with Andrei and get on with acquiring new clients. What do you think of that?'

'I think it sounds marvellous,' I exclaim. 'A fresh start.'

'Absolutely.'

Caroline comes in with a tray of pill bottles and a glass of water. 'Time for your medication, darling!' she says brightly.

I get up. 'Happy Christmas, Mark.' I lean over and kiss him.

'Happy Christmas. Your bonus is on the desk, by the way. Now – have a lovely time with your family and I'll see you back here in January.' He manages a smile.

'Goodbye, dear,' says Caroline. 'If I don't see you, have a lovely time.'

'Goodbye, and happy Christmas, Caroline.'

I ought to feel festive and merry but I realise I'm wiping away tears as I head into the office. Mark is so ill, it's hard to imagine that he'll be any different in the new year. He might never get better. The thought is so awful it makes me gulp, but I fight for control. He needs me to be strong and keep things running. We'll face whatever happens when it comes.

On the desk in the office is a beautiful pale blue box with a plump white ribbon wrapped around it. This must be the bonus Mark mentioned. I'd assumed he meant some shopping vouchers or some cash but he's given me an actual gift. How kind of him. I wonder whether to open it and then decide I'll keep it to open on Christmas Day. Knowing Mark, it's sure to be a beautiful present, and it will be something special to open.

There's also a pile of post that includes a lot of Christmas cards addressed to Mark. He's received dozens already, most from business contacts and clients, from addresses all over the world. Among them I find one addressed to me, with a formal typed label.

*How strange, no one's sent me a card here before! I wonder who it's from.*

I slice open the envelope with Mark's letter opener and take out the card. It's a picture of a Russian icon of the Madonna. I open it and a folded piece of paper slips out onto the desk. Inside there's a printed message that reads: *Happy Christmas and best wishes for the New Year from Andrei Dubrovski.* Beneath that in a scrawling hand written in black ink are the words:

*Beth. Your Christmas Gift. Andrei.*

I pick up the folded piece of paper and open it up. I read it, frowning as I wonder what it means. For one thing, it's dated the 2nd January, which is over a week away. It's titled 'Press Release from the Office of Andrei Dubrovski, embargoed until 2nd January'. I begin to read.

The Office of Andrei Dubrovski announces its intention to sue art dealer Mark Palliser for malpractice and mishandling of affairs after it has emerged that the well- known art expert wrongly identified a work of art as being by the Florentine Renaissance master, Fra Angelico. Mr Dubrovski paid over two million pounds for the work which was later confirmed as a fake by experts at the Hermitage Museum in St Petersburg. Mr Dubrovski was devastated by the verdict and has taken steps to recover the sum he paid for the painting. There are also questions over Mr Palliser's handling of Mr Dubrovski's financial affairs and certain aspects are being investigated with a view to recovering any sums that might be owing.

Mr Dubrovski commented: 'I'm deeply saddened by the end of my professional relationship with Mark Palliser. Unfortunately his mistaken authentication has cost me a great deal of money and I intend to sue for damages and compensation. I hope that further suggestions of financial misconduct will prove to be false.'

Please direct all further enquiries on this matter to the Office of Andrei Dubrovski.

I drop the piece of paper onto the desk with a gasp of horror. So he wasn't bluffing. He intends to do this.

I cover my face with my hands, trying to process what I've just read. But he's given me a grace period. I can only guess that he's going to give me one last chance to change my mind and save Mark.

I think of my friend lying so weak and ill on the bed in the conservatory, and I'm sure that this will kill him.

I take a deep shaking breath, and burst into tears.

Dominic sends a car for me and I climb into its interior, grateful that I'm going to be insulated from the outside. The Christmas cheeriness is too much to bear when I'm feeling so miserable; even the prospect of seeing Dominic is not making me feel much better. The lights blur in front of my eyes as I well up again thinking about the terrible trap I'm in. Dominic persuaded me that I didn't need to worry because Andrei wouldn't carry out his threat but it looks now as though Andrei was in fact deadly serious. He's prepared to sacrifice Mark if I don't do what he wants.

On my way to the rendezvous I wonder, as I've been wondering all day, whether I should tell Dominic that it's all over. I could spin some line about how I don't love him any more, or I could scream and shout, tell him I saw him with Anna last night and accuse him of everything I can think of – and then storm out. Then I would go and live with Andrei, and somehow I would manage to stand it because I'd know that I'd saved Mark, and Dominic too, if Andrei will do as I ask and leave him be. Just when I've resolved that the only way out of this is to concede to Andrei's demands, the car comes to a halt in front of a large, white-fronted house. I look around and realise that we've arrived in Marylebone, just off Wimpole Street.

The driver gets out and opens the door for me, and gestures me towards the huge black front door, a potted bay tree on either side.

I go up and press the large bell push in a brass surround. A moment later, the door swings open and Dominic stands there, handsome in dark trousers and a pale-blue checked shirt that somehow makes his eyes browner than ever.

'You're here!' He's beaming as he opens his arms to me and, despite my resolution in the car to resist him, I throw myself into them, desperate for the comfort of his closeness.

'Hey, Beth, what's wrong?' he says, kissing the top of my head.

I try to speak. I've rehearsed what I want to say in the car and now I ought to deliver my speech with conviction – I need to tell Dominic that it's over and we'll never see each other again – but the reality of being with him shows me the total impossibility that I could ever do it. I'm swamped with guilt because my inability to deny myself the joy of Dominic means that Mark is going to be destroyed. I feel the tears rush up to my eyes again and sob into Dominic's chest.

'You're crying! What is it?' He pulls me inside and closes the door. We're standing in a marble-floored hallway beneath a huge brass lantern.

I look up into his eyes that are full of tender concern. 'Oh, Dominic! It's Andrei. Look!' I wipe away some tears and pull the press release out of my bag and press it into Dominic's hands. He takes it, unfolds it and scans it quickly

'I see,' he says grimly.

'What do you think?' I try not to wail but my voice rises as I say, 'He's actually going to ruin Mark after all! To get back at me!'

Dominic refolds the paper and hands it back to me. 'Don't worry,' he says. 'It's not going to happen.'

'What do you mean? He's prepared this release. It's obvious he's serious. The only reason he's delaying must be to give me one last chance to change my mind.' I grasp Dominic's hand. 'I can't bear it!'

He holds my hands tight in return. 'You're not going to be blackmailed like this, don't you worry. Listen, we've got a visitor or two coming. After that, everything will be clear.'

I shake my head as though waking up and look around. 'Where are we? Where is this place?'

'Do you like it? This is my new house.'

'What?' I stare about the huge hallway. 'Your new house?'

'I think so. I'm still deciding. I wanted to ask your opinion first. What do you think so far?'

I look around. The place seems strange because there's no furniture, except for a few isolated tables, chairs and lamps. 'It's lovely,' I say. Then I look back at him. 'Rather different from Randolph Gardens!'

He smiles. 'Yes. A little bigger. Would you like to look around?'

'I'm not sure, to be honest,' I say, sniffing a little. 'I'm not really in the mood. I'm sorry.'

He takes me in his arms again. 'Hey, don't be unhappy. I promise, it's going to be all right. You'll see.'

'When did you get to London?' I ask him, muffled a little against his shirt.

'Yesterday.' He pulls back so he can look into my face. 'I didn't want to tell you in case what I was doing didn't work out. But I think it's going to be fine and I swear I won't let Andrei hurt Mark – or you.'

I gaze back. *Are you going to tell me about Anna? What happened between you last night?* I remember the way they were laughing together – it's hard to believe what bitterness there's been between the two of them. I wonder whether Dominic really has it in his power to stop Andrei sending out that press release, and starting Mark's destruction.

'Come on,' he says coaxingly. 'Come and see the house. I really want your opinion.'

'Okay,' I say, a little reluctantly. 'I'll look.'

He takes me over the house, full of enthusiasm. It's certainly a wonderful place with five storeys of rooms, all with the graciousness of the Regency style mixed seamlessly with modern comfort and the luxurious touches of beautiful bathrooms, a gym and a cinema room. When we finally return to the ground floor, Dominic is keen to know what I think.

'Well – do you like it?'

'I think it's gorgeous,' I say honestly. 'But it's huge. All this, just for you?'

'Too much?' He looks a little crestfallen.

'It's very grand but . . .' I think about Andrei's chilly palace on the edge of Central Park and then of Georgie's cosy, lived-in brownstone, and I know where I'd rather live. 'Perhaps it would be more homely with some furniture in it,' I say with doubt in my voice.

Dominic starts to laugh.

'What?'

'You're so sweet – and so right. I'm getting carried away. I don't need this house – not yet, anyway.' He kisses me gently on the lips. 'Why don't we look for somewhere together?' he asks.

I almost stop breathing. *Together? Live together?* The idea is a wonderful one that makes me want to dance with joy. Then I rebuke myself. No, he can't mean that. He means he wants my advice looking for somewhere.

'I value your judgement,' he goes on. 'And . . . I want you to feel at home wherever I am.'

'I'd love to help you choose a place,' I say tentatively, not wanting to misunderstand him.

'Beth,' he says, taking my hands in his and standing close to me. 'I want a little more than that. I want—'

A loud noise rings out through the empty hall, making me jump violently.

'Ah,' says Dominic. 'My visitor is here. Don't be shocked, Beth. Wait and see.' He strides over to the front door and opens it. In the doorway is a beautiful silhouette, slender and shapely, with an unmistakable pair of cheekbones. It's Anna. She cranes her neck to accept a kiss from Dominic on each cheek and then sways into the hall on high heels.

'What a perfectly lovely house, Dominic,' she announces. 'Do tell me this is yours.'

'I'm still deciding,' he says with a sideways look at me.

She walks right up to me and fixes me with a look from those slanting green eyes. 'Beth. Hello. How are you?'

'I'm fine, thank you, Anna.' I try to sound cool and composed. 'How are you?'

'Amaaazing,' she purrs. 'As usual.' She spins on her heel and faces Dominic. 'Are you going to offer me a drink?'

'Of course,' he says. 'Champagne?'

'You know me too well. I can't resist.'

'Let's go downstairs.'

We follow Dominic down to the huge kitchen that's been extended into the garden with a wall of glass and is a minimalist creation of white gloss surfaces and polished concrete. He goes to the fridge, takes out a bottle and opens it, pouring the wine into glasses that are waiting on the bench.

I'm still waiting to hear what exactly Anna is doing here, but I'm determined not to leap to any conclusions. I'm going to trust that Dominic knows what he's doing.

He passes each of us a glass of champagne and holds

one up himself. 'To our joint ventures,' he says with a broad smile. 'And success.'

Anna holds up her glass and clinks it against Dominic's. 'To our success.' She turns to me. 'Beth – success.'

I let her clink her glass on mine, but say nothing. I can't forget the fact that she dropped drugs into my drink at the catacombs party, and attempted to sabotage my relationship with Dominic so that she could have him herself.

We all sip our champagne and I feel the bubbles prickling over my tongue.

'So Anna,' Dominic says. 'You remember what we talked about last night. Have you come to any decisions about what you're going to do?'

'I wouldn't be here if I hadn't,' she returns coolly. 'You know that. We just have to be certain that this will work. We can't afford failure.'

'Between the three of us, we can make it work,' Dominic says adamantly. 'Between us, we have the information we need.'

'But you need what I know,' Anna remarks with a coquettish tip of her head. 'I have the key.'

Dominic leans towards her, his eyes suddenly intense. 'And are you going to give me the key?'

'I might.' She flutters her eyelids at him, and I feel a rush of jealousy spiralling up inside me.

*She is completely shameless. I'm standing here and she's flirting with Dominic right in front me! She's unbelievable! Is anything really worth this?* I try to control myself. *Mark is worth this.*

'I don't owe you anything, Dominic,' she says, suddenly still.

'No. But this isn't about me,' he says. 'It's about Andrei.'

A bitter expression crosses her face. 'Yes.' She sounds convinced again. 'Andrei. He's going to be sorry about the way he treated me.' She slides her gaze over to me. 'I've no interest in helping you, Beth, but if that's part of the bargain, so be it.'

I keep quiet, sensing that there is a delicate balance here and I mustn't upset it.

'So,' presses Dominic. 'What can you tell us?'

'I can tell you that Andrei knew that painting was a fake from well before the time he decided to buy it.'

I gasp and despite my resolve not to say anything I can't help my words escaping me. 'He *knew*?'

'That's right,' she says, cocking an eyebrow at me. 'He paid over two million for something he knew was going to be proved a forgery.'

'But *why*?' I say, amazed. 'What could he hope to gain from that?'

She laughs mockingly. 'My darling, you're so naïve. Andrei's money laundering, of course. He's deeply involved with the criminal underworld and he does extremely well out of cleaning the proceeds of drugs and crime, which in turn smooths his path through many of his more difficult deals and makes him more money.'

I stare at her. Then I turn to Dominic. 'Did you know about this?'

'No,' he says firmly. 'Not a thing.'

'He didn't,' says Anna breezily. 'Andrei told only me. He should have remembered that when he decided to throw me aside in the way he did. But I don't think he suspected I would tell you. And . . .' she shrugs '. . . he paid me a lot of money as a severance bonus that he probably thought would buy my silence.' Then she turns to face me. 'The real question is, Beth – did *you* know?'

'Me?' I'm stunned. 'Of course not. Why would I?'

'Because you are the one who is putting the two million back through Mark's accounts, just as has happened with the many dozens of art purchases that Andrei has made over the years.'

I gasp. 'What do you mean?'

'You heard me. Mark has been vital to the whole operation. He's very kindly allowed Andrei to put a great deal of money through his business.'

A white light of anger bursts inside me. 'Are you telling me that Mark is a criminal – a money launderer?' My voice rises. 'There is absolutely no way – Mark is completely honest, an utterly genuine man. He would never do such a thing.'

Dominic extends a hand towards me as if to calm me down, but I'm facing Anna, my eyes blazing.

She shrugs, unmoved by my fury. 'Perhaps he is not a criminal, perhaps he is simply an innocent. But he has facilitated the laundering of a huge amount of money.'

'Another reason why Andrei wants to cut ties with Mark perhaps?' murmurs Dominic.

I turn to him, my eyes stinging with tears. 'You don't believe that Mark's guilty of this, do you?'

'No,' he says gently. 'But if what Anna says is true, Mark is going to be involved whether he likes it or not.'

'So you mean that the only way to stop Andrei destroying Mark is by revealing his criminal activity – and destroying Mark anyway!' I stare furiously at Dominic.

'It might not come to that,' he says.

'I don't see how it can't.'

'It may be that none of this comes out. It all depends how Andrei reacts when we tell him what we know.' Dominic's expression is sympathetic and I can see in his eyes that when we're alone, he'll tell me more. He turns to Anna. 'So you're committed to this?'

'Yes,' she says, with a sudden bright smile. 'Completely.'

We hear the sound of the doorbell echoing through the hall upstairs.

'Ah,' says Dominic. 'I think that might be your reward. Excuse me, ladies.' He goes upstairs and returns a few minutes later. As he comes down the stairs, I see that he's being followed by another man in a dark suit, and a second later the stranger emerges into view and I realise that I recognise him. Just as I'm working out where I've seen him before, Anna shrieks.

'Giovanni!' She races across the room and jumps into his arms. The monk is startled for a moment and then delighted to find a beautiful woman embracing him. They kiss passionately.

Dominic comes over to me, smiling. 'And there's the last piece of the puzzle,' he says. 'Now we know how

260

Anna knew all our secrets. The only person I told was Brother Giovanni. It turns out my confessor was busy doing his own confessing. I always knew that Anna wasn't a one-man woman. She might have wanted me because I refused her favours, but my guess is that a man who's taken a vow of celibacy was even more of a challenge. She's happy to see him again, don't you think?'

I gaze back, not knowing whether to laugh or cry. 'Oh, Dominic!'

He takes me in his arms and hugs me tight. 'We're going to get through this, I promise. All of us.'

# CHAPTER SIXTEEN

Anna and Giovanni leave soon afterwards, obviously keen to go somewhere private and enjoy their reunion. I wonder if Anna has finally given up on Dominic, or whether she's simply happy to play a waiting game. I suppose I have to do the same and just put up with her, considering how badly we need her cooperation.

Dominic shuts the front door behind us and locks it. 'The keys go back to the estate agent tomorrow,' he says. 'This isn't the house for us, is it?'

I look up at him. '*Us?*'

He gazes down. 'I can't think of a future without you in it. Isn't that obvious by now? I don't want to live without you.'

Happiness rises up through me. 'Really?' I whisper.

'Really.'

I can't say anything as I take this in. I think he's saying that our lives are inextricably entwined and that we'll never be apart. The thought is miraculous.

Dominic smiles at my expression. 'We've got lots to talk about. But it's late. I need to get you home.' He pulls out his phone and taps out a message. 'My driver will be here in a minute.'

I watch him for a moment, thinking how much he's changed since I met him. He's now a force to be reckoned with, a man with the power to bring down Andrei Dubrovski. I say suddenly, 'Is Mark going to be all right, Dominic? Can you promise that?'

He takes my hand. 'I can promise that I won't let Andrei spread lies and destroy Mark's reputation. But if what Anna says is true – well . . . I know Mark is innocent but he might have to prove that in court.' He looks suddenly solemn. 'All of us who are mixed up with Dubrovski – we're all tainted. We're all going to have to explain ourselves. But if we're honest and sincere, I believe we have nothing to fear.'

The car draws up at the kerbside and Dominic takes me over, opens the door and helps me in.

'Are you coming?' I ask.

He shakes his head. 'I want to take a walk and clear my head. I've got a lot to think over. You should get some sleep.'

'When will I see you?' I ask, panicked at the idea that we might not be together before I leave for home on Christmas Eve.

'Tomorrow.' He smiles. 'I have something planned. You'll hear from me then.'

'Dominic . . .' I don't want to, but I have to ask. 'Anna . . . you . . . don't . . .?'

He kisses me gently and says, 'You don't even need to say it. Of course I don't. You're the only one for me.'

\*    \*    \*

I'm grateful to be home, and I sleep deeply that night, worn out by everything that's happened. I feel safer, knowing that Dominic is leading the charge against Dubrovski, but I still have strange dreams in which Andrei is chasing me, threatening me and telling me that I'll never escape him – if he's going down, he'll take me with him.

After my vivid dreams I'm glad to wake up in the morning in the safety of my own bed. This is the last day before I go home for Christmas and the holidays begin. I wonder if Dominic can get the situation with Andrei sorted before the 2nd of January and the release of the statement.

When I get to work, Caroline is surprised to see me. 'I thought you were going home today,' she says. 'I wasn't expecting you.'

'I thought I'd come in and just check things over,' I say. The truth is that I want to check the files that cover Mark's dealings with Andrei, just in case there are any clues there. I realise that Caroline looks very downcast. 'Is everything all right?'

'Mark's not well today,' she says, her expression bleak. 'He's running a temperature and he's very croaky. If he's no better later, I'm going to take him to the doctor.' She looks kindly at me. 'If you've nothing more to do, you should leave early, Beth. You could make a start on your Christmas holidays. It's going to be very quiet here.'

'Thank you,' I say gratefully. 'I might do that.'

I go into the office and start looking through all the files to do with Andrei but as far as I can tell, everything is very straightforward and above board, although, of course, knowing what I now know, it seems extraordinary that Mark has agreed to the system of payment and reimbursement that he and Andrei use.

All the time, I'm waiting for Dominic to contact me. It's not until after lunch when I'm about to leave that I get a message.

Rosa. You are needed. Your master requires Christmas cheer. Be at the boudoir in one hour.

My breath comes a little faster in anticipation. I long for the escape into pleasure that being with my master will give me. My stomach clenches pleasantly at the thought. If Rosa's presence is required, I'll be more than happy to supply it.

I arrive at the boudoir before the hour is up, but I know the value of obedience, so I wait quietly until exactly an hour has passed and then knock at the door.

Dominic opens it and steps back to let me in. The hallway is in darkness and as he closes the door, I blink in the sudden gloom.

'Go the bedroom, Rosa, and choose what you think will please me. I'll be there in ten minutes exactly.'

I put down my bag and slip off my coat, and walk across the small hall to the bedroom. Inside, everything is freshly laid out and organised. There is the white leather spanking seat on which Dominic has driven me to such peaks of delight. There is the cabinet with its range of exciting playthings and instruments. There is the closet where Dominic keeps a range of clothes and accessories for me. I can never be quite sure what I will find there. I go over and open the door.

My master requires Christmas cheer. I shall be his own present, to unwrap and enjoy. I take out a bra that doesn't have cups but instead fastens around my breasts with a big black silk ribbon. A pair of matching knickers is the same but with the bow at the back. I put them on and then put on a red silk robe over the top of that. My eye is caught by a pair of high-heeled boots laced almost all the way to the thigh. Very attractive. I pull them on, grateful for a zip along the side that stops me having to lace them. Then I take up a leather collar and fasten that around my neck – Dominic has always liked to see that as a sign of my submission. Then I sit on the bed and wait for Dominic to come in.

After exactly ten minutes the door opens and Dominic enters. He is smartly dressed in dark pinstriped trousers, a shirt and a tie and a waistcoat. He walks over to a leather armchair placed by the end of the bed and sits down, regarding me with a serious gaze. I notice that he's holding a glass of champagne.

'Stand up, Rosa.'

I obey, holding the robe close about me. His gaze travels over me, noting the boots, and he nods. 'Very nice. Please come here.'

I walk over to him and stand obediently before him, waiting for my next instruction.

'Sit on my lap.'

I turn around so that my back is to him and lower myself down so that I'm sitting on his knees. I feel his hand stroke the silken back of the robe, then travel upwards and lift my hair so that he can see the collar.

'That's good,' he breathes. 'I like to see you know your place, Rosa. You like to be humble, don't you?'

'Yes, sir.'

'Do you like to obey me?'

'Yes, sir.'

'You've been very docile this evening, you've done just as I asked with no mistakes. Does that mean no punishment for you?'

'Whatever you think is right, sir.'

He laughs gently. I press back very slightly into his lap and feel a hardness under my buttocks. As I sit back I can feel it grow and throb beneath me. I stretch out one leg so that he can see the pretty boot and the way it encases my leg all the way up above my knee. His breathing thickens as he notices it.

'You're teasing me,' he says. 'What else are you going to do?'

Without a word, I stand up, drawing my fingertips over the woollen surface of his trousers. I let the silken robe drop to the floor so that he can see the black silk bow sitting pertly in the middle of my bottom. He laughs again.

'My little Christmas present. Let me see what delights you're hiding inside.' He pulls the bow and it slips apart to reveal my bottom, soft and curved, the white flesh in delightful contrast to the black leather of my boots. He strokes his hand over it, admiring its firm globes. 'Turn around.'

I turn. He can see my sex, demure for now with a tiny scrap of silk still covering it, my belly and the big black bow over my breasts. He lifts his eyebrows.

'Another present. Bend down so I can open it.'

I lean forward, my breasts rising before his face in soft mounds. He plucks one end of the ribbon and pulls. My rosy nipples and round breasts are revealed and he makes a growl of appreciation. 'You look delicious,' he murmurs. 'Come closer.'

I bring my breasts up towards his mouth. He takes a sip of champagne from his glass and then puts his mouth over my right nipple. I gasp as the cold liquid submerges my nipple. I can feel the bubbles prickling over the surface, then he sucks hard and swallows. The champagne disappears and he releases me. 'Delicious,' he says with a smile. He takes another sip and does the same to the other nipple. Then he dips his finger in his champagne and trails it down my stomach. The cold wetness prickles my skin, and when he reaches the triangle of silk covering my sex, he slides his finger underneath and rubs it over me.

His touch is shiveringly arousing. I can feel a lascivious desire thrumming up inside my clit and in the swell of my sex. He locks eyes with me and sees it in my thoughts.

He reaches down and undoes his trousers, releasing himself so that his erection rears up from his lap. 'Why don't you sit down again? Perhaps you'd like to have a drink of champagne.'

I move forward obediently and he sits up, moving forward to the edge of the chair so that I can put my legs on either side of him. I reach down and hold his penis. It's stiff and hot under my hand. Without a word, I place myself above it, pull the scrap of silk out of the way and sink down slowly, taking it in me in its entirety. Dominic is controlling his breathing as I engulf him, but only just. He lifts his glass of champagne and takes a large mouthful. Then he pulls my head to his and presses his lips on mine. A gush of cool champagne leaves his mouth and floods mine. I take it and drink it, then enjoy the movement of his champagne-flavoured tongue in my mouth. He takes another mouthful of the wine and repeats, letting the fizzing liquid move from him to me. It's delicious, and intoxicating in more ways than one.

As I drink, I move subtly, clenching my inner muscles so that I grip the hot column inside me. I can feel him growing there, getting thicker and harder as I wriggle very slightly to stimulate him.

'Are you pleasing yourself, Rosa?' he asks in a low voice that's freighted with lust. 'Is that why you're wiggling on me like this?'

'Yes, sir,' I breathe out.

He looks down at my booted legs on either side of him and the way I'm sitting on his cock. My breasts press out towards him, the rosy hard nipples begging for him, showing him how hot I am. His eyes glitter with desire.

'Move up and down,' he orders. I begin to rise and sink, taking my weight on the high heels of my boots and then sliding down his length and pressing as hard as I can on his cock. 'That's right. Faster.'

He puts his hands on my hips so that he can shove me up and down on his penis even harder. I love the sensation of him filling me up and taking his pleasure, and I lick my lips and run my hands across my breasts, pinching my own nipples, twisting them lightly. Dominic watches me with appreciation.

'Poor Rosa,' he says, 'you're not getting quite enough pleasure. You must feel free to give yourself what you want.'

I run my hand over my belly as the other plays with my breast and then drop it to where his penis is pounding into me. Above my entrance, my clitoris is standing proud and swollen and I touch it with my index figure, rubbing it in a circular motion.

'That's right. You show me what you want,' breathes Dominic, watching hard as my finger begins to move faster and hard, twirling around the top of my bud. His cock is thrusting into me harder than ever. I pinch hard at my nipple and give little gasps as my finger lights up the sensations in the tip of my bud. 'Make yourself come,' he orders sharply. 'Do it. I want to see it.'

I begin to surrender to the delicious feelings of his penis pounding into me as my fingers drive my pleasure forward, my cunning fingertips knowing exactly how to play with the stiff little pearl to make it throb and tingle under my touch. I rub harder and Dominic takes his fucking up a pace, breathing hard, my actions exciting him.

'Ohhh,' I cry, as the electricity begins to dart through me.

'Come, Rosa, make yourself come,' he says again and I fly out into my climax, shaking and jerking on top of him as my limbs stiffen and the orgasm possesses me.

I finish, panting, still impaled on his stiff penis.

'That was delicious to watch,' he murmurs, smiling as he regards me sinking forward on his erection. 'We're not finished yet.' He leans forward and whispers in my ear, 'I'm going to fuck you hard, on that stool and then on the bed. You're going to come again, believe me, and so am I. But not before I've taken all the pleasure I want from you, my sweet, submissive Rosa.'

I lift my eyes to his and see that they're glazed with desire. The fire kindles in me again. I clench my muscles around the pillar of his cock, still piercing me to the core.

'Yes, sir,' I say softly. 'Whatever you want.'

Dominic is as good as his word and we spend two hours exhausting each other. He's insatiable, hungry to be inside me with his huge erection, and by the time he comes in a huge outpoured climax, I'm stiff and swollen, my sex tender with the pounding it's taken. I feel wrung out and battered by pleasure. We take a long leisurely bath together and Dominic tends me with soap and a soft cloth, treating me like a precious object as he gently ministers to my red-raw sex. Then he pats me dry and we get dressed.

Even though we've been indulging ourselves for hours, it's still only early evening.

'We're going out for dinner,' Dominic says. 'And there's another little surprise for you.'

I'm intrigued and I'm also starving. I feel light and joyful despite the soreness between my legs. The power of sex to send those wonderful mood-enhancing hormones racing through the bloodstream should never be underestimated. I know that there are dark shadows hovering in my life but an earth-shaking orgasm and the pleasure of touching and tasting Dominic's flesh is enough to keep them at bay for now.

When I'm dressed, Dominic says casually, 'Oh, there's something for you in the hall by the way.'

'Really? What?' I walk into the hall and see a large rectangular white box on the floor. It's wrapped with a red ribbon.

'Open it,' says Dominic from behind me.

'Okay.' I go over and pull at the end of the ribbon. It slips gently apart. I lift up the white cardboard lid and see inside a stunning black silk and cashmere coat, edged with black fur at the collar. I gasp.

'You looked wonderful in the coat you wore in New York. You loved it but you gave it back without a second thought. So I wanted to give you one of your own.'

'It's beautiful,' I say, enchanted. I lift it out and

Dominic holds it up for me while I slip my arms into the silken interior. It fits perfectly and is incredibly cosy and warm. 'Thank you, Dominic, I love it!' I hug him impulsively and kiss him on the cheek, while he laughs.

'You're very welcome. Happy Christmas.'

My face falls. 'But I haven't got you anything!'

He runs a finger down my cheek. 'Don't worry about that. You've just given me the most delicious Christmas present I could imagine.'

Wrapped up in my gorgeous new coat, I'm ready to face the chill outside. With my arm tucked inside Dominic's we walk together through the wintery streets to the Mayfair restaurant that Dominic has booked. As we go in and the maître d' steps forward to greet us, Dominic says, 'Are the other guests here yet?'

'They are, sir.'

I give Dominic a puzzled look. I thought that this evening was just for us – and I hope suddenly that the other guests aren't Anna and Giovanni. That's one surprise I think I could do without.

After our coats are taken, we're led through the plush dining room to a white-covered table at the back where I can already make out another couple. As we get closer, I realise with delight who the woman is.

'Laura!'

She gets up, a big smile all over her face, and greets me with a kiss when I reach the table. 'So I finally get to meet the gorgeous Dominic!' she says as he comes up behind me.

'The pleasure is all mine,' he says with perfect charm, kissing her on each cheek. 'Thank you for coming along with Tom. I asked him if he'd see if you'd like to meet at last.'

On the other side of the table, Tom Finlay is standing up, looking both happy and a little bashful. 'Hi, Dominic. Actually, if you hadn't asked us along tonight, I was going to take Laura out anyway – if she wanted to.'

Laura laughs and flushes lightly. 'Well it's all turned out very nicely, then, hasn't it?'

I look at Dominic, my eyes sparkling. He knew I was dying for him to meet Laura and he must have been listening hard when I mentioned that she and Tom had hooked up. The fact we're spending the evening with them means he wants us to be a proper couple, part of one another's world, getting to know each other's friends.

'I thought you might like this,' he murmurs softly to me, a gentle smile on his lips.

'I love it, thank you so much!'

Tom steps forward to greet me. 'Hi, Beth.'

I laugh as we exchange hello kisses. 'Fancy seeing you here. I hope you're well, Tom.'

'Very well.' He looks happily at Laura who smiles back at him with shining eyes.

*So it looks like it's turning out well.* I'm delighted for her, and it's even better that her new boyfriend should be a friend of Dominic's as well. *Perfect.*

\*    \*    \*

We enjoy a wonderful evening of good food, wine and lots of convivial talk and laughter. There is the sense that the holidays have finally begun and we discuss our plans for Christmas. Laura and I are both going back to our respective family homes to spend time with our parents. Tom tells us that he'll be with his twin brother and his family at their home in Scotland. At last I turn my gaze to Dominic. He looks amazing tonight, and he seems happy, strong and confident. I also get the feeling that he's preparing himself, as though he's a soldier who has been called up to fight and this is his last night of freedom before the battle begins.

'What about you?' I ask, fiddling with the stem of my wine glass. 'Have you made your Christmas plans, Dominic?'

He nods. 'Yes. I'm flying out to the States later tonight. I'm joining my sister in New York.' He gives me a meaningful look. 'And I have an important meeting that I have to attend.'

I can guess what he means. *Andrei.* It's time to confront him with all we know, to strike the counter blow and see what happens. Sadness rushes through me. I don't want Dominic to leave me. It feels so wrong that we should be apart for any time at all, but particularly at this time of the year.

*But you're going to your family – there's no question of not doing that,* I remind myself. Then I realise I've been nurturing a little secret fantasy that maybe I can take Dominic home with me, introduce him proudly to my friends and family, show him all the

275

places that meant so much to me when I was younger. That's not going to happen now. I suppress a sigh. *Oh well, it was pretty unlikely. I shouldn't be greedy. I've had so much of him lately.* And I know that big decisions are approaching on the horizon if what Dominic said last night means anything – decisions about where and how we live. That's exciting. It's something to look forward to. I smile and join in the chatter as brightly as I can.

We leave around eleven, and outside in the chilly air we wish one another a happy Christmas.

'I'm taking Beth home,' Dominic says. 'Do you want to come, Laura?'

She shakes her head. 'I'm staying with Tom.' She looks bashful but happy. 'I'll see you in the morning, Beth.'

'See you then.' I kiss her goodbye and wish Tom a very happy Christmas. Then Dominic ushers me into the warm interior of the waiting car and directs the driver to take us back to my flat. I snuggle up to Dominic and watch as the glittering lights of the city fly past the window, enjoying the pleasure of being close to him and trying not to think that soon we'll be apart.

I hope for traffic jams and snarl ups that will keep us together for longer but the roads are clear – lots of people must have already left for Christmas – and we get to the flat quickly. The driver pulls over and we get out, strolling together towards my front door.

'Thank you for a marvellous day, Beth. I loved every moment of it.' He puts his arm around me and drops his lips down to kiss me tenderly as we both remember the panting joy we shared earlier in the day.

'I don't want you to go!' I say, turning to him, suddenly miserable.

'I know – I don't want to leave you either. But it's just for a short time. I'll be back soon, I promise and then our new life can begin.' He hugs me and then says, 'I have a Christmas present for you.'

'Another one? You've already given me this beautiful coat.'

'Yes, another one. I was going to save it for a slightly more romantic moment, but this feels like the right time. And I want you to have it before I go.' He takes out a small black box from his pocket and hands it to me. 'Open it.'

I fumble with the tiny clasp and then lift the lid to reveal a small hoop of diamonds that glitter with extraordinary brilliance in the light from the street-lamps. 'A ring,' I say wonderingly. Dominic is staring at me intently as I regard the beautiful circle of diamonds in their platinum setting. I look at him questioningly. I'm not sure what kind of ring this is, and I don't want to get it wrong.

As if reading my mind, he says softly, 'This is a promise ring. You can wear it wherever you choose.'

I can hardly breathe as he lifts the sparkling ring from its velvet bed and holds it out. I hesitate just for a moment, and then I raise my right hand to him. He smiles and slips the ring down onto my fourth finger where it fits snugly, flashing at me as I move my hand.

'A promise ring,' I say softly, not able to take my eyes off it.

'It's my promise that I'm yours now and that I want us to be together. Whenever you're worried or in doubt, I want you to look at it and remember this promise. Will you do that?'

I throw my arms around him, sobbing and smiling. 'Oh yes, Dominic, I will! Of course I will!'

# CHAPTER SEVENTEEN

The countryside is rushing by the window as the train takes me further away from London and my life. It feels very strange to be going home. The closer I get to my old existence, the more unreal I feel my new one is. Everything I've lived through and experienced begins to feel like a fantasy, something I dreamed.

Only the glitter of the beautiful ring of diamonds on my right hand reminds me that it is all real.

*Why did you get him to put it on your right hand? Why not your left?*

I stare at the sparkling stones and I know I did the right thing. This is, as Dominic said, a promise ring. A promise of amazing things to come. He's asking me to accept his commitment for us to love one another and see what life – real life – together is like. The next step awaits us if we want it.

I think of him now thousands of miles away from me in New York. I can't help a sense of fearful apprehension when I think about him confronting Andrei. When they faced up to each other that day outside Andrei's apartment, they were like two snarling dogs ready to rip one another apart. I dread to think how

279

Andrei will react when Dominic tells him that he is prepared to take him down once and for all.

Running my fingertips over the bumpy surface of my ring, I send up a silent prayer that Dominic will be all right. All I can do now is hope – and wait.

'Beth, oh Bethy!' My mother wraps me in her arms and showers me with kisses. 'I've missed you!'

'I've missed you too. Hi, Dad.' I hug my father too, filled with happiness to be home. 'Wow, it's good to be back.'

My mother stands back and looks at me. 'You've changed!' She frowns. 'I can't see exactly what it is, but you're definitely different.'

'She's grown up,' my father says wistfully.

'I had to, sooner or later!' I say jokily but I know that I'm a different Beth in so many ways. I've seen another world to the one I grew up in, I've travelled and I've worked and discovered resources inside myself I didn't know I had. And . . . I blush a tiny bit to think of it . . . I've learned some pretty amazing things about love and sex as well. It's almost comical to think of how innocent I was when I left home last summer to travel to London, and yet I thought I knew it all. Well, I know a lot more now, that's for sure!

Mum begins to bustle round me. 'Come on, let's get your luggage in your old room, and then we'll have some tea and talk while I get on with this cooking. I've got a mountain to do before tomorrow!'

It's like I've never been away. The house is just the same, a mix of cosiness and chaos, and it's like dozens of other family Christmases – the hot scented fug of baking and roasting, the sound of carols coming out of the radio, the frantic air of organisation as my father is sent on last-minute errands to the butcher's, the log man, the coal man, and my mother does her usual thing of trying to get ahead. My two older brothers, Jeremy and Robert, are stretched out in the TV room, watching Christmas specials with a bowl of crisps in front of them and cans of beer already open, waiting for what Christmas goodies are offered to them. In the sitting room, a tree, hung with all the old familiar decorations including a shabby old blue tinsel star, perfumes the room with pine and a twine of holly decorates the mantelpiece. There are already presents under the tree and the room is full of Christmas cards. It's all just the same.

This year, I'm the one who's different.

That evening we crunch through the frosty village to midnight mass. The voices of the choir soar upwards in the beautiful old tunes and we all join in with the Christmas hymns, belting out 'O Come All Ye Faithful' with all our strength. The church bell starts to chime as we make our way home, ringing in Christmas. A message pops through to my phone.

Happy Christmas, gorgeous girl. I'm thinking of you.
I love you. Dx

Tears start in my eyes even though I breathe a happy sigh and smile.

281

I look up at the clear night sky peppered with sparkling stars. Somewhere, thousands of miles away, it's still daytime. It's still Christmas Eve and he's thinking of me.

'Happy Christmas, Dominic,' I whisper. And I slip my phone back in my pocket so that no one knows about my message. It's for me alone.

Christmas Day is merry and exhausting. After breakfast, we gather by the tree to open our gifts. As I stretch out my hand to take a parcel that my brother Jeremy is passing me, my mother's eagle eye catches the sparkle on my finger.

'What's that, Beth?' She reaches out and takes my hand, gazing down at the circle of diamonds on my finger. 'This is very nice. Who gave it to you?'

'Oh, it's just a bit of costume jewellery,' I say airily. 'From a friend.'

She looks at me suspiciously but I send her a look that I hope translates as: 'I don't want to talk about this right now in front of the others, ask me later!'

Mum seems to understand, though she drops my hand reluctantly and murmurs, 'Those diamonds look real to me!' under her breath. I wish I'd remembered to take the ring off but I know that secretly I couldn't bear to. The ring is my link to Dominic, my promise. I want to be able to look at it at any moment, and remember.

We open our presents, and exchange thanks and kisses. We all have a familiar haul in front of us: the whisky, slippers and handkerchiefs for my father, the soap and scent for my mother, and books, films and music for the rest of us. It's the usual comfortable set of presents from the people we love, and that makes them special. I'm excited that everyone seems to like the gifts I brought back from New York: a silver charm bracelet from Bloomingdale's for my mother, baseball tops for my brothers and a J Crew sweater for my father.

'Hold on,' says my father, and he reaches out for a parcel I put under the tree the night before. 'Who's this for?' He pulls out the beautiful pale blue box wrapped with a white ribbon and examines the tag. 'To darling Beth, Happy Christmas, Love from Mark.' He hands it over to me. 'Something fancy from your boss, by the looks of it.'

I take the parcel and open it slowly, with everyone watching.

'Gorgeous ribbon,' breathes my mother. 'You should keep that. You could use it again.'

I lift the lid of the box and reveal a mound of the softest tissue paper underneath. Holding my breath, I put my fingers into it and find another small box, this time in navy blue watered silk. I open that and reveal inside a perfect miniature painting in an oval gold frame. It must be eighteenth-century; a portrait of a girl with rosy cheeks and pink rosebuds in her powdered hair. One hand is lifted by her cheek and holds another flowering rose as she gazes out of the picture with merry blue eyes and a smile on her red lips.

There is a tiny note next to it in Mark's elegant flowing hand. It reads: *In memory of your Fragonard.*

I gasp. Could this be a Fragonard? It certainly looks like his style, but it can't be possible. A real Fragonard miniature would be worth thousands. There's no way Mark would give me that as a gift. This must be of his school, a painting in his style. Mark has given it to me to remind me of the painting I bought for Andrei, the stunning portrait of the reading girl. I gaze again at the bright rosy face, so perfectly realised by the artist's brush. It's beautiful. I love it.

'Let me see,' says my mother, craning curiously. 'Oh, that's very pretty. What a lovely present! I saw something just like that in the gift shop of the V & A.'

I stare at my painting. I don't think this is from a museum gift shop, but maybe it's better if my parents think it is. They wouldn't like me to accept anything too valuable.

I think of Mark at home with Caroline this Christmas. I wonder how he is and if his fever is any better. I'll call him later, I decide, to wish him a merry Christmas and thank him for this beautiful gift.

In the event Christmas Day is busy, and I spend most of it in the kitchen helping my mother prepare the feast. After an enormous lunch that goes on for hours, we do the traditional family things of playing games and teasing each other over yet more food – cheese, biscuits, chocolates and Christmas cake. There's time for a quick walk around the village, stopping to chat to people we know, as the sun goes down.

When we turn for home, my father and brothers walk on ahead while my mother and I stroll along behind, and I tell her all about New York. I know she's dying to ask me about my ring and I'm just working up to mentioning Dominic when I see a familiar figure in a puffy jacket and a woolly hat, walking along with a girl in a big fluffy white coat.

'Isn't that Adam?' asks my mother, squinting over, trying to make him out in the failing light.

'Oh – yes, I think it is.' I stare over, not quite sure how I feel to see my old boyfriend. It's hard to believe that I once considered him the love of my life. He looks like a stranger now – pleasant enough but nothing special. Compared to Dominic, he seems pallid and ordinary.

'Adam!' calls my mother and waves as he turns to look.

'Mum! Why did you do that?' I hiss, shooting her daggers.

'No harm in letting him see what he threw away,' murmurs my mother, smiling in a satisfied way. Sure enough, Adam has recognised us and is walking over, bringing his reluctant companion with him.

'Hi, Mrs Villiers,' he says as he comes within earshot. He looks at me. 'Hi, Beth.' He gestures to his girlfriend. 'You remember Hannah.'

I look over at her and remember the last time I saw her – she was under Adam with her legs wide open as he pounded in and out of her. 'Yes. How nice to see you again.'

She scowls at me and grunts something, shoving her hands deep in her pockets to indicate her boredom with the situation. I smile at her. I owe her one for deciding to sleep with my boyfriend.

'How are things, Beth?' Adam asks cheerily. 'You're looking really well. You still with that bloke you met in London?'

My mother's eyebrows rise as she turns to look at me.

'Um – yes,' I say, flushing a little. 'Everything's fine, thanks. How are you?'

He nods enthusiastically, his plump cheeks shaking with the movement. 'Yeah, great. Hannah is expecting a little one. We're really excited.'

'Oh.' I look back at the sulky face of his girlfriend. 'That's lovely news. Congratulations. When is it due?'

'In March.' Adam smiles at me. 'I can't wait to be a dad.'

For a moment I have a flash of myself standing here, next to Adam, pregnant and looking forward to life spent bringing up a baby in the village where I grew up. I'm flooded with relief that I've found a different path. It's right for Adam and Hannah, but it's not right for me.

'That's fantastic. Good luck. See you around, Adam,' I say, and my mother and I walk on together, heading after my father and brothers in the distance.

'A man in London?' says my mother in an inquisitive voice. 'I think you've got some explaining to do.'

She gives me a sideways look. 'And if that ring is a fake, I'm Audrey Hepburn!'

I laugh. 'Don't worry, I'm going to tell you everything!'

'I should hope so. I've noticed you've got a different air about you.' She gives me a keen look that has a touch of wistfulness in it. 'You've changed, Beth.'

'You'll hear all about it. I was just waiting for the time to be right, that's all. While the boys are washing up, we can sit down by the fire and I'll spill the beans.' Just then my phone buzzes into life. I pull it out, sure that it's a Christmas greeting from Dominic. He should be up by now and sharing his Christmas morning with Georgie, or with his cousins, or wherever they've ended up. I wonder what he's doing right now, whether he's opening presents or sipping a glass of champagne over breakfast.

The message on my phone reads:

Dear Beth, I'm sorry to give you this news today of all days. but I thought you should know that Mark's been taken into hospital. He's seriously ill. Please call me. Caroline.

My father tries to persuade me not to drive, but I won't listen.

'I have to get to Mark,' I say stubbornly when he attempts to talk me out of it.

'You're upset. You shouldn't get behind the wheel, you're very likely to have an accident if you drive in a state like this.'

'Your father's right,' my mother chimes in, agitated. 'You mustn't go, Beth, I won't allow it. There's nothing you can do for Mark anyway!'

'I can be there for him,' I say, determined. 'He's done so much for me. You can't forbid me, I'm not a child.'

'I can forbid you from taking the car!' declares my mother and we scowl at each other.

Jeremy heaves a big sigh and gets to his feet. 'I can drive her,' he says in his languid way. 'I don't mind.'

'But you've been drinking,' my mother says anxiously. 'We all have!'

Jeremy makes a face. 'I had a couple of glasses of wine over lunch but that was hours ago. I was saving myself up for the pub tonight. But I guess I can take Beth back to London if she has to get there.'

I'm washed over with a wave of relief. 'Oh thank you, Jeremy! I owe you.'

'You certainly do,' he says but with a smile. 'Come on, then, we'd better get going. The roads will probably be all right as it's Christmas Day.'

I run upstairs to get my things.


The journey back to London takes just under two and half hours, which is very good going. Jeremy makes my mother's small runabout car zoom down the motorway at speeds it probably didn't know it was capable of. I'm agitated, watching the miles disappear with what seems like agonising slowness beneath our wheels. It seems to take forever to get back to the city but at last, in the darkness of the evening, we make our way along the roads that lead into the heart of London. I direct my brother through the intricacies of east London and into the centre, where we finally pull up at the Princess Charlotte hospital.

'Thank you, Jeremy,' I say, giving him a grateful look. 'I really appreciate this.'

'You're welcome,' he says. 'Do you want me to wait?'

I shake my head. 'Not unless you want to. I don't know when I'll be going back home. I want to stay with Mark while I can. I can get a taxi home later.'

'Okay, sis. I'll take a walk, stretch my legs and have a coffee and then head home.' He grins. 'I might make it back in time for the lock-in!'

Inside the hospital the mood is subdued. There aren't many staff around and there is the sense that Christmas is happening somewhere else and everybody would like to be there more than here. I check my phone but there are no messages. I texted Caroline to let her know I was coming but there's been no answer from her.

The nurse at the desk looks solemn when I tell her that I've come to see Mark. 'He's in intensive care,' she tells me. 'You can visit, but not for long.'

'What's wrong with him?' I ask, frightened. 'Is he going to be all right?'

'I'm afraid his infection has developed into pneumonia. He's fighting it as well as he can, but the fact that he is so weak already isn't helping.' She looks at me with sympathetic eyes. 'I'm sorry.'

*Sorry?* Why is she sorry already? He's still alive, isn't he? 'What are his chances?' I ask with a shaking voice.

The pause before she answers me is the worst thing of all. 'We're doing our best for him but I'm afraid that he's already so weak, he has very little left to fight with. I don't want to worry you, but things can move very quickly in these cases. Come with me, I'll take you to him.'

Caroline is sitting at Mark's bedside. He's a tiny frail figure, nothing like the dapper, energetic man I once knew, and he's lying asleep in his huge bed, hooked up to monitors and drips, an oxygen mask over his face and a pump hissing in and out as it delivers the air to his lungs. He looks very ill.

'Caroline?' I say gently as I approach. She jumps and looks at me.

'Oh, Beth.' Her eyes fill with tears and her face grows even pinker. 'I was going to tell you not to spoil your family Christmas and to stay with them, but I couldn't. I'm glad you're here.'

I go over and hug her, putting my arms around her broad back and trying to comfort her as best I can. I'm scared when she starts to sob. Caroline is so calm and capable – if she's crying, what does that mean for Mark?

'What do the doctors say?' I ask, trying to soothe her.

She sniffs and takes out a handkerchief to wipe her eyes. 'They say they're doing all they can but it's out of their hands. The next twenty-four hours are critical.

He's so weak already, you see! The cancer . . . they're not even sure now that the tumour they took out was the primary source. It might still be there somewhere, slowly killing him. Beth, I don't know how he can fight the pneumonia as well!' She sobs again into her handkerchief.

I gaze over at Mark's frail body surrounded by machines. 'He can do it,' I whisper. 'I know he can. And he's getting the best possible care. '

'I know, I know.' She looks up at me, her eyes pink and watery. 'All we can do now is hope and pray.'

I sit with Caroline at Mark's bedside for a while, and then she goes off to get some tea and go to the ladies. I'm alone with Mark, feeling helpless. All I can do is speak to him and let him know that I'm here, that I believe in him and that he will get better.

'Mark,' I say, leaning towards him. I wonder if he can hear me over the noise of the machines and the rhythmic hiss of the oxygen pump. 'Mark, it's Beth. I'm with you. I'm willing you to get through this and get better. Do you hear me, Mark? You have to get better! We all need you so much.' I want to hold his hand but I daren't touch him. His hand, thin and grey, has lines inserted into the back of it and I don't want to disturb anything. 'I love my Christmas present, thank you so much. It's beautiful. I'll treasure it so much. I'm so looking forward to us working together next year. We'll have so much fun. And we won't be dancing to Andrei's tune any more.' I gulp back a lump

291

in my throat when I remember what Anna told me. Poor, innocent, honest Mark. He's been duped by Andrei into laundering money for him. His own upright nature has led him into trouble because he trusted Andrei to be the kind of person that he, Mark, is. I try to imagine Mark in court, fighting to clear his name, but it makes me so terribly sad, I can't bear to think of it. Is this what the future holds for Mark? I wish I had the power to make it different, but it's out of my hands now. The truth about Andrei is out.

'Oh Mark,' I whisper. 'I'm so sorry. I feel like I brought all this on you. I didn't mean to. I'd do anything to make it turn out some other way. Please, please, get well again, so we can fight this together.'

There's a kind of sigh that I think for a moment comes from Mark, and then I think that it must be the pump and the hiss of oxygen. The beeps and chirrups from the machinery go on and Mark continues to lie there, silent, unconscious, fighting for his life.

I'm woken from a sleep by a nurse. I come to feeling dazed and bewildered by my surroundings. *Where am I?* Then I remember. I'm here in the hospital and I went to sleep for a while on the chairs in the waiting room while Caroline kept watch over Mark. Later she's going to sleep on the trundle bed in his room while I sit by his side.

'What is it?' I say, shaking my head to clear the sleep away.

'Please come at once,' the nurse says, her face grave,

and I'm instantly awake and on my feet, my stomach twisting with fear as I follow her along the corridor to Mark's room. We go in. There are two more nurses by Mark's bedside, attending to the machines and the drips, muttering numbers and statistics to one another. Caroline is there, leaning over Mark and clutching his hand.

'Oh, Mark,' she sobs. 'Please don't leave me. Please.'

I turn to the nurse. 'Is it . . .?'

She gives me a sad look. 'I'm afraid he's losing his battle. There's very little we can do now.'

'No!' I cry out. I won't let this happen. Mark can't die, he can't! 'Where are the doctors? Can't you operate? Give him more drugs? Do something!'

'The consultant has been here. There's nothing more we can do but make him as comfortable as we can.' She puts a hand on my arm. 'He's not in any pain. He's very peaceful.'

I glance at Mark. How can she say that? His breathing is laboured and torturous, his chest shuddering with every rise and fall. The noise is the worst thing I've ever heard as his infected lungs struggle for breath.

I go to Caroline. She turns to me, tears streaming down her face. 'We're losing him, Beth. He's leaving us.'

'No . . . Oh Caroline, no!' Grief wells up in me like a swollen stream bursting its banks, unstoppable, flowing through me. Tears pour from my eyes as a nurse instructs another to increase the morphine.

We hug each other, sobbing, and then, quite suddenly, we both become calmer. We are still weeping but the hysteria that was threatening to overwhelm us leaves us and the room becomes full of strange serenity. We both look down at Mark and as I stare at him, it seems as though his face changes even though he's still wearing the oxygen mask. His forehead seems to smooth, his face relaxes and the strain seems to leave it.

'Miss Palliser.' A nurse is at Caroline's side, a gentle hand on her arm. 'There's nothing more we can do. Shall we stop the oxygen pump?'

Caroline bites her lip. She can't speak but she nods. The machine is switched off and there is a sense of relief as the rhythmic hiss comes to a stop. The room is quiet as the nurse lifts off Mark's mask, except for the slow rattling breath that he draws in, now unaided.

It's so wonderful to see his face again, without the mask on it. It's still thin and frail but he looks untroubled now, as though he's no longer fighting but preparing to sleep. He looks younger again, more like the old Mark, my smiling, charming friend.

He lets out a slow gravelly breath. It's a long minute before he takes another that is exhaled even more slowly. We wait, Caroline's hand tight over mine, for him to take a breath and at last he does – a short soft breath that finally leaves him on a long gentle sigh.

There is no more. I know that with that last breath, Mark is released from his struggle. He's gone. I hear a low sob from Caroline and I bow my head.

*Goodbye, dear Mark. Goodbye.*

# CHAPTER EIGHTEEN

The flat is cold and dark when I arrive there in the early hours of the morning. My phone is dead. It's long since run out of power and I haven't charged it.

I'm curiously calm as I sit down on the sofa and plug my phone in. So it's over. There will be a million things to think about soon, but before then I can only think over and over of my friend and the fact that he's gone.

My phone flickers into life and starts charging up. After a while, messages and missed call notifications start arriving too. My mother has called several times, and I've missed a call from Laura as well. But there are several missed calls from Dominic and a series of messages, first wishing me a happy Christmas and then growing in agitation as I don't reply.

Where are you, Beth? I'm seriously worried. Call me or I'll be on the first plane out of here and coming to find you.

I check my watch. That was sent two hours ago. I quickly send a reply:

I'm so sorry. I've been in the hospital with Mark. He's dead. I need you so much. Call me when you can. X x x

Then I huddle down on the sofa with a blanket over me, even though my bed is only down the hall. Somehow this seems like the right thing to do. I cry quietly, thinking of my friend, and at last I fall into an exhausted sleep, my phone in my hand so that when Dominic calls me, I'll be able to answer right away.

I wake suddenly to the sound of knocking on the door. I'm confused again – why am I on the sofa in my clothes in the daytime? I look at my watch. It's almost midday. What time did I go to sleep?

The pounding on the door sounds again, and I get up to answer it. I pull it open, blinking, and the next moment I'm engulfed in a huge hug, lifted off my feet with its force and pulled against a strong chest.

'Beth, I'm so sorry. Oh Christ, I'm sorry.'

Dominic's voice is in my ear, his arms are around me, his body is giving me the comfort I've craved so much over the last terrible hours. We stand for a long time, locked in our embrace, unable to say anything else to one another. I want to weep but I'm all cried out. It occurs to me that I must look a sight with swollen eyes and mussed-up hair but I know Dominic doesn't care and neither do I. I need him so much at this moment and it's a relief to lead him through to the sitting room and sit down with him, still pressed tight to him, his strong arm around me.

'How did you get here?' I ask, wonderingly. 'You were in New York!'

'When you didn't answer I decided to get on a plane.'

'On Christmas Day? How did you get a flight?'

He shrugs. 'I chartered a plane. You can do anything if you really need to. And I had to find you and I'm glad I did.' He holds my hands tightly. 'Poor Mark. Can you tell me about it?'

I start to tell him the whole story and even though I thought I was cried out, I can't help weeping as I describe those last hours in the hospital and how Mark took his final breath as I watched.

'I saw his spirit go,' I say, wiping my eyes with a tissue. 'I just knew that he'd gone and that what was left behind wasn't Mark.'

'Hush,' murmurs Dominic, his lips pressed against my hair. 'He's at peace now. Nothing can hurt him.'

'I suppose that's true,' I say wretchedly. I lift my eyes to Dominic's brown ones with their look of tender sympathy. 'Andrei can't do anything to him now.'

Dominic shakes his head. 'No. I suppose Mark can still be investigated, but he'll never know what Andrei was prepared to do to him, and how he was used.'

'That's the only good thing to come out of all of this.' I sigh.

'And what will happen to you now?'

'Me?'

'Your job with Mark.'

I blink. 'Oh my goodness, I don't know. I haven't

thought . . . It seems too soon. I have no idea what arrangements Mark will have made.'

Dominic hugs me again. 'Don't worry about that now. We'll find out in due course.'

I inhale the delicious scent of his body as my nose presses against the softness of his jumper. 'Did you really leave your Christmas just for me?'

'Of course. Although no one was surprised, to be honest. I have a reputation for hot-headedness. I was sorry to leave Georgie but I didn't much mind leaving Aunt Florence and the deadly dull cousins.' He puts his hand under my chin and tilts my head up. 'Listen, why don't you come back with me? I promised Georgie I'd go with her to the New Year ball at some fancy house. Let's go there together.'

I draw in a startled breath. New Year in New York with Dominic? It sounds amazing. 'But,' I say, 'what about my family? I'm supposed to be at home with them. And what about Caroline? I don't want to leave her.'

'There's nothing you can do at the moment,' Dominic says. 'Caroline will need you in a few days, when you've both recovered from the shock and you have to start sorting out the business. But nothing will happen now till after the new year, I promise. And as for your family – let's go and see them now. I'll come with you. I want to meet your parents anyway and now seems like a good time. I can ask for their permission to whisk you away to New York.'

I think about this for a second. It feels wrong to

consider enjoying myself with everything that's happened. 'I don't know . . . it feels disloyal to Mark.'

'Mark always told you to grasp opportunities and enjoy yourself. He wouldn't want you to mope. He'd be telling you that life is short and to seize it while you can.' Dominic gives me a sweet smile and I feel sure he's right.

'Okay,' I say, smiling back. 'Let's do it.'

My mother's face when we arrive in a luxurious black Range Rover is something to behold. I'm not sure where Dominic keeps these cars but he seems to have access to whatever he needs wherever we are in the world, and the powerful vehicle makes easy work of the journey to Norfolk.

'Beth, what on earth . . .?' says Mum, coming out of the house, wiping her hands on a tea towel. My brothers are out and admiring the car almost before we've pulled to a stop, while my father eyes Dominic suspiciously. 'I thought you were in London!'

'I've come back.' I smile at her. 'I want you to meet Dominic. He's my . . . boyfriend.'

It seems like a rather lame word to describe all Dominic is to me and what he's meant, but I can't think of any other.

Dominic steps forward, a smile on his face and at his most charming. 'Hello, Mrs Villiers, it's a pleasure to meet you. Beth's told me so much about her family, I feel like I know you.'

'Mmm,' says my mother, slightly mollified. 'She's told me practically nothing about *you*. But I'm delighted to meet you. Please come in.'

As we go in, she puts her arm around me and gives me a half hug. 'I was so sorry to hear about Mark, darling. We got your message. How very sad.'

'Thanks, Mum,' I whisper.

'But ... I'm very happy to meet Dominic.' She glances over her shoulder to where Dominic is following as he chats to Dad. 'I take it he's the one who gave you that ring, and that rather special glow you've got about you?'

I nod.

'I thought as much. He's very welcome.' She drops her voice down to a whisper. 'And *very* dishy!'

'Mum!'

'Well, he is. I'm just saying. Now let's get tea and you can tell me how long you're staying.'


It's so weird to see Dominic in my family home, like seeing a film star in the local supermarket or a famous landmark at the end of the road. It's incongruous and yet I can't help thinking, well, why not? Dominic seems to be enjoying himself and praises everything from the tea and my mother's very good Christmas cake to the shed my father has in the garden, of which he's given a guided tour.

Later, before he's shown very firmly to the guest room, we have a moment together and I manage to thank him for charming my family so comprehensively. 'It's obvious they really like you!'

'I really like them,' he says. 'And you have a lovely home – a proper home. You're very lucky.' He looks a little wistful. 'Even while my parents were alive, we never had a home like this. Always diplomatic residences behind gates and barbed wire, peopled with servants and full of strangers. I always wanted something cosy and loving like this.'

I hug him, wishing I could give him everything he wants and needs. Then I remember what's hanging over us. 'So – did you fix up a meeting with Andrei in New York?'

He nods. 'It's the reason I need to get back. We'll leave tomorrow if that's all right.'

'Of course. I just want to be with you.'

'And I want to be with you. When all this is over, we can start our lives properly, okay?' He reaches down and touches the ring around my finger. 'Remember our promise?'

I nod and look into his gentle brown eyes. 'I remember.'


Everything seems to run like clockwork the next day, even though I never see Dominic doing much more than tap an email or two into his phone. We leave home in the morning and arrive at the airport where a driver is waiting to take the Range Rover away. We're quickly ushered through check in and into the first-class lounge and not long after that, we're aboard a flight back to the States.

'How do you do it?' I ask, amused.

'I have my ways,' he says with a smile, and we settle down for the journey back. I feel I can relax a little and come to terms with some of what's happened now that I've heard from Caroline. She tells me that she'll be arranging Mark's funeral for the first week of January and that when I get back to the office on the 2nd we can start working out what will happen next. She says nothing about her intentions, so I have no idea whether or not Mark's business will be continuing. That means I might be out of a job. In fact, I think that's the most likely scenario. And if Andrei's money-laundering comes to light and Mark's estate is investigated, that might not be such a bad thing.

We rest, watch films and chat all the way back to America, and Dominic tells me what he has planned.

'We'll stay at my rented apartment,' he says, 'although finding a more suitable place is going to be something I want to get on with as soon as I can. I've arranged to meet Andrei on the 29th and I hope that we'll be able to resolve everything that day. Obviously now that Mark is no longer with us, there isn't the same urgency, but I still need him to back off and leave me – and you – alone. Then we can relax together and go to this ball on New Year's Eve. What do you think?'

'It all sounds great,' I say stoutly. *But it depends on whether Andrei plays ball or not.* And it's hard to imagine how I can be too cheerful and merry on New Year's Eve considering that I'll be flying home to Mark's funeral straight afterwards. I try to put that out of my mind for now. Before then, I have many long and happy hours to spend with Dominic, so that's what I'll think about until real life comes back to get me.

Dominic's apartment is just as I remembered: bare and soulless. I wish we could be back at Georgie's home, where I felt cosy and comfortable despite the short time I spent there. But, I remind myself, this is just temporary. Maybe I can persuade Dominic to move away from the palatial glass type of apartment and towards something a little warmer and more welcoming.

'You don't like it, do you?' he asks as he puts our bags in the bedroom. It's still barely furnished, with just a bed, chest of drawers and a lamp.

I wrinkle my nose. 'Not really, no. It's kind of cold.'

He looks about. 'I know what you mean. Come on. We won't stay here. Georgie's still at my aunt's, I think. She won't mind if we use her house. Would you rather go there?'

'Oh yes,' I say happily. 'A home!'

Dominic laughs. 'A home it is. Let's get going.'

Less than thirty minutes later, we're in the welcoming warmth of Georgie's brownstone. It's so much more cheerful to see books and pictures, and to sit on a cosy sofa with plump cushions.

'Are you sure your sister won't mind?' I call to Dominic, who's taking our bags up to the guest room.

'Of course not,' he calls back. 'She's always on at me to stay more often. She'll be delighted.'

I sigh with happiness when we're together in the sitting room, sipping proper British tea from Georgie's mugs, music playing on the sound system and the fire lit.

'You know what,' Dominic says hesitantly as if unsure whether or not he should broach the subject, 'maybe this is a good time for a fresh start.'

'What do you mean?'

'Of course it's terrible that Mark has passed away. But change was in the air already, and I'm going to be in New York for months at a time. Maybe you could think about joining me here.'

I think about this for a second as I sip my tea. It's what I've longed to hear, but it can't be that simple, can it? 'If you're here for half the year, where are you going to be for the other half?'

He shrugs. 'London, mostly. Plus some other travelling. It will always be like that, it's the nature of my business.'

'Then even if I move to New York,' I say reasonably, 'I'm still going to be away from you for half the year, so what's the difference if I'm in London?'

He sighs. 'I suppose so. I just want us to be together as much as possible.'

'Well, it seems like the only way that can happen is if I give up working altogether so I can be with you all the time. I can't do that. I need an identity of my own. I'm young and I want to work, explore my interests and learn as much about art as I can. I love it. I can't give it up.'

Dominic looks at me seriously. 'I wouldn't ask you

to. But let's think about ways that we can spend as much time together as we can. Do you want that?'

I gaze at his beautiful face. 'Of course I do. You know I do.'

'Okay.' He smiles at me, his full lips curving up into a smile. 'Then let's keep thinking about our options, okay? And I'll get a decent apartment that you actually like as soon as I can. I want you to help me find a place in London too. These are going to be our homes, not just mine.'

I lean over and kiss him. 'Thank you. For everything.'

He smiles at me. 'It's just the beginning.'

That night, in the very comfortable guest suite, we make delicious, tender love. Dominic knows that I'm carrying the weight of sadness and that I have an unspoken burden of guilt over Mark's death. I don't have to say anything, he knows. He understands instinctively that tonight is not the right night for a scene. Tonight I need delicate, sweet, comforting love. When we've shuddered to our orgasms, I start to cry, and he kisses the tears away and holds me in his arms until I'm calm again and ready to face another day.

Georgie comes back from her aunt's the next day, and is full of excitement to see Dominic and me again. She greets me with a huge kiss and gives Dominic a mock stern look.

'I can almost forgive you for leaving me alone on Christmas Day with Aunt Florence now that you've brought Beth back to stay,' she says, and we have a very happy day together, venturing out for a walk around the neighbourhood and ending up at a favourite local restaurant for dinner.

I try to enjoy myself as much as I can but I'm nervous about the coming day. In bed later, in Dominic's arms, I can't sleep.

'Hey, Fidget,' Dominic says, yawning. 'What's wrong?'

'I'm scared. Tomorrow you see Andrei, don't you?'

Dominic pauses and then says quietly, 'Yes.'

'Where are you meeting him?'

'At his office downtown.'

'Will you be safe?'

'I'm sure I will. He won't try anything in his own premises. And he'll know that plenty of people will be aware of my whereabouts. Besides, I'll be wearing a wire and my driver will be nearby. He's ex-SAS and quite tidy in a tricky situation.'

I raise myself up on an elbow and look at him anxiously. 'You think there might be a fight?'

'I'm sure there won't, but I intend to be prepared.' He grins at me, his white teeth gleaming in the half-light, and the brown surface of his skin glimmering where the moonlight falls on it. 'That's why I was such a good Boy Scout.'

I want to laugh about it all but I can't. I know how dangerous Andrei Dubrovski is, and I don't believe for a second that he'll listen to what Dominic has to say and simply become all docile and go off like a little lamb, content to leave us alone.

'Beth. Don't worry. Andrei is a businessman, first and foremost. He'll want to act in in his own best interests and when he sees that cooperation is his only way out, that's what he'll do. I know him very well, believe me.' He yawns again. 'Now, I've got to get some sleep.'

I lie back down, staring into the darkness. Dominic might think he knows Andrei but he hasn't witnessed the way that Andrei spoke to me. I remember the passion in his eyes when he spoke about the life he thought we could have together. I know that it cost a proud man like Andrei a very great deal to make the offer to me, the one to share his life and build a family with him. To have it rejected must have been unbearable. Surely he must hate Dominic even more now, knowing that not only has his one-time employee become his rival in business, but also that he's won the battle for my heart.

*I just wish he'd never decided that for some reason I was the one! Couldn't he tell I wasn't interested?*

But I know that it was precisely because I wasn't interested in his wealth or influence that Andrei was drawn to me. The fact that I loved Dominic made me even more irresistible.

*The damned competitive instinct.*

More than ever, I want tomorrow to be over and for Dominic to be safely back with me. I hate the idea of his walking into Andrei's office, into Andrei's power and control.

*Who knows what the hell Andrei might have planned?*

# CHAPTER NINETEEN

Dominic goes off not long after breakfast. He looks heartbreakingly handsome in his tailored Kilgour suit and a camel coat. Not only does he radiate strength and determination, he also looks in a happy mood.

'I've waited a long time for this,' he says, finishing his coffee as Georgie and I eat our breakfast at the kitchen table.

'For God's sake, be careful, Dom,' warns Georgie. She butters a piece of toast carefully. 'Dubrovski's a slippery customer. Don't take it for granted that you'll be able to best him.'

'Hey, I'll be fine. Candy from a baby!' he says, and winks to show he's joking as he drops a kiss on his sister's cheek. 'I'll see you later,' he murmurs to me as he kisses me goodbye. 'Go out shopping, take your mind off it. I'll keep in touch and be back as soon as I can.'

Once he's gone, driven away in one of those sleek long motors, Georgie and I swap worried glances but we make an unspoken decision not to dwell on it. While we wait for the time to pass, she shows me through old photo albums and tells me about her and Dominic's childhoods. It's lovely listening to tales of the past and imagining Dominic as a small boy but I find it hard to concentrate.

After a while I get up, unable to keep still. 'I'm sorry, Georgie, I'm going to have to go out for a walk. Is that all right?'

'Of course. Will you be okay? Do you want me to come with you?'

I shake my head. 'No. Really. I think I need to be on my own for a bit. I'll be back before too long.'

'Okay. I'll get some lunch ready for us. And maybe this afternoon we can go out and look for something for you to wear to the New Year ball.'

*Maybe. But if we haven't heard from Dominic by then, there's no way I'm going to be able to think about shopping.*

I put on a jacket and go out into the cold wintery day outside. The sky is low and a marbled grey colour, with little in the way of sunshine. It seems to reflect my own mood and I walk along the blocks of brownstone houses, staring at my feet and my mind miles away. I can't help wondering what's happening this very minute between Dominic and Andrei. Are they facing each other down? Yelling? Grappling? Or are they giving one another frosty stares across a desk, keeping their emotions in check as they play the ice-cool businessmen?

*This waiting is killing me!*

For the hundredth time I take out my phone but there's nothing there. I wish I knew how long I was going to have to wait. Then at least I could think about something else.

I walk for a long time and I suddenly realise that I've made my way almost to Central Park. I decide to go in and find a place where I can have a coffee. I'll message Georgie too, and tell her I won't be back for a while.

I find a café in a small clearing and sit down at one of the outside tables. There aren't many people about; perhaps it's too cold for families or perhaps they've gone away for Christmas like so many Londoners do. A waitress comes up and I order a latte. It arrives a few minutes later in a takeaway paper cup, which I wrap my fingers around, grateful for the warmth. When they've defrosted a little, I'll text Georgie where I am and explain I'll be a little late for lunch.

'Do you mind if I join you?' The voice is harsh, gravelly and unmistakable. I look up and find myself staring into the pale blue eyes of Andrei Dubrovski.

I gasp and half stand up in surprise. 'What?! What are you doing here?'

He sits down on an iron chair, his coat incongruously smart against the worn surface of the seat. 'I want to talk to you.'

I'm astonished, breathless. I can hardly believe my eyes. 'But you're supposed to be with Dominic! Where is he?' I look wildly about, as though I'm going to see Dominic struggling in the bushes, kept a prisoner by Andrei's henchmen.

'Don't worry about him,' Andrei says calmly. 'He's at my office as we arranged.'

'But he's been there hours. Aren't you having your meeting?'

'My lawyers are keeping him very busy while I have this little rendezvous with you. I know that Dominic has something to tell me and I have an instinct what that might be. But I want to hear it from you first. I want to hear it from your mouth.'

I gape at him as I sink back into my seat, not knowing what to say. This isn't something I'm ready for. How do I tell a man like Andrei that I know he's busted, a criminal whose activities are about to be exposed?

Andrei is looking at me, his eyes scanning my face, and I realise that there's something like pity in their chilly depths. 'I heard about Mark,' he says. 'I'm very sorry.'

'Really?' I spit back. 'Because I got your charming Christmas card. The one with the press release explaining how you were going to hang Mark out to dry and make sure he was completely ruined in the process. Are you sorry he's dead, or are you just sorry that you're not going to be able to make him suffer the way you'd hoped?'

His face goes flinty. 'Of course I'm sorry. I was fond of Mark. Do you think I'm pleased that he's dead? Do you think I'm a monster?'

'You know what? I really don't know! I don't want to think that, but you've done your best to show me that you're cold and ruthless so I'm beginning to believe that's what you are!'

'I know what I want and I try to get it. I don't wish people to be hurt in the process but it sometimes happens,' he snaps back.

'Maybe it would happen less if you didn't involve innocent people in your money laundering!' I retort.

There's an awful pause while this hangs in the air between us. Andrei's face is rock hard. Then he speaks.

'So that is what Dominic intends to accuse me of.'

'He knows. I know. You used Mark as a conduit. You took advantage of his trusting nature and then you were prepared to destroy him.' I shake my head in disbelief. 'I think it's time you dropped your man of compassion act. You're a nothing but a selfish crook.'

Andrei leans back in the small iron chair and folds his gloved hands across his stomach. 'You believe this then.'

'Of course. We have a pretty unassailable witness and I'm sure the proof will all be there in Mark's files.'

'And the price, I assume, for silence on this matter is that you and Stone are left in peace.'

I nod. 'It was going to be for Mark too – but it's too late for him now.'

'I have ways of ensuring your silence. And Dominic's. And Anna's – I assume she is the witness you spoke of.'

'Yes, you could dispose of us, I assume that's what you mean. But we've all made witnessed statements to be passed to the police in the event of our deaths.' This is a bluff but I hope it sounds plausible.

He stares at me again, his expression unreadable. Then he says at last in tones of finality, 'I see.' He leans towards me, his eyes suddenly urgent. 'It's not too late, Beth. You can still leave him and come away with me. I promise you a life you will never have with Stone.'

'I know.' I smile coolly at him. 'That's what I'm afraid of.'

We hold one another's gaze for a long time and then Andrei sighs.

'I understand everything now. Dominic has it in his power to destroy me and I'm sure he's enjoying it. I do not need him to tell me this to my face and it will give me just a little pleasure to deny him that. You may tell him that the field is clear. I will not stand in his way, in business or in personal matters. You've made your choice of your own free will and I will respect it. I will leave it up to you what you do with the power in your hands.' He gets up. 'I wish it could have been different.'

I can't help feeling a strange tenderness for this man, despite everything. We have been through a lot together. 'Perhaps it could have been, once,' I say. 'But in the end, you made sure that it could never be, as soon as you tried to force me to do what you wanted.'

He gives a light laugh. 'The tyrant's fatal flaw. I wish you well, Beth. Will you wish me the same?'

'Of course. I wish you everything you truly want in life. I wish you love.'

He looks very sad suddenly, his blue eyes a well of grief. 'And you have already found it. You're lucky. I've spent over half a lifetime looking for it and never come near it yet.'

313

I stand up too and hold out my hand. 'Goodbye, Andrei. Good luck.'

He looks at my outstretched hand for a moment and then takes it. He smiles. 'Good luck to you. And goodbye, Beth. I don't know if we will meet again. I suspect not.'

I say nothing more. We have said all we need to. I watch as he turns his back on me and strides away across the park. I wonder what he intends to do now. Then I realise that it's not my problem any more. My heart is suddenly light. I pull out my phone. Still nothing from Dominic. No doubt the lawyers are enjoying wasting his time, making him prepare for a meeting that will never happen.

Call me as soon as you are out.

I send the message off and sit back in my chair, waiting for a reply as I gaze out over the wintery park.

'So Andrei was intending to see you all the time?'

Dominic is striding about Georgie's sitting room, his face both confused and furious. 'I spent hours in his fucking boardroom being made to read papers and sign affidavits! And all the time, he wasn't even in the goddamned building!'

Georgie gives me a sideways look, shrugs her shoulders and turns her eyes to heaven. I smile back. I like Georgie a lot.

Dominic stops pacing and turns to face me. 'How the hell did he know where you are?'

'He seems to be rather good at tracking me down,' I say simply. 'But having someone watching your sister's house is probably not beyond him.'

Dominic shakes his head and then laughs. 'I've got to hand it to him. He knows how to wrong-foot me. I was so looking forward to rubbing his nose in it. I should have guessed that he wouldn't let that happen.'

He makes me go through every part of my interview with Andrei again and together we analyse it.

'Well, at least he understands exactly what we have on him,' says Dominic. 'And good thinking about that signed witnessed statement. We should all do that, just to be on the safe side, though I don't really believe we have anything to fear from Andrei now. He knows there's too much evidence stacked up against him. If he gets taken down he'll risk his criminal networks, and those are people he really won't want to piss off, believe me.'

'Then we're free?' I ask, hardly able to believe it.

'Free.' Dominic smiles at me.

'Are we duty-bound to tell the police?' I ask, frowning. 'I mean, he's laundering money. He's helping gangs and supporting their activities. Aren't we guilty as well if we let him carry on?'

Georgie says, 'Beth's right, Dom. You don't really have a choice about this. Andrei's been laundering money all over the place.'

Dominic fixes me with a serious look. 'Of course that's the right thing to do. But it means Mark's name will certainly be dragged through the mud. And Anna and I – and even you – will have to stand up in court and bear witness against Andrei and his underworld friends. That could be dangerous. You need to think hard about that.'

'I will,' I say slowly. 'I will think about it. I'll think about what Mark would have wanted and what I think is best.'

'Okay,' Dominic says. He smiles at me. 'But let's take our time before we make any heavy decisions. The day after tomorrow is New Year's Eve. We've got a party to go to. It's time to see out the old year and welcome the new.'

I smile back. This year has been the most incredible of my life. And I have a feeling that the year to come will be even more amazing.


The scene before me is like something in a fairy story. In a huge marbled ballroom beneath a many-tiered chandelier, a mass of people is whirling, skirts flying, polished shoes glinting, as they dance to the orchestra that plays from the stage. It's a beautiful spectacle and I'm entranced by it as I stand watching from the balcony. I'm also breathless, as a few moments ago it was me down there on the dance floor, my emerald silk dress floating round me as Dominic spun me around in his arms, humming along to the waltz as we went.

He comes up and hands me a glass of champagne. 'Here you are,' he says with a smile. 'Your refreshment. Are you having a good time?'

'Amazing,' I say. 'It's so lovely to look at.'

'The old-fashioned New Year's Eve ball. You know what, it's nearly midnight. Come with me.' He leads me away from the balcony and opens a door to small terrace with a view over the city. We step out into the night air. 'I thought you'd like one last look at the city before we go home tomorrow.'

'It's been incredible,' I sigh. I can't help feeling wistful. Next week is Mark's funeral. He won't see this new year arriving, or anything else. No matter how upsetting it would be to see his business brought down, I'm sure he'd rather have been alive.

Dominic takes off his tailcoat and slips it over my shoulders. He places a kiss on my lips. 'I want you to live with me, Beth. I want us to be together all the time. When we get home, I want us to find a place we both love where we can build a life together.'

I thrill to everything he's saying. 'That's what I want too,' I say gently. 'But not at the expense of my career and my work.'

'I understand that,' he says. 'It might mean that we're apart some of the time – but we'll always know that we share a home, that we're joined in our hearts.'

I nod. 'Yes.' I put my arms around him and pull him tight. 'I'm so happy. It's been a bumpy ride but we've made it.'

Dominic puts his arms around me and we stand like that together for a while, enjoying our closeness. Then he says, 'Hey, they're getting ready for the countdown inside. We'd better go back in. We don't want to miss the New Year.'

We go back through the door into the ballroom. Below us the orchestra has stopped playing and the crowd are watching a clock on the wall as the hands inch round to midnight. As it reaches its last few seconds, everyone begins to chant: 'Five, four, three, two . . .'

As they yell, 'One!' and cheer, Dominic kisses me. When he pulls away, his eyes are shining. 'Happy New Year, Beth.'

'Happy New Year!'

The orchestra bursts into 'Auld Lang Syne' but we don't sing along. We're too engrossed in our own private world, lost in the pleasure of our kiss.

# CHAPTER TWENTY

Mark's funeral is very well attended. In the Chelsea church, the pews are full and the mourners are a particularly elegant crowd, the men very well turned out in dark suits and waistcoats, and the women in black, their jackets given a touch of richness with diamond brooches and pearl necklaces. Some are wearing hats, others a small spray of black feathers or soft wool berets in deference to the cold weather.

Caroline greets me as I come in. She looks awful, not at all like her usual pink-faced self, but she is composed and happy to see me. She directs me to one of the sidesmen for a services sheet and I realise that the tall man in the gold-rimmed spectacles is James.

'Hello, dear girl,' he says quietly as I come up. 'I was hoping to see you today. How are you?'

'All right,' I say, managing a smile. The sight of Mark's polished coffin at the top of the aisle surrounded by flowers is like a stab to my innards. I'm feeling shaky and grief-stricken all over again.

'Bear up, old thing,' he say sympathetically and puts a steadying hand on my arm. 'It's a bad business. Poor Mark. He went much more quickly than any of us expected.'

'Do you think it was bound to happen?' I ask, staring up at him beseechingly.

'From what I understand, the cancer was much further advanced than they suspected at first. He would have had a miserable time undergoing radiotherapy and goodness knows what else, and the result would have been much the same. Perhaps it was kinder to go quickly without enduring all of that.'

'But wouldn't he have wanted more time?'

James looks grave. 'You know Mark. He loved elegance and beauty. He wouldn't have liked what he was reduced to at all. Not one bit.'

'Perhaps you're right.'

James pats my arm comfortingly and then hands me an order of service. 'Here you are. Sit anywhere you like. Is Dominic with you?'

I nod. 'He's taking a call outside. He'll be here in a minute.'

'He never stops. I'll come and find you afterwards at the wake. I want to talk to you when I've got all this out of the way.'

'Of course.' I make my way to an empty pew and take my place. I hope I look as elegant as Mark would have wanted. I'm wearing a black suit, high heels and a small cloche hat with a diamond arrow pinned on it. I think Mark would have liked the arrow in particular. While I'm waiting for Dominic, I read over the order of service. It's a lovely, old-fashioned service and I know all the hymns.

The choir is about to come in when Dominic slips into the pew beside me. 'Sorry,' he murmurs. 'That was Tom. I had to take it. Amazingly enough, several obstacles in the way of my purchase of the Siberian iron ore mine have disappeared.' He shoots me an amused look. 'Funny that.'

'Shhh,' I say, frowning. Then the organ strikes up and the choir enters as the congregation rises to its feet and begins to sing.

It's a beautiful service. When the choir sings 'The Lord's My Shepherd' I feel the hot sting of tears in my eyes, but mostly it's a celebration of Mark's life and work. His friends stand up to give a joint address that is funny and poignant at the same time. Caroline gives a short speech about Mark's life and how much she is going to miss him. There are prayers and then another hymn. After the blessing and dismissal, we watch the coffin being taken back down the aisle to the hearse that's waiting outside. The family goes with it to the crematorium and the rest of us walk a short distance to the wake, which is held in a small but beautiful and polished pub, as only pubs in Chelsea can be.

'That was a very moving service,' Dominic says as we follow the rest of the congregation along the road, our black clothes and hats drawing looks from passers-by. 'Dear old Mark. I'm glad he had a send-off like that.'

'It's a testament to a person that so many people wanted to be there and say such nice things,' I reply. 'I was lucky to know Mark.'

'He was a big fan of yours,' says Dominic. 'And with good cause.'

At the pub, Bloody Marys and Bull Shots are being offered to the guests along with wine or soft drinks. I take a Bloody Mary and sip at its spicy warmth as I look around for James. I spot him over by the fireplace chatting to Erland, and when he sees me, he beckons me over. I leave Dominic talking to a fellow guest and make my way across the room to him.

'Well, hello there,' he says. 'I'm glad I've got you to myself at last. Erland, go and get me another drink, there's a love.'

When Erland has gone, James says, 'Has Caroline had a word with you?'

I shake my head. 'Not yet. I've been to the office since I got back but she said she didn't want anything done until after the funeral. I suppose that we'll be starting work again on Monday. Has she spoken to you?'

James nods. 'She has. Mark has appointed her and me as executors of his will and he's left instructions that we are to continue running the business as we see fit in the event of his death.'

'Oh,' I say, puzzled. 'So what does that mean?'

'Well, we've still got to thrash it out but Caroline has indicated that she wants to keep the business going, and she wants me to help do that.'

'Can you do that? On top of running the gallery?'

He fixes me with a beady gaze. 'If you help me, I can. Caroline showed me your notes of what you did in New York. It looks as though you did an excellent job of networking and finding pieces of interest. The finances are in a very healthy state too – Mark was certainly good at buying cheap and selling high. I think that between us, we can make a decent fist of keeping Mark's legacy going. And if Caroline wants to in the future, she'll have a healthy business to sell. But . . .' James looks solemn. 'There's a catch. Mark always spent a good deal of time in New York, and the American side of things was very important to him. I can't do all that, I have to be here where I can keep an eye on the gallery. Can't go jaunting off all the time. So you'll need to be prepared to spend a bit of time Stateside. Can you do that?'

I stare at him, my eyes lighting up as the implications sink in. 'I'd love to do that!'

James smiles. 'Good.'

My own smile fades a little as I remember what Dominic and I still have to decide – whether or not we are going to turn Andrei over to the police. If we do, that means my rosy future running Mark's business with James may not come to pass after all.

'Everything all right?' asks James.

'Yes, fine,' I say. Now is not the time to start going into all that with James. Erland comes back clutching two glasses of champagne and hands one to James.

'Hello, Beth,' he says in his lilting Norwegian accent. 'How are you? Wasn't the service lovely?'

'It was. Really lovely.' I smile at him. 'It's exactly what Mark would have wanted.'

Erland's eyes suddenly move towards the door. 'Wow,' he mutters. 'Who's that? I didn't notice her at the church!'

I turn to look. There is Anna, stunning in a clinging black dress and a hat with a veil that covers her face to the nose, drawing attention to her bright red lips. She's looking around for someone and when she spots Dominic, she begins to walk over to him.

'Excuse me,' I say, and leave James and Erland as I go over to intercept her. 'Hello, Anna.'

She gazes at me with a look of sardonic amusement. 'Ah, Beth. How nice to see you. If you don't mind, I need to speak to Dominic.'

'Of course. Let's find him together.'

As soon as Dominic sees us approaching, he moves away from the man he's talking to and leads us into a small room off the main bar.

'Hello, Anna,' he says politely. 'You've decided to join us.'

'Yes. I wanted to raise a glass to Mark, a man who was always most civil to me. But I also wanted to let you know something rather important. According to my contacts, Andrei is in the process of winding up his presence both here and in America.'

'What?' Dominic stares at her, astonished.

Anna nods her head, her dark veil bobbing and her eyes glittering underneath it. 'That's right. For some reason, he appears to be retrenching, and removing himself from this country, and from the States.'

'I see,' mutters Dominic. He shoots me a look. 'Clever of him. He's getting out of the way so that even if we go to the police, there's nothing they can do about it.'

'You mean, he's leaving?'

'Exactly. He'll have people cleaning up after him right now.' Dominic frowns. 'Thanks for letting us know, Anna. This changes quite a few things. If you'll excuse me, ladies, I've just got to go outside and make a call.'

He strides out, reaching for his phone and leaving Anna and me together. She watches him go and then turns to me, a smile playing around her red lips.

'It looks as though you two are very happy together,' she says.

'Yes, we are – thank you,' I say, sounding stiff even though I don't want to.

'Good, good. And I'm very happy with Giovanni. In fact, we please each other so much, he's going to leave the monastery, just for me. Isn't that nice? So you're quite safe from me now. I've lost interest in Dominic – and to be honest, he was beginning to bore me anyway.' She leans closer to me, her eyes sparkling. 'By the way, did you ever find out what happened in the caves, Beth?'

'I found out you drugged me,' I retort, angered by the memory despite my relief that she has decided to give up pursuing Dominic. 'And I also found out that I didn't make love to Andrei, so my conscience is clear.'

'Then if it wasn't Andrei,' she says, her low voice playful and rather dangerous, 'who was it?'

'It was Dominic, of course,' I say coolly.

'Was it?' She laughs.

'Of course it was.' I feel a stab of cold fear. Is she trying to imply that it was another man altogether? She once tried to make me believe that it was she herself who had made love to me but that was impossible.

'You told Dominic you made love to him in the caves.' She laughs again.

'What's so funny?' I demand.

'Then he must really love you. Because, you see, he knows that he didn't make love to you.'

'He didn't?' Clammy shock dampens my palms.

She shakes her head, giving me a pitying look from behind her veil. 'No. But he thinks you made love to someone. And he's never said a word about it. So you see . . . he must really love you.'

My head is in a whirl as I try to process this. 'Then . . . who?' I cry. Anna turns to go and I stop her with a hand on her arm. 'Please, Anna – who? You've got to tell me.'

She stares at me for a moment and then she says in a cold voice: 'It was no one. You didn't make love to anyone.'

I can't believe it. I remember that night, those sensations, the cold wall, the hot skin against mine, the blissful feeling of being taken hard by the man whose face I couldn't see . . .

'No one?' I whisper.

She tilts her head close to mine and says quietly, 'I gave you a very powerful sexual stimulant. I've used it successfully on many people and on those with a particularly lubricious character, it can have a surprising effect. It is possible to hallucinate sexual encounters and to experience them almost as if they were real. Like a dream in which you come, but a thousand times more vivid. I'm sure you have those, don't you, Beth? I know you do.' She drops her voice to a whisper. 'I saw you.'

She gives me a brilliant smile and turns on her heel, walking out with a swing of her hips and leaving me gaping after her.

Dominic finds me there a few minutes later when he returns.

'Are you all right? Where's Anna?' He looks at me more closely. 'You look like you've been hit over the head. Are you okay?'

'Yes . . . yes . . . I'm fine.' I'm still slotting everything in place and working it out. I realise suddenly that Dominic has never accused me of anything or demanded to know the truth about what happened in the catacombs. He must have realised that in my drugged state I couldn't be held accountable for my actions. He might believe I fucked someone in the caves thinking it was him, and he's decided to let it go. Anna is right. He must love me.

I hug him close, treasuring him more than ever.

'Hey,' he says, 'are you sure you're all right?'

I nod. One day I'll tell him the truth. Not now – but one day soon.

'I've been talking to my lawyer in the States,' Dominic says. 'He doesn't think there's much point in us pursuing Dubrovski right now. As long as he's clearing up his operation and getting out, we'll be making trouble for ourselves without a hope of getting him. So his advice is to let sleeping dogs lie.'

'So Andrei gets away with it,' I say, suddenly furious.

'Not really. He's lost more than he gained. And . . .' Dominic brushes his lips against mine. '. . . He doesn't get the thing he wanted most of all. You.'

I relax into his arms and let him hold me for a moment.

Then I look him straight in the eye. 'You're sure you want me, aren't you, Dominic? After everything?'

He picks up my hand and we both look at the hoop of diamonds sparkling on my finger. 'There's my promise,' he says softly. 'You're still wearing it. As long as it's on your finger, it holds good. Of course I want you. I love you. I adore you.' He kisses me and I revel in the sweetness and passion in his kiss.

'And Rosa?' I say wickedly, pressing my lips to his ear.

'I'll always love Rosa too,' he murmurs throatily. 'She's so sweet and always so naughty! I don't know if she'll ever learn her lesson . . . but most of all, I love Beth. My gorgeous, clever, funny, talented, sexy Beth.'

I laugh. 'I love you too.' Then, with a gentle kiss to his jawline, I whisper, 'Sir . . .'

Our eyes meet and we smile knowingly, the smile of our shared secrets and our shared passions. I shiver lightly at the thought of our next rendezvous and the lessons I might be compelled to learn.

A speech is starting in the other room. They are going to toast Mark in his favourite champagne. Dominic takes my hand and we go to re-join the others.

# EPILOGUE

The parcel arrives for me care of Mark Palliser.

'As though whoever it is doesn't know he's dead,' remarks James as he props it up in the office. 'You'd think they'd know. His obituaries were in all the papers, after all. And you sent out the official notification, didn't you?'

I nod. We had cards printed at the Queen's stationers and sent out to all Mark's clients. The condolence cards sent back are on every surface.

'It's addressed to me, anyway,' I say. 'So perhaps it's just a mistake.'

'Shall we open it?' James gets some scissors off the desk and starts to slice carefully away at the wrapping. Underneath there is bubble wrap and below that is a wooden case sealed shut with metal ties. It takes all of James's strength to cut through them so that we can open it.

At last James lifts the wooden top and there is one final layer of softest cotton. He lifts that, and I gasp.

It is the painting of the girl reading that I bought for Andrei's bathroom in Albany. It is a stunning masterpiece by Fragonard himself, a portrait so lifelike and moving that I've always imagined the girl is just about to turn the page of her book.

James whistles and says, 'Oh my Lordy. Look at this. Is this what I think it is?'

I nod, my eyes wide. 'The Fragonard. But James – why would Andrei send this to me?'

James laughs. 'Who knows? But I'll tell you something, it's the best present you're ever going to get!'

I stare at the picture. I have no idea why Andrei would give me this precious painting unless it was somehow to protect it. But why this one, among all his treasures? Perhaps it's because it is the only one I chose for him myself. I wonder if he knows that all his art will be taken from him, when justice inevitably catches up with him, whenever that day may be.

I remember Mark's present to me of the tiny miniature. Suddenly it occurs to me that that tiny painting is a real Fragonard too. For some reason, Mark gave me a real painting, worth thousands. A strange thought floats into my mind. Did Mark suspect that Andrei was using him all along? Was he too protecting one tiny precious work of art by giving it to me?

'Beth? Are you all right?'

I look up. 'Yes. I'm fine. I'm not sure what to do with this. It should be in a museum really.'

'Maybe.' James puts his head on one side and looks at it. 'But I know where it would look beautiful. What about that adorable Chelsea house you and Dominic are going to buy? Won't it look amazing in the drawing room?'

I think about the sweet little cottage we've found and how pretty the painting will look above our fireplace. Every time I imagine our home, I feel a surge of warmth and excitement.

'Or how about your New York pad?' James says wickedly. 'Or haven't you chosen that yet?'

'Not yet,' I say with a laugh. 'We're going to stay with Georgie for the time being, even if it doesn't quite fit with Dominic's idea of himself as a Park Avenue kind of guy.'

'Take her home with you,' James urges. 'She's yours. I know you love her.'

I look at the painting's lavender and yellow tones, the girl's delicate skin, the kink in her little finger where she holds her book.

'Why resist?' smiles James. 'What would Mark say?'

I smile back. 'All right, I will. She can hang in the cottage and remind me of an incredible time in my life.'

'Good girl. You deserve her. Now, let's put her away for now, and get on with the rest of our work. I want to go through your New York itinerary.'

I watch as James puts the cotton covering back over the portrait. The girl vanishes beneath the soft white sheet. We can store her in the box room where Mark kept his paintings on their way to be packed or unpacked. Like the ring that sparkles on my finger, something tells me that she is another kind of promise.

But, try as I might, I can't think of what.

# ACKNOWLEDGEMENTS

Once again, I owe a great deal to my editor, Harriet, and copyeditor, Justine – thank you both for your hard work. I'm thankful to everyone at Hodder, particularly the amazing production department, and to Lucy for her wonderful efforts in publicity.

Thank you to Lizzy and Harriet, my agent and her splendid assistant, for everything they do on my behalf.

Thank you to my friends and family for all their support, and to my husband for not minding when I vanish for long stretches into another world. I couldn't do it without you.

Most of all, thank you to the wonderful readers of these books who've told me how much they've enjoyed reading about Beth and Dominic. I feel so happy to have shared them with you and to have received such encouraging messages on Twitter. Thank you all so much!

If you haven't read the first two books in
Sadie Matthews' thrilling and provocative
*After Dark* series, then indulge yourself with
a teaser extract from book one,

# *fire*
# *after*
# *dark*

Find out how it all began . . .

# THE FIRST WEEK

# CHAPTER ONE

The city takes my breath away as it stretches beyond the taxi windows, rolling past like giant scenery being unfurled by an invisible stagehand. Inside the cab, I'm cool, quiet and untouchable. Just an observer. But out there, in the hot stickiness of a July afternoon, London is moving hard and fast: traffic surges along the lanes and people throng the streets, herds of them crossing roads whenever the lights change. Bodies are everywhere, of every type, age, size and race. Millions of lives are unfolding on this one day in this one place. The scale of it all is overwhelming.

*What have I done?*

As we skirt a huge green space colonised by hundreds of sunbathers, I wonder if this is Hyde Park. My father told me that Hyde Park is bigger than Monaco. Imagine that. Monaco might be small, but even so. The thought makes me shiver and I realise I'm frightened. That's odd because I don't consider myself a cowardly person.

*Anyone would be nervous*, I tell myself firmly. But it's no surprise my confidence has been shot after everything that's happened lately. The familiar sick feeling churns in my stomach and I damp it down.

*Not today. I've got too much else to think about. Besides, I've done enough thinking and crying. That's the whole reason I'm here.*

'Nearly there, love,' says a voice suddenly, and I realise it's the taxi driver, his voice distorted by the intercom. I see him watching me in the rear-view mirror. 'I know a good short cut from here,' he says, 'no need to worry about all this traffic.'

'Thanks,' I say, though I expected nothing less from a London cabbie; after all, they're famous for their knowledge of the city's streets, which is why I decided to splurge on one instead of wrestling with the Underground system. My luggage isn't enormous but I didn't relish the idea of heaving it on and off trains and up escalators in the heat. I wonder if the driver is assessing me, trying to guess what on earth I'm doing going to such a prestigious address when I look so young and ordinary; just a girl in a flowery dress, red cardigan and flip-flops, with sunglasses perched in hair that's tied in a messy ponytail, strands escaping everywhere.

'First time in London, is it?' he asks, smiling at me via the mirror.

'Yes, that's right,' I say. That isn't strictly true. I came as a girl at Christmas once with my parents and I remember a noisy blur of enormous shops, brightly lit windows, and a Santa whose nylon trousers crackled as I sat on his knee, and whose polyester white beard scratched me softly on the cheek. But I don't feel like getting into a big discussion with the driver, and anyway the city is as good as foreign to me. It's my first time alone here, after all.

'On your own, are you?' he asks and I feel a little uncomfortable, even though he's only being friendly.

'No, I'm staying with my aunt,' I reply, lying again.

He nods, satisfied. We're pulling away from the park now, darting with practised agility between buses and cars, swooping past cyclists, taking corners quickly and flying through amber traffic lights. Then we're off the busy main roads and in narrow streets lined by high brick-and-stone mansions with tall windows, glossy front doors, shining black iron railings, and window boxes spilling with bright blooms. I can sense money everywhere, not just in the expensive cars parked at the roadsides, but in the perfectly kept build-ings, the clean pavements, the half-glimpsed maids closing curtains against the sunshine.

'She's doing all right, your aunt,' jokes the driver as we turn into a small street, and then again into one even smaller. 'It costs a penny or two to live around here.'

I laugh but don't reply, not knowing what to say. On one side of the street is a mews converted into minute but no doubt eye-wateringly pricy houses, and on the other a large mansion of flats, filling up most of the block and going up six storeys at least. I can tell from its Art Deco look that it was built in the 1930s; the outside is grey, dominated by a large glass-and-walnut door. The driver pulls up in front of it and says, 'Here we are then. Randolph Gardens.'

I look out at all the stone and asphalt. 'Where are the gardens?' I say wonderingly. The only greenery visible is the hanging baskets of red and purple geraniums on either side of the front door.

'There would have been some here years ago, I expect,' he replies. 'See the mews? That was stables at one time. I bet there were a couple of big houses round here once. They'll have been demolished or bombed in the war, maybe.' He glances at his meter. 'Twelve pounds seventy, please, love.'

I fumble for my purse and hand over fifteen pounds, saying, 'Keep the change,' and hoping I've tipped the right amount. The driver doesn't faint with surprise, so I guess it must be all right. He waits while I get myself and my luggage out of the cab and on to the pavement and shut the door behind me. Then he does an expert three-point turn in the tight little street and roars off back into the action.

I look up. So here I am. My new home. For a while, at least.

The white-haired porter inside looks up at me enquiringly as I puff through the door and up to his desk with my large bag.

'I'm here to stay in Celia Reilly's flat,' I explain, resisting the urge to wipe away the perspiration on my forehead. 'She said the key would be here for me.'

'Name?' he says gruffly.

'Beth. I mean, Elizabeth. Elizabeth Villiers.'

'Let me see . . .' He snuffles into his moustache as he looks through a file on his desk. 'Ah, yes. Here we are.

Miss E. Villiers. To occupy 514 in Miss Reilly's absence.' He fixes me with a beady but not unfriendly gaze. 'Flat-sitting, are you?'

'Yes. Well. Cat-sitting, really.' I smile at him but he doesn't return it.

'Oh yes. She does have a cat. Can't think why a creature like that would want to live its life inside but there we are. Here are the keys.' He pushes an envelope across the desk towards me. 'If you could just sign the book for me.'

I sign obediently and he tells me a few of the building regulations as he directs me towards the lift. He offers to take my luggage up for me later but I say I'll do it myself. At least that way I'll have everything I need. A moment later I'm inside the small elevator, contemplating my heated, red-faced reflection as the lift ascends slowly to the fifth floor. I don't look anywhere near as polished as the surroundings, but my heart-shaped face and round blue eyes will never be like the high-cheek-boned, elegant features I most admire. And my fly-away dark-blonde shoulder-length hair will never be the naturally thick, lustrous tresses I've always craved. My hair takes work and usually I can't be bothered, just pulling it back into a messy ponytail.

'Not exactly a Mayfair lady,' I say out loud. As I stare at myself, I can see the effect of everything that has happened lately. I'm thinner around the face, and there's a sadness in my eyes that never seems to go away. I look a bit smaller, somehow, as though I've bowed a little under the weight of my misery. 'Be strong,' I whisper to myself, trying to find my old spark in my dull gaze. That's why I've come, after all. Not because I'm trying to escape – although that must be part of it – but because I want to rediscover the old me, the one who had spirit and courage and a curiosity in the world.

*Unless that Beth has been completely destroyed.*

I don't want to think like that but it's hard not to.

Number 514 is halfway down a quiet, carpeted hallway. The keys fit smoothly into the lock and a moment later I'm stepping inside the flat. My first impression is surprise as a small chirrup greets me, followed by a high squeaky miaow, soft warm fur brushing over my legs, and a body snaking between my calves, nearly tripping me up.

'Hello, hello!' I exclaim, looking down into a small black whiskered face with a halo of dark fur, squashed up like a cushion that's been sat on. 'You must be De Havilland.'

He miaows again, showing me sharp white teeth and a little pink tongue.

I try to look about while the cat purrs frantically, rubbing himself hard against my legs, evidently pleased to see me. I'm inside a hall and I can see already that Celia has stayed true to the building's 1930s aesthetic. The floor is tiled black and white, with a white cashmere rug in the middle. A jet-black console table sits beneath a large Art Deco mirror flanked by geometric chrome lights. On the console is a huge white silver-rimmed china bowl with vases on either side. Everything is elegant and quietly beautiful.

I haven't expected anything else. My father has been irritatingly vague about his godmother's flat, which he saw on the few occasions he visited London, but he's always given me the impression that it is as glamorous as Celia herself. She started as a model in her teens and was very successful, making a lot of money, but later she gave it up and became a fashion journalist. She married once and divorced, and then again and was widowed. She never had children, which is perhaps why she's managed to stay so young and vibrant, and she's been a lackadaisical godmother to my father, swooping in and out of his life as it took her fancy. Sometimes he heard nothing from her for years, then she'd appear out of the blue loaded with gifts, always elegant and dressed in the height of fashion, smothering him with kisses and trying to make up for her neglect. I remember meeting her on a few occasions, when I was a shy, knock-kneed girl in shorts and a T-shirt, hair all over the place, who could never imagine being as polished and sophisticated as this woman in front of me, with her cropped silver hair, amazing clothes and splendid jewellery.

*What am I saying? Even now, I can't imagine being like her. Not for a moment.*

And yet, here I am, in her apartment which is all mine for five weeks.

The phone call came without warning. I hadn't paid attention until my father got off the phone, looking bemused and said to me, 'Do you fancy a spell in London, Beth? Celia's going away, she needs someone to look after her cat and she thought you might appreciate the chance to stay in her flat.'

'Her flat?' I'd echoed, looking up from my book. 'Me?'

'Yes. It's somewhere rather posh, I think. Mayfair, Belgravia, somewhere like that. I've not been there for years.' He shot a look at my mother, with his eyebrows raised. 'Celia's off on a retreat in the woods of Montana for five weeks. Apparently she needs to be spiritually renewed. As you do.'

'Well, it keeps her young,' my mother replied, wiping down the kitchen table. 'It's not every seventy-two-year-old who could even think of it.' She stood up and stared at the scrubbed wood a little wistfully. 'I think it sounds rather nice, I'd love to do something like that.'

She had a look on her face as if contemplating other paths she might have taken, other lives she might have lived. My father obviously wanted to say something jeering but stopped when he saw her expression. I was pleased about that: she'd given up her career when she married him, and devoted herself to looking after me and my brothers. She was entitled to her dreams, I guess.

My father turned to me. 'So, what do you think, Beth? Are you interested?'

Mum looked at me and I saw it in her eyes at once. She wanted me to go. She knew it was the best thing possible under the circumstances. 'You should do it,' she said quietly. 'It'll be a new leaf for you after what's happened.'

I almost shuddered. I couldn't bear it to be spoken of. My face flushed with mortification. 'Don't,' I whispered as tears filled my eyes. The wound was still so open and raw.

My parents exchanged looks and then my father said gruffly, 'Perhaps your mother's right. You could do with getting out and about.'

I'd hardly been out of the house for over a month. I couldn't bear the idea of seeing them together. Adam and Hannah. The thought of it made my stomach swoop sickeningly towards my feet, and my head buzz as though I was going to faint.

'Maybe,' I said in a small voice. 'I'll think about it.'

We didn't decide that evening. I was finding it hard enough just to get up in the morning, let alone take a big decision like that. My confidence in myself was so shot, I wasn't sure that I could make the right choice about what to have for lunch let alone whether I should accept Celia's offer. After all, I'd chosen Adam, and trusted him and look how that had turned out. The next day my mother called Celia and talked through some of the practical aspects, and that evening I called her myself. Just listening to her strong voice, full of enthusiasm and confidence, made me feel better.

'You'll be doing me a favour, Beth,' she said firmly, 'but I think you'll enjoy yourself too. It's time you got out of that dead-end place and saw something of the world.'

Celia was an independent woman, living her life on her own terms and if she believed I could do it, then surely I could. So I said yes. Even though, as the time to leave home came closer, I wilted and began to wonder if I could pull out somehow, I knew I had to do it. If I could pack my bags and go alone to one of the biggest cities in the world, then maybe there was hope for me. I loved the little Norfolk town where I'd grown up, but if all I could do was huddle at home, unable to face the world because of what Adam had done, then I ought to give up and sign out right now. And what did I have to keep me there? There was my part-time job in a local cafe that I'd been doing since I was fifteen, only stopping when I went off to university and then picking it up again when I got back, still wondering what I was going to do with my life. My parents? Hardly. They didn't want me living in my old room and moping about. They dreamed of more for me than that.

The truth was that I'd come back because of Adam. My university friends were off travelling before they started exciting new jobs or moved to other countries. I'd listened to all the adventures waiting for them, knowing that my future was waiting for me back home. Adam was the centre of my world, the only man I'd ever loved, and there had been no question of doing anything but being with him. Adam worked, as he had since school, for his father's building company that he expected one day to own himself, and he was happy enough to contemplate living for the rest of his life in the same place he'd grown up. I didn't know if that was for me, but I did know that I loved Adam and I could put my own desires to travel and explore on hold for a while so that we could be together.

Except that now I didn't have any choice.

De Havilland yowls at my ankles and gives one a gentle nip to remind me that he's there.

'Sorry, puss,' I say apologetically, and put my bag down. 'Are you hungry?'

The cat stays twined around my legs as I try and find the kitchen, opening the door to a coat cupboard and another to a loo before discovering a small galley kitchen, with the cat's bowls neatly placed under the window at the far end. They're licked completely clean and De Havilland is obviously eager for his next meal. On the small white dining table at the other end, just big enough for two, I see some packets of cat biscuits and a sheaf of paper. On top is a note written in large scrawling handwriting.

*Darling, hello!*

*You made it. Good. Here is De Havilland's food. Feed him twice a day, just fill the little bowl with his biscuits as if you were putting out cocktail snacks, lucky De H. He'll need nice clean water to go with it. All other instructions in the useful little pack below, but really, darling, there are no rules. Enjoy yourself.*

*See you in five weeks,*

*C xx*

Beneath are typed pages with all the necessary information about the cat's litter tray, the workings of the appliances, where to find the boiler and the first aid kit, and who to talk to if I have any problems. The porter downstairs looks like my first port of call. My porter of call. Hey, if I'm making jokes, even weak ones, then maybe this trip is working already.

De Havilland is miaowing in a constant rolling squeak, his little pink tongue quivering as he stares up at me with his dark yellow eyes.

'Dinner coming up,' I say.

When De Havilland is happily crunching away, his water bowl refreshed, I look around the rest of the flat, admiring the black-and-white bathroom with its chrome and Bakelite fittings, and taking in the gorgeous bedroom: the silver four-poster bed with a snowy cover piled high with white cushions, and the ornate chinoiserie wallpaper where brightly plumaged parrots observe each other through blossomed cherry tree branches. A vast silver gilt mirror hangs over the fireplace and an antique mirrored dressing table stands by the window, next to a purple velvet button-back armchair.

'It's beautiful,' I say out loud. Maybe here I'll absorb some of Celia's chic and acquire some style myself.

As I walk through the hallway into the sitting room I realise that it's better than I dreamed it could be. I imagined a smart place that reflected the life of a well-off, independent woman but this is something else, like no home I've ever seen before. The sitting room is a large room decorated in cool calm colours of pale green and stone, with accents of black, white and silver. The era of the thirties is wonderfully evoked in the shapes of the furniture, the low armchairs with large curving arms, the long sofa piled with white cushions, the clean line of a swooping chrome reading lamp and the sharp edges of a modern coffee table in jet-black lacquer. The far wall is dominated by a vast built-in white bookcase filled with volumes and ornaments including wonderful pieces of jade and Chinese sculpture. The long wall that faces the window is painted in that serene pale green broken up by panels of silver lacquer etched with delicate willows, the shiny surfaces acting almost like mirrors. Between the panels are wall lights with shades of frosted white glass and on the parquet floor is a huge antique zebra-skin rug.

I'm enchanted at this delightful evocation of an age of elegance. I love everything I see from the crystal vases made to hold the thick dark stems and ivory trumpets of lilies to the matching Chinese ginger pots on either side of the shining chrome fireplace, above which is a huge and important-looking piece of modern art that, on closer inspection, I see is a Patrick Heron: great slashes of colour – scarlet, burnt orange, umber and vermillion – creating wonderful hectic drama in that oasis of cool grassy green and white.

I stare around, open-mouthed. I had no idea people actually created rooms like this to live in, full of beautiful things and immaculately kept. It's not like home, which is comforting and lovely but always full of mess and piles of things we've discarded.

My eye is drawn to the window that stretches across the length of the room. There are old-style venetian blinds that normally look old-fashioned, but are just right here. Apart from that, the windows are bare, which surprises me as they look directly out towards another block of flats. I go over and look out. Yes, hardly any distance away is another identical mansion block.

*How strange. They're so close! Why have they built them like this?*

I peer out, trying to get my bearings. Then I begin to understand. The building has been constructed in a U shape around a large garden. Is this the garden of Randolph Gardens? I can see it below me and to the left, a large green square full of bright flower beds, bordered by plants and trees in the full flush of summer. There are gravel paths, a tennis court, benches and a fountain as well as a plain stretch of grass where a few people are sitting, enjoying the last of the day's heat. The building stretches around three sides of the garden so that most of the inhabitants get a garden view. But the U shape has a small narrow corridor that connects the garden sides of the U to the one that fronts the road, and the single column of flats on each side of it face directly into each other. There are seven altogether and Celia's is on the fifth floor, looking straight into its opposite number, closer than they would be if they were divided by a street.

*Was the flat cheaper because of this?* I think idly, looking over at the window opposite. No wonder there are all these pale colours and the reflecting silver panels: the flat definitely has its light quota reduced being close to the others. *But then, it's all about location, right? It's still Mayfair.*

The last of the sunshine has vanished from this side of the building and the room has sunk into a warm darkness. I go towards one of the lamps to turn it on, and my eye is caught by a glowing golden square through the window. It's the flat opposite, where the lights are on and the interior is brightly illuminated like the screen in a small cinema or the stage in the theatre. I can see across quite clearly, and I stop short, drawing in my breath. There is a man in the room that is exactly across from this one. That's not so strange, maybe, but the fact that he is naked to the waist, wearing only a pair of dark trousers, grabs my attention. I realise I'm standing stock still as I notice that he is talking on a telephone while he walks languidly about his sitting room, unwittingly displaying an impressive torso. Although I can't make out his features all that clearly, I can see that he is good looking too, with thick black hair and a classically symmetrical face with strong dark brows. I can see that he has broad shoulders, muscled arms, a well-defined chest and abs, and that he is tanned as though just back from somewhere hot.

I stare, feeling awkward. Does this man know I can see into his apartment like this while he walks about half naked? But I guess that as mine is in shadow, he has no way of knowing there's anyone home to observe him. That makes me relax a little and just enjoy the sight. He's so well built and so beautifully put together that he's almost unreal. It's like watching an actor on the television as he moves around in the glowing box opposite, a delicious vision that I can enjoy from a distance. I laugh suddenly. Celia really does have it all – this must be very life-enhancing, having a view like this.

I watch for a while longer as the man across the way chats into his phone, and wanders about. Then he turns and disappears out of the room.

*Maybe he's gone to put some clothes on*, I think, and feel vaguely disappointed. Now he's gone, I turn on the lamp and the room is flooded with soft apricot light. It looks beautiful all over again, the electric light bringing out new effects, dappling the silver lacquer panels and giving the jade ornaments a rosy hue. De Havilland comes padding in and jumps on to the sofa, looking up at me hopefully. I go over and sit down and he climbs onto my lap, purring loudly like a little engine as he circles a few times and then settles down. I stroke his soft fur, burying my fingers in it and finding comfort in his warmth.

I realise I'm still picturing the man across the way. He was startlingly attractive and moved with such unconscious grace and utter ease in himself. He was alone, but seemed anything but lonely. Perhaps he was talking to his girlfriend on the phone. Or perhaps it was someone else, and his girlfriend is waiting for him in the bedroom and he's gone through there now to take off the rest of his clothes, lie beside her and drop his mouth to hers. She'll be opening her embrace to him, pulling that perfect torso close, wrapping her arms across the smooth back . . .

*Stop it. You're making it all worse.*

My head droops down. Adam comes sharply into my mind and I can see him just as he used to be, smiling broadly at me. It was his smile that always got me, the reason why I'd fallen in love with him in the first place. It was lopsided and made dimples appear in his cheeks, and his blue eyes sparkle with fun. We'd fallen in love the summer I was sixteen, during the long lazy days with no school and only ourselves to please. I'd go and meet him in the grounds of the ruined abbey and we'd spend long hours together, mooching about, talking and then kissing. We hadn't been able to get enough of one another. Adam had been a skinny teenager, just a lad, while I was still getting used to having men look at my chest when I walked by them on the street. A year later, when we'd slept together, it had been the first time for both of us – an awkward, fumbling experience that had been beautiful because we'd loved each other, even though we were both utterly clueless about how to do it right. We'd got better, though, and I couldn't imagine ever doing it with anyone else. How could it be so sweet and loving except with Adam? I loved it when he kissed me and held me in his arms and told me he loved me best of all. I'd never even looked at another man.

*Don't do this to yourself, Beth! Don't remember. Don't let him keep on hurting you.*

I don't want the image but it pierces my mind anyway. I see it, just the way I did on that awful night. I was babysitting next door and had expected to be there until well after midnight, but the neighbours came back early because the wife had developed a bad headache. I was free, it was only ten o'clock and they'd paid me for a full night anyway.

I'll surprise Adam, I decided gleefully. He lived in his brother Jimmy's house, paying cheap rent for the spare room. Jimmy was away so Adam planned to have a few mates round, drink some beers and watch a movie. He'd seemed disappointed when I said I couldn't join him, so he'd be delighted when I turned up unexpectedly.

The memory is so vivid it's like I'm living it all over again, walking through the darkened house, surprised that no one is there, wondering where the boys have got to. The television is off, no one is lounging on the sofa, cracking open cans of beer or making smart remarks at the screen. My surprise is going to fall flat, I realise. Maybe Adam is feeling ill and has gone straight to bed. I walk along the hallway towards his bedroom door; it's so familiar, it might as well be my own house.

I'm turning the handle of the door, saying, 'Adam?' in a quiet voice, in case he's sleeping already. I'll go in anyway, and if he's asleep, I'll just look at his face, the one I love so much, and wonder what he's dreaming about, maybe press a kiss on his cheek, curl up beside him . . .

I push the door open. A lamp is on, the one he likes to drape in a red scarf when we're making love so that we're lit by shadows – in fact, it's glowing darkly scarlet right now, so perhaps he's not asleep. I blink in the semi-darkness; the duvet is humped and moving. What's he doing there?

'Adam?' I say again, but more loudly. The movement stops, and then the shape beneath the duvet changes, the cover folds back and I see . . .

I gasp with pain at the memory, screwing my eyes shut as though this will block out the pictures in my head. It's like an old movie I can't stop playing, but this time I firmly press the mental off switch, and lift De Havilland off my lap onto the sofa next to me. Recalling it still has the capacity to floor me, to leave me a sodden mess. The whole reason for coming here is to move on, and I've got to start right now.

My stomach rumbles and I realise I'm hungry. I go through to the kitchen to look for something to eat. Celia's fridge is almost bare and I make a note that grocery shopping will be a priority for tomorrow. Searching the cupboards, I find some crackers and a tin of sardines, which will do for now. In fact, I'm so hungry that it tastes delicious. As I'm washing up my plate, I'm overtaken suddenly by an enormous yawn. I look at my watch: it's still early, not even nine yet, but I'm exhausted. It's been a long day. The fact that I woke this morning in my old room at home seems almost unbelievable.

I decide I'll turn in. Besides, I want to try that amazing-looking bed. How can a girl not feel better in a silver four-poster? It's got to be impossible. I go back through to the sitting room to turn out the lights. My hand is on the switch when I notice that the man is back in his sitting room. Now the dark trousers he was wearing have been replaced by a towel tucked around his hips, and his hair is wet and slicked back. He's standing right in the middle of the room near the window and he is looking directly into my flat. In fact, he is staring straight at me, a frown creasing his forehead, and I am staring right back. Our eyes are locked, though we are too far apart to read the nuances in one another's gaze.

Then, in a movement that is almost involuntary, my thumb presses down on the switch and the lamp obediently flashes off, plunging the room into darkness. He cannot see me any more, I realise, although his sitting room is still brightly lit for me, even more vivid than before now I'm watching from the dark. The man steps forward to the window, leans on the sill and looks out intently, trying to see what he can spy. I'm frozen, almost not breathing. I don't know why it seems so important that he doesn't see me, but I can't resist the impulse to remain hidden. He stares a few moments more, still frowning, and I look back, not moving but still able to admire the shape of his upper body and the way the well-shaped biceps swell as he leans forward on them.

He gives up staring and turns back into the room. I seize my chance and slip out of the sitting room and into the hall, closing the door behind me. Now there are no windows, I cannot be seen. I release a long sigh.

'What was all that about?' I say out loud, and the sound of my voice comforts me. I laugh. 'Okay, that's enough of that. The guy is going to think I'm some kind of nutter if he sees me skulking about in the dark, playing statues whenever I think he can see me. Bed.'

I remember De Havilland just in time, and open the sitting-room door again so that he can escape if he needs to. He has a closed litter box in the kitchen which he needs access to, so I make sure the kitchen door is also open. Going to turn out the hall light, I hesitate for a moment, and then leave it on.

I know, it's childish to believe that light drives the monsters away and keeps the burglars and killers at bay, but I'm alone in a strange place in a big city and I think that tonight, I will leave it on.

In fact, even ensconced in the downy comfort of Celia's bed and so sleepy I can hardly keep my eyes open, I can't quite bring myself to turn out the bedside lamp. In the end, I sleep all night in its gentle glow, but I'm so tired that I don't even notice.

The second novel in Sadie Matthews' provocative romance series will take you one step closer to the bittersweet edge of passion.

# secrets
# after
# dark

*Ours was a love bound by power . . .*

Falling in love with Dominic changed me. I relinquished myself completely and placed my heart and my trust in Dominic's hands, but in one exquisite, excruciating moment he abandoned his control. Anguished by his actions, he has locked those darkest desires inside, unable to share my conviction that it would never happen again.

Now it's not only Dominic who craves that delicate, seductive game of give and take, of walking the line between pain and pleasure, abandon and release. Persuading Dominic to let those secret parts of himself unravel will be the biggest risk I've ever taken, but I can't resist. Even if it means we fall apart . . .

*Provocative and sophisticated, exhilarating and seductive, the* After Dark *series is a compelling pleasure we should all indulge in . . .*

**HODDER**